PRAISE FOR *THE BEST MAN PLAN*

"An irresistible blend of sweetness and heat. . . . Erin is an appealing, resilient heroine (who's also not above dressing a puppy in a tutu), and empathetic, attentive Jason will make romance readers swoon. This is a treat."
—*Publishers Weekly*

PRAISE FOR JACI BURTON AND HER NOVELS

"Jaci Burton's stories are full of heat and heart."
—*New York Times* bestselling author Maya Banks

"A wild ride."
—#1 *New York Times* bestselling author Lora Leigh

"Jaci Burton delivers."
—*New York Times* bestselling author Cherry Adair

"One to pick up and savor."   —*Publishers Weekly*

"Jaci Burton's books are always sexy, romantic and charming! A hot hero, a lovable heroine and an adorable dog—prepare to fall in love with Jaci Burton's amazing new small-town romance series."
—*New York Times* bestselling author Jill Shalvis

"A heartwarming second-chance-at-love contemporary romance enhanced by engaging characters and Jaci Burton's signature dry wit."
—*USA Today*

TITLES BY JACI BURTON

• • • • •

BOOTS AND BOUQUETS SERIES

The Matchmaker's Mistletoe Mission
(an eNovella)

The Best Man Plan

The Engagement Arrangement

BROTHERHOOD BY FIRE SERIES

Hot to the Touch

Ignite on Contact

All Consuming

HOPE SERIES

Hope Smolders
(an eNovella)

Hope Flames

Hope Ignites

Hope Burns

Love After All

Make Me Stay

Don't Let Go

Love Me Again

One Perfect Kiss

PLAY-BY-PLAY SERIES

The Perfect Play

Changing the Game

Taking a Shot

Playing to Win

Thrown by a Curve

One Sweet Ride

Holiday Games
(an eNovella)

Melting the Ice

Straddling the Line

Holiday on Ice
(an eNovella)

Quarterback Draw

All Wound Up

Hot Holiday Nights
(an eNovella)

Unexpected Rush

Rules of Contact

The Final Score

Shot on Gold

THE
Engagement
ARRANGEMENT

JACI BURTON

JOVE
New York

A JOVE BOOK
Published by Berkley
An imprint of Penguin Random House LLC
penguinrandomhouse.com

Copyright © 2021 by Jaci Burton, Inc.

ISBN: 9780451491305

First Edition: June 2021

Printed in the United States of America
1 3 5 7 9 10 8 6 4 2

Book design by Alison Cnockaert

For A—I hadn't expected to lose you.
I still expect my phone to ring
and for us to chat about all the things.
You were always there for me,
and my life has less light in it now that you're gone.
Thank you for being the best
big sister I could have ever asked for.
Love you always and I'll see you again someday.

CHAPTER

· · · · · ·

one

AN IRISHMAN NEVER left a glass of whiskey unfinished, and Finn Nolan was as Irish as the green hills of his former homeland. He propped his booted feet up on the Bellinis' front porch railing to finish off the last of his whiskey before heading back to his own house for the night. He rolled the amber liquid around in his glass, then frowned as he saw headlights cutting into the darkness in front of him.

It was late. His boss, Johnny Bellini, had gone inside for the night. As far as he knew, everyone in the house had already gone to bed. Normally Finn would have headed to his place on the Bellini property, but Johnny had wanted to chat and Finn enjoyed his company, so he'd hung out long past dark.

The car pulled down the long gravel drive. He decided he'd wait and see if maybe someone had made a wrong turn. The lights were off on the front porch so they couldn't see him as they stopped in front of the house.

Recognition dawned as he saw Brenna Bellini open the passenger door of the Mercedes, followed by some tall, professionally dressed dude exiting the vehicle's driver's side.

The guy walked around the car and Brenna held up her hand.

"Don't," she said.

"At least let me walk you to the door."

"Don't bother. It's clear this date is over."

"Why? Because I asked you to come home with me?"

"No. Because you're a class A, narcissistic asshole whose primary interest is in yourself. Go get in your car and take yourself home, Jerry. I'm sure you and your hand will have a lovely finish to the night together."

Jerry looked offended. "Hey. I can get a lot of women."

"Then go get them. A whole harem of them." When he continued to stand there, she shooed him with both hands. "Go."

Jerry lifted his chin, muttered something Finn couldn't hear and got in his car. Brenna waited, arms crossed, while he drove away.

Finn smirked. The one thing he knew about Brenna Bellini was that she could take care of herself.

"What a dick," she muttered as she made her way up the stairs, stopping when she caught sight of him.

"Bad date, huh?" Finn asked.

"How long have you been out here?"

"The whole time." He pulled his feet from the porch railing and stood. "Why do you keep going out with such losers?"

She shot him a glare. "What do you know about my dating history?"

"I hear things."

"Where?"

"Here and there."

"From my sisters?"

He shrugged. "Here and there."

She rolled her eyes and started toward the front door.

"You deserve better, Brenna."

She looked over at him. "Damn right, I do."

He walked over, stopping in front of her. Damn, she smelled good, like a vanilla cookie. He wanted to taste her. And kiss her. Her gorgeous red hair streamed out behind her in the breeze, and he itched to run his fingers through it, to see if it felt as soft as it looked. But he'd never once touched Brenna Bellini.

Except in his fantasies.

"Then why don't you give a good guy a chance?"

She looked him up and down. "What? You think you're the right guy for me?"

"Why not? I'm a better guy than those jackasses you keep going out with. Stop playing with those boys you're not interested in and let a real man into your life."

She shook her head. "Not a chance in hell, Finn. First, you work for my family, and second . . ."

His lips curved as she trailed off, unable to finish the sentence.

"Go on . . ."

"And second . . . you're like family."

"Nah. I'm not your family and you know it. I'm the man you've always wanted, always needed, but never knew it. Until just now."

He saw her breath catch, her eyes widen, her lips part. He knew if he pulled her into his arms and kissed her, she wouldn't object. But the one thing Brenna needed was a slow-burn romance, and he intended to give it to her. She deserved that.

He tipped his cowboy hat toward her. "Good night, Brenna."

He turned and walked down the steps and around the side of the house, enjoying the quiet of late night, the glow of fireflies dancing around him. He'd lived on the Bellini property since he was eighteen years old, after his ma died and, since he had no other living relatives, Ma's childhood best friend, Maureen Bellini, had flown him from Ireland to come live with them. After that, Johnny and Maureen Bellini had become family to him. Brenna's sisters Erin and Honor had become like sisters.

But Brenna? She'd never been family. She'd been something else entirely. The first time he'd laid eyes on Brenna, with her beautiful red hair and unusual hazel eyes and hellacious temper, she'd lit a fire in him that over a decade later had yet to be extinguished.

Not that she'd ever known that. He'd never wanted her to know. Until now.

At first, he'd been too young, too unsure of himself, too tongue-tied around the fierce beauty. And then they'd both grown up and he'd watched her fall in love with and marry that shithole Mitchell Walker. Mitch had never appreciated the fine woman he'd had. He'd taken her for granted, ignored her in favor of his business, and then he'd lost her.

She'd needed time to grieve the end of her marriage, to get back on her feet, to regain her confidence. She'd gotten back out there and started dating again, but she found fault with every one of the guys she dated.

As he turned the corner and headed down the path toward his place, he smiled. He knew why none of those guys had lit a spark under Brenna. Because none of those men knew her like he did, knew what she needed.

He was the flame to her tinder, and it was time he lit the match.

• • • • • •

BRENNA TOSSED HER purse onto her bed and stared at the full-length mirror leaning against the wall. Her face was flushed with a pink glow, her pulse still racing after that comment from Finn.

What the hell had that been about? He was the one she always wanted but never realized, or some such nonsense? Where had that come from? After her useless date tonight, she'd felt empty and disappointed. But a few words from Finn on the front porch and she was lit up like a bonfire.

She was not interested in Finn Nolan. Like, not at all.

Liar, liar, because your panties are on fire.

"Shut up," she whispered to herself. She took off her dress and hung it up, went into the bathroom to wash off the remnants of her terrible date, then climbed into bed to read a book. But she couldn't concentrate, Finn's words still pinging around in her head.

Was he the guy she'd always wanted, always needed, but had never realized it?

Stop playing with those boys you're not interested in and let a real man into your life.

She pulled her legs in toward her chest and wrapped her arms around them, thinking about how he'd looked when she'd walked up the steps. His long, jean-clad legs stretched out, his cowboy hat tipped low across his brow, hiding his magnificent stormy gray eyes. And that Irish lilt to his voice—that alone could melt a woman's clothes right off her. He needed a haircut, all that rich, silky black hair spilling out from underneath his hat, making her itch to run her fingers through it while his mouth crashed down on hers and his tongue—

Whoa.

Okay, maybe she had an attraction. And maybe she always had. She still remembered when he'd first arrived on the ranch. He'd been eighteen then, and she'd been seventeen. He'd been lanky and shy and oh so heartbroken about his mother's death that her heart had just about broken with him. But he had a smile that lit up the entire state of Oklahoma.

Oh, she'd fought that attraction with everything in her. After all, Mom had trusted all of them to take care of Finn, to treat him like family. And when he'd loosened up and become part of the family, she'd held that attraction she'd felt to herself, while Finn had come out of his shell and laughed and made friends and had girlfriends and treated her just like he treated everyone else.

Then Mitchell had come along, distracting her with his sweet talking and empty promises of happily-ever-after.

What an eye opener that had been. Happily-ever-after was for fairy tales. That was why she worked the winery and left the wedding stuff to her sisters.

She rolled her eyes, realizing that thoughts of Mitchell were like buckets of cold water all over her libido, dousing her hot fantasies of Finn.

With a sigh of disgust, she turned out the light and climbed under the cool covers.

She and Finn weren't meant to be, anyway. He worked on the vineyard, they saw each other every day, and the two of them fooling around would be a recipe for disaster.

There. Fantasy effectively ended.

It was never going to happen.

CHAPTER

· · · · · ·

two

Finn slung his hammer into his tool belt and stepped away from the building he was putting an addition on, removing his hat to wipe the sweat from his brow. He unscrewed the lid from his jug and swallowed several gulps of water.

August in Oklahoma sucked. It was hot as fuck this morning, the sun beat down on him and there wasn't a single cloud in the sky. And it wasn't even eight a.m. yet. He'd deliberately started early so he could beat the heat. Hell of a lot of good that had done him. Today was going to be brutal.

It was days like this that made him miss the small town in Ireland where he'd grown up. He missed the clouds and the chill and the salty air of the sea. At times it felt like it was only yesterday that he'd walked along the coast, looking out every day at the amazing power of all that water crashing against the shore or taking a boat out to do some fishing with his da.

Other times it felt like a lifetime ago.

Damnú aír. He raked his fingers through his hair. No point in thinking of what had been. He was damn lucky to be here, grateful to the Bellinis for a home of his own and a roof over his head. He'd had no one back then after Ma had died. Now he had a family.

He went to the barn to grab some supplies for his project. He had to pass the main house, and while walking by he heard singing. Following the sound, he saw Brenna on her hands and knees, working in the dirt at the side of the house.

He cocked his head to the side and smiled, admiring the view. She was dressed in shorts and a cropped top, her smooth skin glistening with sweat as she used a trowel to dig out vegetables from the garden she tended.

Damn but she was beautiful, even sweaty and slinging dirt. Her hair was swirled up in a bun on top of her head, small curling red tendrils escaping and teasing her neck. All he could think about was how much he wanted to press his mouth to her nape.

Among other parts of her.

She shook the dirt off the potatoes and tossed them into a bin, then inched over to pull some peppers.

"Garden looks good, eh?" he asked.

She jumped back and straightened, shooting a pissed-off look in his direction. "Jesus, Finn. You could have made some noise to let me know you were there."

"Just did." He moved in closer, then crouched down to her level. "What're you harvesting this mornin'?"

"Potatoes. Carrots. Peppers. Onions."

"Need some help?"

She frowned. "Don't you have a job to do?"

"Yeah. Don't you?"

She lifted her chin. "I'll get to it. You should go do your job."

"Was on my way to do that and I heard you singing. You have a beautiful voice, Brenna."

"Uh-huh."

She stared at him, giving him her classic Brenna glare as if that would somehow scare him off. He'd never once been scared of her, so that never worked. "Do you need some help or should I just watch you?"

"What are you? Some kind of stalker?"

He laughed and got down on his knees beside her, taking the trowel from her hands. "I can't rightly be a stalker since I live here, can I?"

"I . . ." She kept glowering at him while he harvested the vegetables. "Don't do that."

"Do what?" he asked as he plopped the vegetables in the bin. "Help you? Kneel this close to you? Exist?"

"All of those things."

He laughed. "Trying to be rid of me, *álainn*?"

"Don't do that, either."

"What? Talk to you?"

"No. Talk to me in Gaelic. It's . . . it's . . ."

He arched a brow, waiting for her answer.

"Just . . . stop it."

She had a smudge of dirt on her face. He wiped his hand on his jeans, then swept his thumb over her cheek. "You had some dirt there."

She didn't pull away, just kept staring at him with those amazing eyes and dark lashes that always made his pulse kick up.

"Thanks."

He got up and grabbed the bin, then held out his hand

for her. She looked at his hand for a few seconds, then let
him haul her to her feet.

He handed her the bin.

"Thank you for the help. Not that I needed it."

"No, you didn't. You don't need anyone, Brenna. But
you might want someone. Sometime. Don't forget I'm
here."

He turned and walked away, smiling as he did.

That had gone well.

BRENNA TOSSED THE bin of vegetables on the kitchen
counter with a loud thud.

"What's that all about?" their cook, Louise, asked. "Did
some of the veggies go bad?"

"No, they're all ripe and fabulous."

Louise gave her a curious look as Brenna left the
kitchen.

She went upstairs and headed straight for the shower.
She was covered in sweat, dirt and consternation, all of
which needed washing away.

After showering, she put on panties and a sundress,
which was just about all she could stand to wear in this
unbearable heat. Kneeling shoulder to thigh with Finn
hadn't helped her internal heat situation, either.

How dare he interrupt her self-isolation, the time of day
when she got into her own head and enjoyed digging in her
vegetable garden? Didn't he know that was one of her favorite things to do—alone?

Men. Always getting in her damn way.

She went downstairs and fixed herself a glass of ice water, then closed herself in her office to do some paperwork.

Growing and harvesting grapes was a year-round job.

With the weather ever changing from year to year, it was her job to decide what they would plant and when. A bad decision could ruin a crop for the following year, and cost Red Moss Vineyards a ton of money.

They weren't a huge winery by many vineyard standards. They couldn't compete with the California vineyards by any stretch of the imagination. But her parents had been in the vineyard business for over twenty years, and Brenna had been working in it with her dad since she was a little girl. Growing grapes had always held an interest for her. There was a science to it that she found fascinating. Types of grapes and yield and managing weather conditions, so much of it was out of her control. Yet she loved everything about it.

Her sister Honor knocked on the doorjamb. "You ready for the meeting?"

She hated meetings. "I'll be there in a sec."

"Okay. See you there."

She gathered up her notes and her laptop and headed into the dining room, which had the biggest table in the house. When all three of the sisters joined the winery and wedding business, Mom and Dad had had the offices built on, but they'd all decided the dining room table would suffice as the conference room for meetings. Plus, they could eat snacks there, and who didn't like snacks?

Dad was busy in the wine cellar and hated coming to morning meetings anyway, so typically Brenna attended them so he didn't have to unless it was necessary. If there was something earth-shattering that he needed to be informed about, she'd let him know.

Mom handled the overall organization of both family businesses. Erin handled the budgets of the wine and wedding business, making sure invoices went out accordingly, and Honor was the Bellini Weddings planner. And though Brenna's primary function was with Dad on Red Moss Vineyards, she also worked with Honor on supplying wine for the weddings they held on-site.

Honor came in and took her seat. Mom was on a call in her office and had held up one finger as Brenna had walked by, so she knew their mother would be in shortly. Which meant they'd just have to wait for Erin. Since she lived with her fiancé, Jason, now, she had to drive to the house every day. She came running in a few minutes later, her dog Agatha trailing in behind her.

"Sorry I'm late," she said, tossing her things on the table and brushing her dark hair away from her face. "Jason had an early surgery and I forgot to set my alarm and then Agatha took forever to get ready." She ended with a smile.

"Oh, sure," Brenna said. "Blame the dog."

Agatha bounded over to Brenna for her morning scratch behind the ears. She plopped her fluffy butt right on top of Brenna's right foot, wagging her tail back and forth.

Brenna smiled down at the furry pup. "Don't let her blame you because she and loverboy stayed up late last night fooling around."

"Hey," Erin said. "Not true."

"The telltale blush on your cheeks says otherwise," Honor said, then laughed.

"Sometimes I hate having sisters."

"No, you don't," Brenna said. "We're the best thing to ever happen to you."

Erin sniffed. "If I hadn't had two sisters I'd have had more shoes."

Honor snorted. "That's probably true. You are the shoe queen around here."

"Hey," Erin said. "And you're the one who loves clothes."

"Guilty," Honor said. "And Brenna buys all the books and pretty bracelets."

"Now that I think about it," Brenna said, "without you two I could have had it all. The shoes, the clothes, the books, the bracelets—everything."

"But you wouldn't have had us," Honor said. "And you'd have missed out on all our sisterly shenanigans."

"Point taken."

"All right, girls," their mother said as she walked into the room, so used to the three of them bickering it rolled right off her. "Can we get started now?"

Agatha bounded out of the room, no doubt to bug Louise for treats or to go looking for their dad.

"Okay, to get things started," Erin said after taking a seat, "I've sent out the invoices for last weekend's super successful weddings."

"With happy brides and grooms for both," their mom said.

Honor smiled. "They were lovely weddings, weren't they?"

"They were," Erin said. "We did well on both of those. Also, I've made adjustments on a couple of budgets. The Harrison/Landell wedding on the twenty-seventh added thirty-six guests, and the Mathison/Blue wedding on November sixth wants ice sculptures and ten more cases of cabernet."

"We'll need more wine for Harrison/Landell," Brenna said.

Honor nodded. "I think so."

Brenna pulled up the order forms for the weddings on her laptop and added additional wines to make sure they stocked appropriately. "Got it."

Mom always held the agenda, so she looked to Brenna next. "What have you got, Brenna?"

She didn't need to read a report to give the information she needed to. "The vineyards are in good shape for harvest. All the grapes are strong. No diseases. Those in fermentation look amazing, and we're bottling like crazy. The chardonnay is especially tasty. Our yields are going to be fantastic this year. Dad's really happy with every stage."

Mom smiled widely. "Yes, he's especially pleased. It's a good year for the grapes."

"That's great news," Erin said. "I can't wait for harvest."

Harvest was always an especially fun time of year. "Me, too," Brenna said.

"You're up, Honor," their mother said.

Honor opened up her notebook and slid her laptop in front of her. "Okay. I met with three couples last week and took them on a tour of the grounds, to include the reception barn and the vineyard. All three scheduled weddings."

"That's fantastic," Brenna said.

"I know, right? Well, four weddings were scheduled, actually."

Mom frowned. "Four?"

Erin grinned. "She means that Jason and I have set a date for our wedding."

A loud chorus of excited cheers went up.

"When?" Mom asked.

"The Richmond/Lisbon wedding moved to next year, so I slipped into their October slot."

Brenna blinked. "You mean October as in two-months-from-now October?"

Erin nodded. "Yes."

Their mother just stared, openmouthed, with nothing to say.

"Holy shit." Brenna opened the wedding schedule to

check the slot. It was mid-October, which was actually less than two months away since they were already well into August. "Erin, are you insane?"

Erin shrugged. "We were going to plan it for next spring, but I was supposed to marry Owen in the spring and I don't want a repeat of that disaster. Plus, Clay and Alice are getting married next May and I want to be able to focus on their wedding without mine getting in the way."

Brenna waved her hand back and forth. "First, as if that disaster could ever happen again. Your relationship with Jason is solid. You two love each other. Second, you juggle like no one I've ever seen."

"I know," Erin said. "The idea of this wedding being like my . . . nonwedding is ridiculous. Still, it's in my head and I don't want it to be. And besides, if anyone can pull a wedding together in two months, it's this family."

"This is true," Honor said. "I promised her we could do it. Obviously, we have the venue sewn up. And wine. And we have all the connections to prod and push the vendors to make sure we get everything else in line quickly."

Erin nodded. "We've got this. It's doable."

Honor was already making furious notes. "I can handle this."

"No, we will handle this," Brenna said. "As a family. Whatever you need on the wedding side, Honor, we'll all pitch in and help."

Honor gave her a grateful look. "Thanks."

Wow. Her sister was getting married. This year. Brenna did not see that coming. What a whirlwind this was going to be.

"Which just leaves me to get the dress," Erin said. "Er, dresses, since there will be bridesmaids, of course."

"A wedding in two months," Brenna said. "Only this family would try to make that happen."

"Not try," Erin said. "We're going to do this, right?"

Mom shook her head. "My child, you are nothing if not a constant surprise. All right. If everyone agrees, then we'll make it work. No, we'll more than make it work. We'll make it perfect."

Erin looked around the table. "I won't deny that this will be difficult."

Brenna shrugged. "I'm in and I'll do whatever it takes. After what you went through with Owen, you deserve your happily-ever-after, however you want it."

"What Brenna said," Honor said. "You know I can make this happen for you."

Erin clapped her hands together. "I love you all so much. Thank you for supporting Jason and me."

"How does Jason feel about all of this?" Brenna asked.

"He'd happily go to City Hall and marry me there tomorrow. And he's all on board for the October wedding. He wants whatever makes me happy."

"Which is why he's the one for you, honey," Honor said. "So when do we go dress shopping?"

Erin laughed. "Obviously as soon as possible."

"Okay," Mom said. "Let's get out our calendars and we'll make some plans."

They did just that, picking a day that week where they could clear their schedules.

"That's not all the news I have."

Everyone stared at Honor.

"There's more?" Brenna asked.

Honor nodded. "Yes, and this one will affect you, Brenna."

Brenna shot her a curious look. "In what way?"

"Esther Brown's wedding next weekend."

Brenna nodded. "Right. I'm a bridesmaid." She and Esther had been friends since high school. She'd been honored when Esther not only chose their vineyard to have her wedding but then asked Brenna to be a bridesmaid.

"Exactly. Her matron of honor, Vanessa, is seven months pregnant and lives in Portland. She planned to be here but her pregnancy just became high risk because of high blood pressure and her doctor advised against travel, so she can't make it to the wedding. Which means Esther's had to come up with a replacement."

"Oh, that's too bad," Mom said. "She must be so upset about that."

"They both are. However, Esther also happens to be best friends with Allison Walker, who's going to be Esther's replacement matron of honor."

Erin looked over at Brenna. "Oh, crap."

Brenna rolled her eyes. Since Allison was married to Brenna's ex-husband, that meant Mitchell would be there, too. There was no way Allison would show up on Bellini property without him. "Won't that be fun."

She ran into Mitchell now and then at events, but it wasn't like they actually . . . talked or anything. In fact, they hadn't had an in-depth discussion since the day he'd moved out of their condo, effectively splitting up their marriage. Which was . . . four years ago? Then less than a year after their divorce had been finalized he'd married Allison. No mourning period for him.

Not that she'd mourned him. At all. Much.

"Are you going to be all right with this?" her mom asked.

Brenna shrugged. "I'm fine with it. Business is business, so we'll deal with it just like any other wedding."

"There's more," Honor said.

Brenna braced herself.

"Go ahead."

"Esther and Brock want to make an entire weekend of it, here at the vineyard. Wine tasting with the wedding party on Thursday, rehearsal dinner on Friday, then the wedding on Saturday followed by brunch with the family and wedding party on Sunday morning."

"Oh, that's a lot of Mitchell," Erin said, wincing. "And a lot of Allison."

Mom shook her head. "Absolutely not. How dare she—"

"Mom," Brenna said. "You have to remember this isn't Mitchell making these plans. It's the bride and groom. They chose Bellini Weddings and Red Moss Vineyards. I'm sure they never even made the connection."

"More likely Allison just wants to dig in the knife and vomit her happiness all over you."

"Erin." Their mother shot Erin a glare. "Not that I don't disagree, but that was vile."

"And not untrue," Honor said. "We all know Allison's motivations. She'd always had it out for Brenna, even in high school."

Brenna couldn't disagree with that. Some women never grew out of their high school pettiness. Brenna and Allison had been friends in high school. Close friends. Until Brenna had been asked to junior prom by Dean Cullen, one of the most popular boys in the school, and Allison had never forgiven her. How was Brenna supposed to know Allison had a crush on the guy if she had never told Brenna about it? It wasn't like Brenna had even flirted with Dean. Okay, maybe she'd eyed him in the halls, but who wouldn't have wanted to go out with the hottest tight end on the football team? Every girl did back then. Never in a million years did she think Dean would ask the dorky bookworm over the super cool cheerleader. She'd been as shocked as Allison had been. After Allison had informed her of how upset she was, Brenna had told her she'd turn him down.

But it had been too late, and Allison blamed her, had accused Brenna of going behind her back to get Dean to ask her to prom when she'd known all along that Allison had liked him, which had been utterly ridiculous. And totally wrong. And had pissed her off—and to be honest, hurt her feelings. So she'd gone to prom with Dean just for spite.

Of course, she'd had a terrible time, because Dean was a prime douchebag who'd brought booze and had only been interested in getting laid, and thought Brenna would be more than eager to let him into her panties. He'd been so wrong about that.

Boys. She should have known better. She'd called her dad to pick her up and left Dean in the dust.

It had been an awful night, and Brenna had lost one of her best friends in the process.

Brenna often wondered if Allison had hooked up with Mitchell after their divorce to get back at her. Given how long Allison could hold a grudge, it wouldn't surprise her in the least.

"Look," Brenna said. "It's just a wedding, and four days of events will make for excellent income for us. We'll deal with it. I'll deal with it. Mitchell and I are ancient history."

"If you're sure," her mom said.

Brenna lifted her chin. "Totally positive."

She'd make this work. She'd get through those four days, smile, do her job, be the best bridesmaid she could be, and show Mitchell and Allison that she was thriving and happy.

But single. She knew Allison would toss several digs in about that.

She'd have to figure out an angle so she wouldn't have to hear *Oh, poor Brenna can't get a guy after Mitchell dumped her.* She knew how Allison's mind worked. And Mitchell would just follow along.

She'd be damned if she'd be gossip fodder for Allison and her friends.

She needed a plan.

And she knew just the person to help her.

CHAPTER
······
three

Finn stood under a lukewarm shower for about ten minutes, letting the water rinse off the sweat and grit from his body. After today's work, it felt good. He scrubbed his body down, washed his hair and got out. After drying off, he pulled on a pair of jeans and went to the fridge to grab a beer. He popped it open and took several long swallows of the cold brew, sighing in pure pleasure.

He was about to sit down and relax for a few when he heard a knock on the door, which surprised the hell out of him. Normally no one bothered him at his place after hours.

He went to the door, even more surprised to see Brenna standing there. She looked pretty as ever, her hair piled high in a ponytail. She wore a yellow sundress that highlighted her creamy skin.

"Brenna. What are you doin' here?"

She gaped at him for a few seconds, then said, "We need to talk."

He shrugged. "Sure. Come in."

He shut the door and followed her inside. She turned to face him. "I've got a problem and I think you're my perfect solution."

This was new. Normally she avoided him like he carried some kind of plague. "Okay. What can I help you with?"

"My ex-husband and his wife are going to be here on the property for a wedding next weekend. A wedding where I'm one of the bridesmaids."

"Mitchell's coming here? That's a surprise."

"Tell me about it. Anyway, his wife, Allison, is a friend of mine from high school. Ex-friend, I guess you could say. She and I had a falling-out. She blames me for—well, anyway, that story doesn't matter. She's the matron of honor in the same wedding. As you can imagine, it is going to be a nightmare having to be around them."

He crossed his arms and studied her. She was pacing back and forth and seemed very uncomfortable. And frantic, which wasn't like her. Normally, Brenna was cool and had everything under control. Obviously this whole Mitchell-and-Allison thing had her rattled.

"What do you need me to do for you?"

She leveled her gaze at him. "I need you to be my fiancé for four days."

He arched a brow. "Say that again?"

"They're going to be here for four days. Around me all the time. In my business. Driving me crazy. I need you to pretend to be engaged to me so I don't have to deal with the 'Oh, poor Brenna is all alone' shtick from Allison."

"Who gives a shit what Allison or your ex thinks? You're an independent woman, Brenna. And a successful one at that. Look at all you've accomplished since high school. You run a vineyard, for Chrissakes."

"I know that."

"And you sure as hell don't need a man at your side to prove your worth."

"I know that, too. It's just . . . will you do it or not?"

He shrugged. "Sure. Do I get to kiss you in front of them?"

"Absolutely not."

He knew that would get to her. "How about holding hands?"

"I . . . that'll be fine."

"We should set some ground rules."

She frowned. "Like what?"

He stepped forward and smoothed his hand down her arm. "Like knowing whether I can touch you like this."

Her breathing increased. He saw it when her breasts rose and fell more rapidly. Not that he watched her breasts or anything, but it was hard not to notice her deep inhales and exhales. She didn't step away or ask him to stop, so he continued to touch her, keeping his movements light, easing his fingertips across her neck, to her jaw, teasing her earlobe.

She shivered, but it wasn't revulsion. It was excitement. He liked that.

"They'd expect an engaged couple to be familiar with each other's touch."

"Right," she whispered.

"So touch me, Brenna."

She reached out, hesitated. "You should put a shirt on."

"Why? I'm clean."

"That's not what I mean. Your chest . . ."

"Is what?"

"Bare."

"It is." He took her hand and laid it on his chest. Now he was the one breathing heavily as the coolness of her palm splayed across his pecs.

"You're shaking, Brenna."

She snatched her hand away. "I am not. And anyway, it's not like you're going to be bare-chested in mixed company."

"True enough. But if you start shaking every time you stand next to me, no one's going to believe we're engaged. Or anything else." He picked up her hand and massaged it between his. "You need to relax."

"I *am* relaxed!"

She'd yelled the words at him, which made him smile. "Are you?"

"Okay, maybe not. But I just came up with this idea today. It's not like I've had the time to settle it in my head."

"You don't have to do it at all, you know," he said, keeping her hand between his, getting her used to his touch. "You can just be yourself. Proud. Single. Telling them both to go fuck themselves."

She laughed at that, and he felt the tension in her hand ease. But then she shook her head. "No. I'll have enough to deal with that week without Allison's annoying voice buzzing in my ears about how I can't get a man. It's just four days, Finn. We can do this for four days, can't we?"

"Sure we can."

"Okay." She pulled her hand from his and then held it out to his for a regular handshake.

She was joking, right?

"Then it's a deal?"

He arched a brow. He might agree to do this, but he wasn't going to make it easy for her. "It's a deal. Should we kiss?"

She laughed and headed to the door. "Nice try, but no."

She turned the knob and opened the door. "Thanks for doing this, Finn. You're a good friend."

She closed the door behind her.

His lips curved and he went into the bedroom to grab his shirt.

Friend his ass. The way she reacted to him had nothing to do with friendship and everything to do with a woman who was attracted to a man.

And he wasn't going to let that one lie. If Brenna wanted to pretend to be engaged for four days, then they were going to have to get close.

Really close.

Besides, she could have asked anyone to be her fake fiancé. But she'd asked him. Why was that? He already knew the answer, but did Brenna?

This was going to be fun.

CHAPTER

. . . . . .

four

THERE WAS NOTHING more fun than wedding dress shopping, as long as Brenna wasn't the one trying on said wedding dresses. She'd already had one disaster of a marriage and never intended to make that colossal mistake ever again.

Erin and Jason, though? They were perfect for each other. Other than her parents, she'd never seen two people more in love. Like, sickeningly in love. She couldn't help but be happy for her sister. After what she'd gone through with her ex, Owen, Erin deserved some happiness. Even if Owen dumping her two days before their wedding had been for good reasons. They'd all worked it out and everyone was back to being friends now. Owen was just about finishing up with his chemotherapy treatments and seemed to be on the road to beating his cancer.

Now it was Erin's time for her happily-ever-after. They had all finished up work early that day, then piled into Mom's SUV and took off for the city.

"I've already made contact with two bridal shops that

are willing to work with me on such short notice," Erin said. "I'm really lucky because normally they require a minimum of six months, preferably a year."

"You'll have to get a dress off the rack, though, right?" Honor asked. "It'll be too late to order one."

Erin nodded. "Yes, but that's all right. I can't have everything I want and I know that. And if the dress needs alterations, I know a wonderful seamstress who's agreed to do the job."

Brenna was glad Erin was so at ease about this. And she knew her sister was organized to the max, so if something needed to be done, it would.

They got to the first shop forty minutes later and parked in the lot.

"Are you nervous?" Brenna asked as they all got out of the SUV.

"Well, it's not my first time trying on wedding dresses."

Brenna laughed. "True. And hopefully it'll be your last time."

"No hopefully about it. This is definitely my last."

"It had better be," Mom said. "My heart can't take any more stress."

Erin wrapped her hand around their mother's arm. "Trust me, Mom. Jason will be standing at the end of the aisle on our wedding day."

"I know he will, *cailín leanbh.*"

They walked into the store and were greeted by a tall, dark-haired woman by the name of Alexandra. Erin introduced everyone to her.

"Erin, it's nice to meet you and your family," Alexandra said. "I'm ready to get started if you are."

"I am."

Erin had told them she'd sent some ideas to Alexandra

earlier in the week, so she'd already pulled some dresses for her to try on. They took seats and waited while Erin went into the dressing room.

The first dress was lace and tulle and looked totally overwhelming on Erin's slender frame. They all thought it was a no, including Erin.

The second dress was a very pretty satin and clung to her curves.

"It's pretty," Brenna said.

"Agree," Honor said. "It's pretty."

Mom shook her head. "Too plain. You need something more wow."

Erin smoothed her hands down the dress. "It is nice and I like the fit, but I agree it needs something . . . more."

"Back to the dressing room," Alexandra said.

The third dress was entirely too poofy. The volume swallowed her up.

"Absolutely not," Erin said as soon as she looked at herself in the mirror.

Even Alexandra wrinkled her nose. "You're right. Let's move on. I think I have one you're going to love."

After Erin left, Brenna turned to her mom and sister. "Have you noticed she's trying on dresses that look absolutely nothing like her first wedding dress?"

"Can you blame her?" Honor asked. "She wants nothing to remind her of that first disaster, including the dress."

"It was a beautiful dress," Mom said.

"Yes, it was," Brenna said. "But it wasn't the right dress. Or the right guy."

"True that," Honor said.

Brenna knew how that felt. She'd had a lovely dress for her first wedding. If she was going to get married again—which she wasn't—the last thing she'd want to wear would be anything resembling her first dress. It would seem unlucky somehow.

"She'll pick the right dress," Mom said. "The one that's meant to be hers."

A few minutes later, Erin floated out on a dress that made them all gasp. A white crepe with off-the-shoulder lace sleeves, it clung to her body and floated down to a mermaid shape, with a lace cathedral train. When Erin stood up on the platform with her back to them, they all gasped again.

The back was adorned with see-through lace and crepe buttons and Brenna could swear this dress was made just for Erin because it fit her as if it had been created for her body. If it was going to need alterations, they would be very minor.

"Damn," Honor whispered.

Brenna caught the telltale glitter of tears in Erin's eyes as she stared at herself in the full-length mirrors.

"Erin," their mother said. "That dress is breathtaking."

She finally turned. "I love it. I love it so much."

"It's perfect, Erin," Brenna said.

"It's you, honey," Honor said. "It fits you perfectly and you look like a princess."

Mom nodded. "I agree."

"Isn't it amazing?" Alexandra asked. "The alterations on this would be minimal. And she looks like a million bucks in this dress."

Brenna couldn't argue.

Mom stood up and went over to get a closer look, then took Erin's hand. "Well?"

"I can't imagine loving another dress as much as I love this one. I can see myself wearing it when I marry Jason. This is the one."

They all clapped and Brenna and Honor got up and went over to her to hug her. Erin changed, filled out the paperwork and paid for the dress.

"While we're here we should look for dresses for you two and for Mom," she said.

Brenna rolled her eyes. She was going to be a bridesmaid again. Not her favorite thing, but she'd do what she had to do since her sister was the bride-to-be this time.

In the end, it hadn't been difficult at all to find dresses. Erin had already chosen her bridesmaid colors, and the store had a wonderful inventory. Honor and Brenna tried on a few and found a couple of styles that looked amazing on both of them, which was quite a feat considering they had two completely different body types. Brenna was curvier and taller than Honor, but Erin said as long as the colors of the dresses were the same, they could wear different styles. She wanted Alice in the wedding as well, which meant once Alice flew back to town from Los Angeles she'd have to come and pick out a dress as well. But the fabric and color would be the same and the styles were similar, and now that was taken care of with a minimal amount of fuss. Even Mom had found a dress she liked. All in all, a good shopping day.

After that they were starving, so they hit up a restaurant in the city and celebrated with margaritas.

Brenna raised her glass. "Here's to finding a wedding dress, Erin."

Erin raised her glass as well. "I'll definitely drink to that."

They sipped their drinks and rehashed their workdays, then put in their food orders.

"Erin, you crossed quite a few things off your wedding to-do list today," Honor said. "Wedding dress, bridesmaid dresses, mother-of-the-bride dress. That's a huge accomplishment."

"It is. More than I planned to accomplish, actually. I'm ahead of schedule now. We could probably move the wedding up to September."

Honor frowned. "That's not funny."

Brenna laughed. "Actually, it's pretty funny."

"That's because you only have to supply the wine. I have to do everything else."

Erin grasped Honor's hand. "Hey, not true. I told you I'm handling all of this."

"As if I'd let you. You've had enough stress already. Just being the bride is stressful."

"And I'm not one of your typically scheduled brides. I've got this, Honor. I'll handle it."

"We'll all handle it," their mom said. "As a family. It's not one person's job, Honor. It's not just your job. It's all of ours. Understood?"

"Yes, Mom," Honor said.

"Hey," Erin said. "When we meet on Monday I'll astound you with my wedding checklist. You'll see how much I've already got checked off. Jason and I are nailing down cakes and a deejay this weekend."

Mom looked from Erin back to Honor. "See? Not just your job."

Honor raised her hands in acquiescence. "Fine. Okay. I can see you do, in fact, have this, Erin."

Erin smiled. "Good. So stop stressing over me. I'm not doing this alone. I not only have all of you, I have Jason, who for some reason is totally pumped about wedding planning."

Brenna grinned. "Because he's crazy in love with you."

"He is. Isn't that amazing?"

"Not so amazing," Mom said. "It's what you deserve."

Erin laid her head on their mom's shoulder. "I love you."

They ate dinner, which was another amazing thing because who knew dress shopping could work up such an appetite? Brenna cleaned her entire plate of salmon and asparagus tips, then had cheesecake for dessert. By the time they got back to the house, she needed to walk off dinner. She hugged Erin, who had to leave for home, then went upstairs and changed out of her dress and into a pair of shorts and a tank top before slipping into her tennis shoes. Even though the sun had set, it was still oppressively hot. There was no breeze and the humidity was high. It wasn't even like she was moving at a fast clip, just needing to walk.

She'd meant to discuss her ludicrous fake fiancé plan with her mom and her sisters tonight, but they'd been so busy discussing everything else, it hadn't come up.

Or maybe she was just a coward, and the whole idea was stupid and she should give it up.

She should do just that. Forget the thought of pretending to have a fiancé, and go about her business as a successful single woman. Finn had been the one to suggest that, and he was probably right.

Though she could already picture Allison's smug expression that she'd have to live with for four freaking days. Brenna had been married to Mitchell before. She knew from experience that he wasn't someone to brag about.

Still, they'd been divorced for four years. What exactly had Brenna done with her life since then?

Not much. She'd moved back home, where she still lived. She worked at the winery, which she'd been doing when she was married to Mitchell. And . . . and . . .

And nothing.

She looked around at her surroundings, realizing that for some reason she'd ended up at Finn's place. His lights were on, so he must be home. She hesitated, thought about turning around and heading back to the house. Just as she did, she caught sight of him walking up the path from the other side. She couldn't exactly hide from him since he'd already seen her, so she continued her walk, hoping he wouldn't think she'd been coming to his place. Which maybe she subconsciously had been for reasons she couldn't fathom.

"Out for a stroll?" he asked as he stopped in front of her.

"Yes. I had a big dinner that I'm walking off."

"I hope you didn't have a date. I frown on my fiancée going out with other men."

She rolled her eyes. "Funny. I went shopping for a wedding dress for Erin."

"Jason told me they moved up the wedding. It'll be tight."

"We'll get it handled."

"I have no doubt."

She looked at him, realizing he had a rifle at his side. "What are you doing? Squirrel hunting?"

"No. Taking a walk. I heard some noises out by the pond so I took the rifle to check it out."

She peeked around him. They sometimes got trespassers since their property butted up against public land where hunters or kids might wander. "Find anything?"

"No. But I'll keep an eye out."

Brenna knew the family liked having Finn on this side of their land because he kept an eye on potential trespassers. He'd already run off teens several times who'd come out to party in the woods. Nothing like a tall, lean, but well-muscled badass carrying a rifle to scare the bejeezus out of you and keep you from thinking of ever doing it again.

"It's a good hiding place to hang out," she said as she continued to walk.

Finn slung the rifle over his shoulder and walked with her. "Yeah? You've been there?"

She shrugged. "I did my share of partying there when I was a teen."

"In the woods. Over there."

"Of course. Didn't have to leave the family property, and it was easy to sneak my friends in over the property fence. Plus . . . easy access to wine."

He slanted a grin at her. "Aren't you the sly one?"

She shrugged. "I had my moments. And some fun. Until the night Dad caught us."

"I definitely want to hear that story."

They had made their way to the pond. There was a bench with a comfortable back, so they took a seat there. She was glad she remembered to put bug spray on before she left the house so she wouldn't get eaten up by mosquitoes.

"I was seventeen. It was me and William, the boy I was dating, then my friend Rachel and her boyfriend, Oliver, and four other friends. I snuck three bottles of chardonnay from the cellars and stored them in an ice chest in the woods, then met my friends at the fence. They climbed over and we ate chips and drank the wine, laughed and had a great time. Got totally blitzed on that chardonnay, too. And then Rachel and Oliver decided they wanted to go skinny-dipping in the pond."

He motioned with his head. "This one?"

She nodded. "Yes. I didn't think that was a good idea since the moon was full and it was too light out, but we were all drunk so we decided to go for it. I was down to my underwear when Dad walked to the edge of the pond."

"Oh, Christ. What happened?"

"Everyone grabbed their clothes and scattered, including William, leaving me standing there to face my dad, alone in my underwear."

Finn winced. "That had to be awkward."

"Like you would not believe. He turned away from me and told me to get dressed, then he walked with me to pick up the bottles of wine we'd left in the woods. He informed me that I owed him for the wine, and he wanted to know the names of everyone who'd been there with me besides William and Rachel, both of whom he already knew. I wasn't about to snitch on my other friends.

"The next morning Mom called William's and Rachel's parents to let them know what had gone down. I was mortified."

"That's rough. How did your friends react?"

"Rachel was okay. William broke up with me and said I snitched on him, which of course I didn't."

"And your other friends?"

"Oh, they were fine since they didn't get in trouble, but I got grounded for a month. Like, home-from-school-and-straight-to-my-room grounded. With no phone or TV privileges."

"Ouch."

"Then I got banned from the winery for three months. That hurt more than getting grounded."

"I'm sure it did. Lesson learned, though, huh?"

"Yeah. I learned not to skinny-dip during a full moon. And not to get my wine from the family winery."

He tilted his head back and laughed, his full, sexy timbre vibrating all the way from his chest. Lord, she could listen to that laugh all night long.

"You're a feisty one, Brenna. I never knew you had a wicked streak."

"That was in my youth."

"Oh, in your youth, huh? So, what? You're old and wise, now?"

"Wis*er*. I learn from my mistakes."

He tilted his head to study her. "Like your ex?"

She stared out over the pond. "I don't want to talk about him."

"Sometimes talkin' about things helps you put them in the past."

"Oh, trust me, he's well in the past."

"Right. That's why I'm your pretend fiancé."

She wagged her finger at him. "Not yet you aren't. And only for four days."

"I'm very hurt by you shutting me out, Brenna. After we get married we need to work on our communication skills."

She laughed. "Yeah. I'll put that high on my list." She stood. "I'm going to walk."

He got up. "I'll go with you."

"You don't have to."

"I don't mind."

The way he smiled at her could light up the sky. It made her heart flutter, threw her off balance, and she did not like being off balance.

"I'm just going to head back to the house. There's no need."

"You're avoiding me."

She patted his shoulder. "Now you're getting the hint. Good night, Finn."

He gave her a knowing grin. "Night, Brenna. When you fall asleep tonight, think of me."

She rolled her eyes and walked away, taking the path that led toward the house. By the time she made it back she definitely felt better. She walked up the steps to the porch and went inside, up to her room, and closed the door.

After stripping off her clothes, she climbed into bed and grabbed a book to read, but damn if visuals of a sexy Irishman didn't invade her thoughts.

Get out of my head, Finn. I don't want you there.

She tried to focus again, but his easy smile was right there, his gray eyes studying her intently whenever she spoke. She couldn't help but think about the way he walked with such predatory grace, his incredible mouth, all that silky hair just begging to be tugged on while he was inside her, thrusting deep—

Dammit. She tossed the book on her nightstand, slid down in her bed and stared up at the ceiling.

Now she was hot. So. Damn. Hot.

She blew out a breath and willed her body to cool down. Her body did not comply.

Finn had been living on the property for more than ten years. Why was he front and center in her mind now? Why was she completely and inexplicably in lust with him all of a sudden, out of nowhere?

She knew what she had to do to get him out of her head. Go on a few dates with some new guys. Maybe even get into a relationship, and then she could banish Finn from her thoughts. There was nothing like the focus of a new guy to get her attention off someone who was strongly on her mind. And Finn was most definitely in her thoughts lately. Like, all the time.

And she didn't want him there.

After this farce of a fake engagement was over, that was exactly what she'd do. She'd go find some guys to have some fun with, and then Finn would be out of the picture for good.

Easy enough. Now she had a plan and she could get back to her book.

CHAPTER

· · · · · ·

five

FINN HAD LOVED building things since he was old enough to hold a hammer, when his da had brought him into his shop to let him tinker and play with discarded pieces of wood. When he was six, he'd built his first birdhouse. When he was ten, Da had let him build a new house for the dogs by himself. He'd built all kinds of things, learning something new every time. His da had been a master woodworker. When he was fifteen, he'd helped carry Da's coffin to the gravesite, knowing he'd never stand shoulder to shoulder with his father in the woodshop again.

Three years later he'd lost his mum, then left Ireland to live with Maureen and Johnny and their three daughters. Sure, he'd known Maureen Bellini. She'd often traveled to Ireland to visit with his ma, even when he'd been a small boy. Maureen and his mother had a close friendship—a lifelong one, according to Ma. It had helped that he at least knew who she was when she'd come to the funeral and offered to give him a home with her family when he'd had no one left.

But, still, a hell of a whirlwind for a kid consumed with grief and loss. But the one thing his da had taught him was never to feel sorry for himself, to pick himself up and carry on. A lesson he'd always held on to. Because he might have only had his parents for a short while, but he knew he'd been loved, so what the hell did he have to feel sorry about?

The best way to honor his parents was to do well in life, and he figured he'd done that. He had master carpentry skills, though he'd never be as good as his father. But he had also taught himself how to make a damn fine whiskey. His da would be proud.

Today he finished the last wall in the addition, then began to create the shelves that would line one of the walls.

"Do you like sweating or is this some form of self-torture?"

He turned and grinned at Jason, Erin's fiancé and one of his best friends. "Sweat's good for the soul."

"That's what I try to tell myself when I'm doing pregnancy checks on cattle in ninety-degree heat, like today."

Jason stepped into the building and Finn wrinkled his nose. "Yeah, you stink, man. You must have been doing ranch calls today."

"Everybody gets their turn, and this was my day for it." Jason looked around the oversized space that would soon be the new storage building for the wedding business. "It's looking good in here. Lots of space."

"They need it for all their arches and props and whatchamacallits they use for the weddings."

Jason laughed. "Yeah, those things."

"You here to see Erin?"

"Nah. I called her on the way over. She told me she's busy today. She and her sisters are going over invitations after work and she doesn't have time for me. She said she'd see me when she got home. So I dropped Puddy off with her so Agatha and Puds could hang out, and she'll bring both the dogs home. I thought maybe you, me and Clay could go have dinner and play some pool tonight."

"Good plan. I'm just about to finish up here. You talk to Clay?"

Jason nodded. "Yeah, he's gonna meet us at the pool hall. I have a change of clothes in the truck so I'll shower here."

"Okay. I'll put things up here then go shower and change and then meet you at the house."

"Sounds good."

Jason left and Finn cleaned up his work area, put away his tools, then headed to his place. He stripped off the clothes that were sticking to him like a second skin and went straight into the shower. The semicool water felt great pouring over his head and body, washing away all the sweat and dirt that clung to him. He put on a clean pair of jeans and a T-shirt, then added his going-out boots before making his way to the main house.

He walked in through the back door, never needing to knock. Louise was in there making dinner. He leaned in to take a deeper smell of whatever was in the pot on the stove.

"Something smells good."

"Chicken for tomorrow night's dinner since everyone is scattered tonight."

"Oh, good. It's my favorite."

She nudged him with her elbow. "Everything is your favorite."

He laughed. "That's true."

"You're going out tonight?"

"Yes, ma'am. With Jason and Clay."

"You boys behave."

"I always behave."

She rolled her eyes. "Sure you do."

He kissed her on the cheek, because Louise and her husband, Marcus, were as much family to him as the Bellinis. Louise had kept him well fed through the years, and Marcus was a handyman on the property, so he'd continued his education on woodworking with him. Finn was indebted to both of them.

He made his way down the hall. Brenna was coming down the stairs, so he paused. She was wearing a sundress and sandals, the dress swishing around her gorgeous legs.

She frowned. "You're dressed up."

"You mean I'm clean."

"Same thing." She made it around the foot of the stairs and stopped in front of him. "Where are you headed?"

"Dinner and to play some pool with the guys."

"I see." She studied him. "What guys?"

"Jason and Clay."

"They should keep you out of trouble."

He laughed. "Yeah? Why would you think that?"

"They're both engaged. That means no picking up women."

"Hey, they're the ones who are engaged. I'm not. Except fake engaged to you."

She shook her head. "Only for four days, remember?"

"Right." He picked up her hand and rubbed it between his. "Unless you want me to remain faithful to ya, in which case I'll be on my best behavior tonight."

She frowned. "Why would I care what you do?"

"Because you like me, Brenna Bellini. And you don't want me to kiss other girls."

She jerked her hand away. "Go. Kiss other girls. I don't care."

But she did care, and he saw it in the flash of anger in her beautiful eyes.

"Who's kissing other girls?"

Honor had come out of her office.

"Not me," Finn said, giving Brenna a wink.

Brenna waved her hand. "Not like I care what he does." She walked away, leaving Finn and Honor standing there.

"What was that all about?" Honor asked.

"She likes me. She just doesn't realize yet how much."

Honor looked down the hall where Brenna had disappeared. "Oh, really."

"Yup. We're even going to be engaged next week."

Honor blinked, then her eyes went wide. "Wait. What?"

"Oh, she knows all about it. In fact, it's her idea. You should have her tell you about it."

"I definitely will."

Jason came down the stairs along with Erin, then looked over at Finn. "Hey, you ready?"

"Yeah."

"Have fun," Erin said as she came down the hall, stopping to give Jason a kiss. "But not too much fun."

Jason laughed. "I'll see you at home. I love you."

"I love you, too."

They headed out the door. Finn looked back, realizing that Brenna had returned and was standing outside on the porch with her sisters, watching them. Watching him.

He smiled.

THE MEETING WITH the prospective bride and groom went well. After touring the grounds and discussing their needs and what Bellini Weddings could provide, along with the budget and a taste of Red Moss Vineyard wines, the couple booked their wedding for September of next year and paid a deposit.

After the couple left, they went over wedding invitations. Erin had narrowed it to a few, but they all easily chose one favorite. Then, they decided they'd go out for pizza since Louise and Marcus had the night off.

Brenna changed into a pair of capris and a short-sleeved shirt, then slid into sandals and pulled her hair into a high ponytail. She met her sisters downstairs.

"Are you riding with us, Erin?" Honor asked.

"Yes. I'll come back here after dinner and pick up Agatha and Puddy."

The dogs sat at their feet, tails wagging expectantly.

Erin waved her hand at the dogs. "Go play."

They ran off, nudging each other on the way.

"The training is going well, I see," Brenna said.

"Since I moved in with Jason the two of them are the best of friends. And for some reason training two pups is so much easier. It's like they try to one-up the other to see which one is the best dog." She rolled her eyes.

Brenna laughed. "They're both the best dog."

Erin looked lovingly at both of them as they lay in the hallway wrestling over a toy. "I know."

"I'm ready if everyone else is," Honor said, keys in her hand. "And hungry."

They headed out toward the city, stopping at their favorite pizza place. They'd been coming to Hideaway Pizza since they were little, and all three of them agreed it was still the best pizza in the city.

They ordered iced teas and looked over the menu. The one thing they couldn't agree on was what type of pizza to order.

"Paradise Pie," Brenna said. "I love the chicken and spinach and garlic."

Erin shook her head. "Chicken Florentine. The pesto sauce with grilled chicken and mushrooms is the best."

They looked to Honor, who sighed. "Why do I always have to be the tiebreaker?"

"Because you don't care what we order," Brenna said. "You like everything here."

"That's true. Then you'll let me decide?"

"Absolutely," Brenna said.

"Yes," Erin added.

"Okay, fine. We're ordering a small size of both."

Brenna shook her head. "Ever the peacemaker, aren't you, Honor?"

Honor beamed a smile. "I try."

When their server returned, they ordered salads and Honor gave the pizza orders. They rehashed their meeting with the prospective bride and groom they'd met with tonight until the server brought their salads. Brenna grabbed her fork and dove in. She was so hungry and the salad was just what she needed.

"So, Brenna," Honor said. "Finn tells me the two of you are engaged."

Erin choked on her sip of iced tea, grabbed her napkin and wiped her mouth. "Excuse me, what?"

Honor continued, "He said you're going to be engaged next week or something along those lines?"

Well, hell. She had meant to lay it out in more explainable terms. Damn that Finn anyway.

"Not really engaged. Just pretend engaged and only for four days."

"Pretend engaged?" Erin looked at her. "What the hell is that?"

"Explain, please," Honor said.

"You know I'm in Esther's wedding next weekend. And now Allison and Mitchell are going to be there."

"Right," Erin said. "Continue."

Brenna waved her fork in the air, hoping this would come out in a way that made perfect sense. "Anyway, I know Allison. She'll be all over me about being single. I don't want to deal with it—or with her—so I've enlisted Finn to be my fake fiancé for the duration of the wedding weekend."

Honor and Erin stared at her and didn't say anything, so she assumed they were in agreement. She went back to eating her salad.

"That's the most ridiculous thing I've ever heard," Erin said.

"Why, Brenna?" Honor asked. "You don't need to pretend to be engaged. Who cares what Allison thinks, anyway?"

"I don't. Not really. I just want a hassle-free four days. They'll think I'm engaged and Allison can go away and bother someone else."

"Do you really think you're less than because you don't have a guy?" Erin asked.

"No, of course not. I'm doing great. I love my job. I have all kinds of things to keep me busy. My gardening, my books, genealogy research. I love my life."

"Again," Erin said. "Why do you have to pretend that you're not complete without some fake fiancé?"

"That's not what this is about. It's about not being harassed by Allison, and by my ex-husband who'll do anything Allison tells him to. Shouldn't I be spared that annoyance?"

"You should be," Honor said. "But you know we'll have your back. We wouldn't let Allison give you a hard time."

"At the expense of the bride?" Brenna asked. "Allison is Esther's matron of honor. We have to keep the bride happy, and me bitch-slapping the matron of honor won't make Esther's wedding the one of her dreams, will it? This is my solution."

Honor looked to her. "You have a point. Not a great solution, but a point."

"Well, damn." Erin chewed thoughtfully for a minute. "Okay, your idea might be a dumb one, but I'll support you."

"So will I."

"Thank you."

Their pizzas arrived and they dug in. Brenna felt a lot better now that her sisters knew about her engagement arrangement with Finn, and that they supported her, even if it was reluctantly.

She'd still have to inform her parents, which she knew was not going to go over well. But her parents would go along with the plan, probably as reluctantly as her sisters had.

Erin picked up her phone and sent a text, then smiled when she got a ping in return.

"Jason said he's jealous we had pizza."

"But I'll bet they had greasy burgers," Brenna said.

Erin sent another text. It took a few minutes for Jason to reply, and then Erin nodded. "They did."

"Just as good, then," Honor said. "Nothing beats a great burger, followed by beer and pool."

"We should go meet them and play some pool," Erin said.

"Why would we want to do that?" Brenna asked.

Erin shot her a look. "Because it's fun? Because Jason's there and I might want to see him?"

Honor shrugged. "I like pool."

Brenna rolled her eyes. "Fine. We'll go."

"Great." Erin smiled. "But first I want to eat another slice of pizza."

They finished eating, paid the bill and climbed into the car, then drove a couple of miles over to the pool hall and went inside.

It was nicely air conditioned, and there were plenty of pool tables to accommodate the crowd. Fortunately there weren't a ton of people there, so Jason and the other guys were easy to spot.

Erin went right over and put her arms around Jason, who seemed surprised and happy to see her.

"Hey, babe. I'm glad you came."

"We were close and I thought I'd kick your ass in a game of pool."

"Oh, you did, huh? Well, you can try."

Brenna watched Finn prepare to take a shot. Actually, she was watching the way his shoulders bunched up as he leaned over the table, the deftness of his fingers as they curled around the cue, the muscles on his forearm as he steadied for the shot, and wow, why was she even interested in every part of his body anyway?

She looked around the place, trying to zero in on a guy—any guy—who might capture her interest. There were several good-looking men in the place. One or two actually looked her way. One gave her an inviting smile.

She felt nothing. No spark, zero interest. Not like when Finn came up and stood close to her giving her a smile of his own, the kind of smile that made a woman's insides quiver.

"Hey," he said.

Just one word. Insides. Quivering.

Damn that man.

She turned away and smiled at Clay. "How's it going?"

"Good."

"Is Alice in L.A.?"

He nodded. "She has a few meetings, but she'll be back this weekend."

"Sorry I'm late. I hear I missed burgers."

They all turned to see Owen, Erin's ex-fiancé, walk in.

"You also missed two games already," Clay said. "Which you'd have lost anyway."

Owen laughed. "You'd like to think that."

"Hey, Owen," Erin said. "How are you feeling?"

"Good, thanks. Finished up another round of treatment this week so we'll see how the testing goes. Every time I do a round I'm hoping I'm finished."

"We all hope that," Honor said, grasping his arm and holding on to it. "You look good."

He smiled at her. "Thanks. I feel pretty good, too."

The whole situation with Owen had been a disaster. First him walking out on Erin practically at the altar and disappearing on her, only to find out he fled because of his cancer diagnosis and not handling it well at all. But after they talked it out they both realized they weren't right for each other anyway. And Erin forgave him, which Brenna gave her a lot of credit for because she didn't know if she could have done that. The rest of the family had come around as well. The important thing right now was for Owen to get well. Being mad at him for dumping Erin was one thing. Losing him was not acceptable.

They'd all been friends since they were kids. You just didn't abandon a friendship, especially once Erin had explained that Owen breaking up with her had led her to

Jason, whom she loved more than anyone she'd ever loved before.

Sometimes things worked out right in the end, even if they started out all wrong.

"You gonna try to play?" Finn asked.

Brenna arched a brow. "Oh, I'll play. And I'll beat you."

Finn shaded a crafty smile at her. "We'll see, lass."

Once the guys finished their game, they grabbed another table and formed two teams. Honor, Owen and Clay played at one table, and Jason, Erin, Brenna and Finn played at another.

Brenna had been taught to play pool by her dad, and she loved the game. She'd played in college, too, and for some reason guys seemed to think women weren't good at pool.

They were wrong.

She won the first game. Erin won the second.

"Shit," Jason said after Erin sank the last ball. She batted her lashes at him.

"Maybe you'll get lucky on the next game," Erin said. "Or maybe not."

Finn gave them a run for their money on their third game, because he wasn't a slouch, either. Neither was Jason. They were all pretty evenly matched.

In the end, Finn won that game. He turned and gave Brenna a smile.

"Good game," she said.

"I'm out." Erin put up her cue. "I'm tired and I need to go get the dogs."

"We'll go," Honor said.

"No need," Jason said. "I'll drive her back to the house to get the dogs."

"You sure?" Brenna asked.

"Hey, I have to follow my lady home and make sure she gets there safely."

Erin rolled her eyes, but leaned against Jason. "Unnecessary, but thanks."

Clay left, too, leaving just Honor, Owen, Brenna and Finn. They ended up grabbing drinks and sitting at a table.

"How's your energy level, Owen?" Honor asked.

"Better now than it was at the beginning of treatment. I'm back at the brewery and, other than appreciating naps more now than I ever have before, I've been getting my stamina back."

"Hey, never discount a nap," Honor said. "They're good for you."

"Trust me, I listen to my body now. And I'll feel even better when the chemo is done with. My numbers have looked really good, so I'm hoping I'm reaching the last of the treatments."

"We all hope that," Brenna said.

Honor looked over at Brenna and Finn. "We should hit up the Screaming Hawk now that Owen is back to work."

"I'm always down for beer," Finn said.

Brenna nodded. "I like beer."

"Great. We'll make a plan and do it."

"I'd love to see you there. I've . . . missed my friends."

"Hey, you're still our friend and that's not going to change," Honor said.

"Thanks. I know that, but I'm trying to stay out of the way. Jason and Erin need their time together."

Brenna couldn't imagine how awkward it must be for Owen. His breakup with Erin meant also breaking up with a family he'd been a part of since they were children. And with his cancer treatments, they hadn't seen much of him lately.

She didn't envy his position.

"We're Erin's sisters," Brenna said. "We'll always be there for her. But we're your friends and that isn't going to change, Owen."

"I appreciate that. More than you know."

"Hey, buddy," Finn said. "We've got your back. And I've got a need for some of that crisp lager you serve."

"I've got it. You just have to show up."

"Then we'll make a plan," Honor said.

Now that Honor was in charge of scheduling it, Brenna knew it would happen.

They finished their drinks and everyone got up to head out.

Owen hugged Brenna and Honor, then said good-bye to Finn and left. Finn walked with them to their vehicle.

"See you at the house," he said.

"Okay," Brenna said, feeling a little weird that he was waiting for them to leave like this was some kind of date, which it wasn't.

Honor just smiled and said thank you, so they climbed into their vehicle and headed back to the house.

"You and Finn make a good couple," Honor said as she drove.

"We are not a couple."

"The way he looks at you tells me otherwise. And I saw you watching him every time he took a shot when we were playing pool."

"I can hardly ignore him. He's part of our group."

"Yes, he is. But no one else in our group stares at his ass. Except you."

"I did not stare at his ass."

Honor went silent and it irked her.

"Nothing's going on between Finn and me."

Honor's lips curved. "Okay, I believe you."

"I mean, sure, he's incredibly hot and all, and that accent is enough to make any woman fall into a dead faint at his feet. He's around all the time and it was just convenient to ask him to pretend to be my fiancé because we know each other so well and he wouldn't get the wrong impression. And he gets me and my weird quirks, you know?"

"Of course. Perfectly reasonable."

She crossed her arms and stared out the window, feeling irritated with her sister but not understanding the reason for it.

"Why would it be a bad idea for you and Finn to get together, Brenna?"

"Because I don't want to."

"You don't like him?"

She'd be lying if she said she didn't have an instantaneous chemical reaction to Finn whenever she saw him or was around him. But those feelings were new and made her feel raw and just a little bit scared. She hadn't had feelings like that for a guy in a very long time.

"I like him just fine. It's just that he's different from the guys I usually date."

Honor let out a soft laugh. "You find fault with every guy you've gone out with since you and Mitchell got a divorce."

"Finding a decent man is difficult."

"Not when he's right in your own backyard. Like, literally."

She shook her head. "Finn and I are not a good match."

Honor drove through the gates of their property. "Why not? He's fun and attractive and smart and a good guy. And everyone in the family adores him. He obviously likes you. What would be so wrong about giving it a try with him?"

Brenna shifted in her seat to face her sister. "And what happens if I do give it a try and it doesn't work out? Does Dad fire him?"

"Of course not."

"Exactly. Then I have to face that weirdness every day. No, I know better than to have a romance in my own backyard. I'll restrict my dating life to well outside the grounds of the family property lines."

"I can see your point there. But what if it could work out and you didn't give it a chance? You could be missing out on something—on someone—amazing, Bren."

"I just don't think I can take the chance on failing again. I haven't been lucky in love."

Honor pulled in front of the house and parked. Finn was leaning against the porch rail. She smiled and reached out to squeeze Brenna's hand. "Maybe your luck is about to change."

They walked toward the stairs and Honor walked up. "Night, Finn."

"G'night, Honor."

Brenna stopped. "You didn't have to wait for us."

"I wanted to make sure you got home safely."

"Well, thanks." She started up the stairs, then stopped, compelled by . . . something she couldn't name. She turned to him. "You do realize that you and I are not . . ."

He cocked his head to the side, waiting.

She walked down so she was level with him. "We're not . . . actually dating or anything."

"Noticed that."

"Okay, I just wanted to make sure that was clear."

"Are you asking me out, Brenna?"

She frowned. "Of course not."

"You want me to ask you out."

"No. I don't know. Why? Were you going to ask me out?"

"I'd like to take you out. Would you go if I asked you?"

"No. I don't know. Maybe."

He laughed. "That's a lot of answers to one simple question. Go on a date with me, Brenna."

Her stomach was doing a wild dance and her pulse fluttered all over the place, which it absolutely did not do whenever a guy asked her out. She was always calm and rational when it came to dating. Why was she never calm or rational around Finn?

She blamed his amazing hair.

She blew out a frustrated breath. "Fine. We'll go out."

"It's not an execution, Brenna. It's a date. I promise we'll have fun."

"You can't promise that."

"Yes, I can."

She'd withhold judgment until said date. Which probably wouldn't happen anyway.

"Okay, we'll see."

"We will. And you'll have fun." He continued to smile as if he held the key to successful dating. Which he decidedly did not.

"I'm going inside now."

"Good night, Brenna."

She walked up the stairs, refusing to continue to gape at him. Because in his jeans and boots and all that . . . hair, she could look at him all night. And what good would that do her?

"Good night, Finn."

She went inside and closed the door, headed up to her room and kicked off her shoes, then lay back on her bed.

She could not believe she'd just agreed to go on a date with Finn.

What was she thinking? Wasn't it bad enough she'd con-
cocted this ridiculous fake fiancé scheme?

Where is your head, Brenna?

She sat up and sighed.

She wasn't thinking with her head lately.

And that was the problem.

CHAPTER
······
six

Finn's plan for taking Brenna on a date had to be put on hold, because an unexpected repair project got dropped into his lap that kept him working double time. He never minded that because he liked staying busy, but it did put a crimp in his plans with Brenna.

Though it seemed as if she'd been avoiding him the past several days. He could swear that any time she saw him coming, she'd pivot and walk in the opposite direction.

They did have three weddings last weekend, so he knew they were busy as well, and her ex-husband and his wife would be showing up at the vineyard tomorrow, so she likely had other things on her mind besides a date with him.

Which didn't mean that Finn intended to forget that she'd agreed to it. He'd bided his time—for years, actually. Now he had a chance to show Brenna he was the right guy for her. He didn't intend to waste the opportunity.

He'd repaired the broken barn door and repainted both of them, and added new hinges as well so they looked brand new. He fixed some of the fence where the horses grazed, and despite the August heat, it had felt good to be outside.

Now all he wanted was some of Louise's lemonade, so he trekked toward the house and walked up the back steps, inched his head inside the door.

Louise wasn't in the kitchen so he wiped his boots on the mat and went in, washed his hands in the sink, grabbed a glass and some ice and opened the fridge, his mouth watering as he reached for the pitcher.

Thank the heavens for Louise, who always had a full pitcher of freshly made lemonade in the summer. He filled his glass and drank greedily, downing the first glass and going for a refill.

"Thirsty?"

He looked up and nodded at Brenna as he took another long swallow. "Yeah. It's hot as hell outside."

"I've been in the winery all day. A little warm in there, too."

You could never tell by looking at her. She wore her hair wound up in a bun on top of her head, and she had on a sundress. Her skin glistened with a subtle glow, but hell, she wasn't a sweaty mess like him.

He got out another glass and filled it with ice and lemonade and handed it to her.

"Thanks." Unlike him, she took a sip of the lemonade. "Mmm, good. What would we do without Louise?"

"I'm grateful for her, for sure. How was your day?"

"Productive. I did some forecasts and put out the call for people for the harvest."

"You usually bring in a big crowd for that."

She nodded. "I think we'll have enough. Even the customers want to come out for harvest."

"Hey, it's good times." He grinned.

"Yes, it is." She took another few swallows of her lemonade, her throat working as she did, making Finn tighten. He wanted to stroke the slender column of her throat, then lick the droplets of sweat from her collarbone. And kiss her. She pressed her lips together, then licked her bottom lip. God, he really wanted to kiss those full lips and suck her tongue. Suck her clit. Make her come. He'd bet she was a screamer when she came. He wanted to make her scream over and over again.

He cleared his throat and emptied his glass, hoping the cold liquid would squelch his lusty thoughts.

"Are you ready for tomorrow?" she asked.

He shrugged. "I'll do what I'm told. Stand where you want me. Touch whatever parts of you that you ask me to."

He caught the way her breasts rose when she inhaled deeply.

"There will be no touching. Of any of my parts."

"Whatever you say, love."

"Just be by my side. Pretend to . . . I don't know, act like a fiancé."

"Never been one of those before. How do they act?"

"My last one was an ass. Don't act like him."

"Noted. So I should be affectionate, but don't touch you. And don't act like an ass. Got it."

She rolled her eyes and put her glass in the dishwasher. "It'll be fine," she mumbled. "It'll all work out."

He came up next to her and slid his glass next to hers. "It will be fine. As long as you relax around me."

She tensed up. "I am totally relaxed."

"Yeah, sure you are. Every time I come close you freeze up. How are they gonna believe I'm your guy if you do that?"

She blew out a breath and grasped the sides of the sink. "You make me nervous."

He turned her to face him and swept his fingertips over her collarbone. "Why?"

"I don't know."

"You've known me a long time, Brenna. You can trust me."

Her eyes were clear and filled with that trust as she tilted her head back to look at him. If they weren't in the kitchen of her family's house where anyone could walk in, he'd pull her into his arms and kiss her. But there was a right time for those kinds of things, and when Finn kissed Brenna, it was going to be the right time.

He stepped back. "Just think of this whole thing as a fun game, and a way for you to stick it to your nemesis."

She nodded. "That is a good way to put it."

"See? Already better, isn't it?"

"Yes, thanks."

"Happy to help. I gotta go. Just let me know what you need me to do tomorrow, and I'll be on board."

"Okay. I'll see you at dinner tonight?"

He turned and offered up a grin. "Do I ever miss dinner?"

Now she smiled and his world turned upside down.

He walked out and realized if he wasn't careful around Brenna, his heart could be in real trouble. He needed to remind himself that she wasn't invested at all in him, just this whole game she was playing. She might have agreed to go on a date with him, but Brenna was skittish.

And that meant taking things slow.

For both of them.

Thoughts of Brenna stayed in his head the rest of the day, and as he made his way back to his place to clean up before dinner. He almost missed the flash in the woods beyond the house, but he had his eyes open and his ears aware, because he'd always thought of himself as guardian of the family's property.

He went into the house and grabbed his rifle. It was still light outside, which wouldn't prevent someone from breaching the property line. He'd run off teenagers before who were looking for a place to hang out, and this was a nice secluded spot. A verbal warning generally took care of that. But you never knew who you might run into in the woods, and Finn wasn't taking any chances.

He crept slowly around the water and toward the thick trees, ignoring the sweat pooling at the small of his back. As he entered the woods he stilled when he saw the bushes move, raising his rifle.

"I've got a gun trained on you and I'll use it if you come at me. I'm giving you ten seconds to get the hell out of here."

He waited, mentally counting to ten. He didn't see anyone running. But someone or something started to come closer.

He lowered his rifle when he saw a dirty creature inching his way.

It was a dog. He crouched down to see that the poor little thing was filthy and looked like it hadn't been fed in a while.

"Hey, buddy, you lookin' for some food?" He held out his hand, not wanting to scare it into running off.

The dog came a little closer, whimpering. Finn wrinkled his nose. The dog stank.

"You need a bath. And a good meal. I'll bet I can help with both of those. Wanna come to my house?"

The dog looked up at him with soulful brown eyes that hit Finn right in the stomach.

He stood, slowly. "Come on. Let's go."

He hoped the dog would trust him enough to go with him. He walked back toward the house, happy to see the dog following him, though he was keeping a respectable distance.

First, he needed food, so as soon as they got to the house Finn went inside. The dog didn't come in, but he waited on the porch while Finn filled a bowl with water and took that outside. The dog lapped greedily. While the dog drank his water, Finn went back into the house and looked through his cabinets and fridge. He didn't have any dog food, but he did have some eggs and bacon. He quickly scrambled up a few eggs and fried the bacon, threw them on the plate, waited for them to cool down some, which only took a minute, then hoped the dog would still be there when he walked out onto the porch.

The dog was still sitting there. The water bowl was empty, trails of muddy water dripping down his chin.

"Here you go, buddy. Try this out."

He laid the plate down and the dog gobbled up the food like he hadn't eaten in days. Judging by the ribs Finn could see, it had probably been longer than that.

Finn crouched down after the dog had licked the plate clean. "Who threw you out like you were nothing but garbage, huh? What asshole would do that?"

He reached out his hand and let the dog sniff him. He wagged his tail and licked Finn's fingers.

"You like that my fingers smell like bacon, don't you? Wanna come inside and see about having a bath?"

He got up, took the plate with him and looked at the dog. "Come on, buddy, let's go inside."

He crossed the threshold, figuring the dog would either follow or not but Finn wasn't going to force it.

The pup was tentative, but he came in, making Finn's heart do a little leap. He didn't know why. Was he actually thinking about keeping this dog?

Hell yes, he was. No one had taken care of this guy, which meant he was now Finn's responsibility.

The dog followed Finn all the way into the bathroom and studied him with his head cocked to the side while Finn turned the water on.

Okay, he seemed interested in the water. That was a good thing.

"Wanna get in there? Do ya?"

When Finn built the house he didn't put in a tub, figuring he never took baths and wouldn't need one. So he just had a walk-in shower. Bathing the dog would have been easier with a—

The dog walked right into the shower and stood under the water as if he knew he stunk like the worst thing Finn had ever smelled.

"Okay, then. Let's shower." Finn knew the only way to get the dog clean was to get in there with him, so he stripped down, grabbed the handheld and made sure the dog was totally wet, then took shampoo and started lathering him up.

The funny thing was, the dog seemed to really enjoy it. Maybe he was tired of stinking, too.

After he rinsed the dog, he grabbed a large towel and dried him off. The dog shook himself and water flew everywhere.

"Thanks a lot, dude."

Finn dried off, too, though he'd have to take another shower later. The important thing was getting the dog clean. He looked at the shower floor. It was covered in dirt and twigs and God only knew what else. Obviously he'd have to clean the shower, too. But at least the dog looked better.

He was pretty, if too thin. Finn would take care of that. He'd have to take him in to the veterinarian to be checked

out. He didn't even know if he'd had any shots. He was glad
Jason was a vet so he knew the dog would be well cared for.

The first thing he had to do was get him checked out. If
he was microchipped and just lost, he'd have to find his
owner and return him.

And didn't that hit him like a gut punch. He'd grown
attached already.

If he wasn't chipped or lost, he'd get food and supplies
for him and make the dog feel welcome and at home.

The dog lay on the bathroom floor and calmly watched
while Finn cleaned the shower, then washed himself. After
he dried and dressed, he picked up his phone and called
Jason, who fortunately answered his cell.

"Are you at the clinic today?"

"Yeah."

"A stray dog wandered onto the property. I got him
cleaned up but he's really thin. Can I run him in for you to
check him over?"

"Sure. I'll be here and I've got some time."

"Thanks. I'll be there in a bit." He hung up, got dressed
and headed out to his truck. The dog had already decided
to follow him everywhere, so he assumed it would be the
same, though he didn't know about riding in the truck.

The dog hopped right in.

"Good dog," Finn said, ruffling the fur on his head. He
was yellow and fuzzy and looked to be a cross between a
golden retriever and a Labrador. "You're a damn handsome
fella. I don't know why someone didn't want you, but obviously whoever it was sucked as a human."

The dog leaned over and licked his face. Finn laughed.

"How about a ride to see our friend, Jason?"

The dog just looked at him.

"You need a name, too." Finn studied him, the way his

head tilted sideways, the intelligence and life he saw in those big brown eyes.

"Murphy. That's your name."

The dog's ears perked. Finn grinned.

"You like that name, huh, Murph?"

His tail whipped back and forth.

Finn put the truck in gear. "Murphy it is. Let's go get you checked out and fixed up, then we'll buy you some food and toys."

BRENNA WAITED ALL through dinner for Finn to show up. When he didn't, she was at first irritated, then concerned.

Finn never missed dinner with the family. But she didn't want to bring it up because . . . well, why would she? It wasn't like they were dating or he was anyone special to her.

He obviously just had other plans. But when they were talking in the kitchen earlier that day, he'd told her he'd be there.

And then he hadn't shown up.

So after dinner, instead of going to her office to work, or into the library to read or to do some research, she'd gone up to her room to pace and think and stew and generally annoy herself.

Just walk down to his place and find out what's going on, dumbass.

Right. *What if he had a date or something and brought her to his place and you walk in on that?* Then she really would be a dumbass. No way was she doing that.

Instead, she went downstairs to the library and picked up a book on medieval forms of armor and sat in her favorite reading chair, paging through amazing photographs and descriptions. After thirty minutes, she couldn't remember a single page she'd read.

Dammit. She got up, put the book away and walked out the back door, feeling ridiculous the entire walk to Finn's place.

He probably wasn't even home. He was out on a date or something.

But as she rounded the corner and saw all of his lights on, she had hope. And when she saw him sitting on his front porch, she also saw a flash of yellow bouncing around near his feet.

Was that a . . . dog?

When she heard a bark, she knew for sure it was. And when it saw her, instead of running toward her, it ran to Finn.

Interesting.

"Oh, hey, Brenna," he said, getting up from his chair. He put his hand on the top of the dog's head. "Meet Murphy."

"You got a dog."

"Well, I found a dog. He was hiding out in the woods. A stray."

She arched a brow. "Are you keeping him?"

"Yeah. I already took him in and Jason gave him an exam. He's not microchipped and no one's been looking for him, so I guess he's mine now. He's healthy. For sure underfed so I got him some good food and he got his vaccinations and worming today."

The dog went over and picked up a toy and brought it to her, his tail wagging back and forth. She took the toy and the associated slobber that came with it. "And toys, too."

Finn grinned. "Well, yeah. The poor guy has been all alone. He needs love and attention. And lots of toys to cuddle up with."

Her heart did a little lurch at seeing this side of Finn. She knew he loved animals. She'd seen him with Erin's dog

Agatha and how the dog followed him around. But this was new. He'd always talked about his love for animals, how he'd had a dog when he was a kid and how much he'd missed having one around.

Finn motioned her to one of the chairs, so she took a seat and he sat on the other chair.

"You've got a dog of your own now. How old is he?"

"Jason said he's barely out of the puppy stage, not more than a year old. He minds well, so he should be easy to train. I think right now it's because I gave him food."

"And some love. From the looks of him, he hasn't had nearly enough of that. Have you, Murphy?" She wiggled the stuffed rabbit and Murphy pounced, obviously wanting her to throw it. She did, and he bounded over to grab it, then came back up on the porch and lay down with the toy.

She looked over at Finn, who was staring at the dog with such love in his eyes it made her heart ache.

"We missed you at dinner."

"Oh, yeah. Sorry. I should have called but between the vet and then the pet store for food and toys and stuff for Murph, I kind of forgot about the time."

"Did you eat anything?"

He shrugged. "I snacked."

"You're probably hungry."

"I'll make do with whatever I have here."

"I'll be right back."

He frowned. "Where are you going?"

"I have to do something. I'll be right back, Finn." She got up and walked back to the house, went into the kitchen and checked the fridge. She knew there'd be leftovers—there always were. She packed up a container and made her way back to Finn's place. He was still sitting outside, throwing a ball to Murphy, who was pretty good at fetch because he brought it right back to Finn.

"I brought you something to eat. We had pork chops, mashed potatoes and carrots for dinner." She handed him the containers.

"Damn. Now I'm hungry."

"Then you should eat."

"Would you come inside with me?"

She should leave. It would make sense for her to do that. "Sure."

"Come on, Murph." He walked in and she followed, the dog right next to her, his stuffed bunny firmly held in his mouth.

Okay, the dog was adorable. As was his owner.

"Want something to drink?" he asked.

"Wine if you've got it."

He grinned. "I've got it." He uncorked a chardonnay from the fridge and poured her a glass, set it down, then warmed up the food in the microwave.

They sat at the table while he ate and taught Murphy table manners, instructing him to go lie down. It took a few tries, but eventually he got the hint and went to the corner of the kitchen with his bunny, circled a few times and went to sleep.

"He's cute, Finn."

Finn swallowed his food and took a drink of water. "You should have seen him when I found him in the woods. He was covered in dirt and God did he smell bad. I had to clean the shower after I washed him."

She laughed. "That bad, huh?

"I went in there with him and I had to shower after I showered. Yeah, that bad."

She looked over at Murphy, all fluffy and cute as he slept. "Poor guy. How does someone just dump a dog? Same thing happened with Erin when she found Agatha. I don't get people."

He stabbed a piece of his pork chop and shook his head. "Some folks just suck."

"I hope whoever did that to Murphy ends up miserable and alone."

He lifted his glass. "I'll drink to that."

They clinked glasses.

"What breed is he?"

"Jason said probably a mix of golden retriever and Labrador, with maybe something else thrown in."

"He sure is cute. He'll be even cuter when he gets a little meat on his bones."

"Jason recommended a good dog food that should help with that."

Her lips curved. "Bring him around Louise—and my dad—and they'll make sure he gets extra scraps."

He laughed. "I don't plan to leave him here at the house. He follows me pretty well so far. He can come to work with me."

"On the days Agatha comes to work with Erin, she'll love having a playmate."

He got up and took his empty plate to the sink and washed it and the container, then put them in the dish drainer.

Brenna got up as well and brought her empty glass to the sink. Finn took it from her hands.

"Want a refill?"

"No, I should go. I have . . . things to do."

He laid the glass in the sink and took her hand. "Yeah? What things?"

"Just . . . stuff."

He was rubbing his fingers over her hand and her body instantly ignited, throbbing in all the wrong places. Or right places. Either way, being close to him like this had her wiring all messed up. She took a step back.

"Anyway, I'm glad you got a dog. Now I won't worry about you being all alone down here."

He walked her to the door. "You worry about me?"

"No."

His lips curled into a smile. "Yeah, you do. That's why you came to check on me."

"That's because you're fa—"

He pressed his fingers to her lips. "Don't call me family, Brenna. You and me, we're not like that and you know it."

She had been leaning against the door and he moved in closer. He was right. He had never been family. It had always been a convenient excuse to avoid him, because when he'd first shown up she'd been a riot of emotions around him and didn't know how to act. It had made her mad that this hot boy was coming to live with her.

She hadn't understood her feelings back then. Now she did. But all those years ago, her only recourse had been to steer clear of him.

She couldn't ignore him now, no matter how hard she tried.

"I have to go, Finn."

He stepped back and opened the door. "See you tomorrow, Brenna."

She left and walked down the path toward the house, her whole body feeling as if it were on fire.

Why, of all the men she knew, had she asked Finn to act as her fake fiancé? Especially now, when her body had come to some sort of fiery awakening whenever she was around him.

It was going to be a long four days.

CHAPTER
······
seven

Brenna never spent time staring into her closet. She went in, chose her outfit for the day and was done with it. She wasn't a clothes kind of woman. She went for comfort. Of course bracelets were another thing entirely, because she loved bangles of all kinds. Beads and silver and threaded bracelets, she could spend a long time staring at her bracelet drawer, trying to decide which ones to wear that day. But clothes? Eh. Just grab something comfortable and put it on.

Today, however, was different. Esther and the members of the wedding party and immediate families were going to be here this afternoon for the official kickoff to the four-day wedding extravaganza, and on today's agenda was the wine tasting. They'd already set up the tasting area earlier in the day, and Brenna had chosen several wines for them to sample. There'd be snacks to go along with the tasting.

Which meant as a member of the wedding party, Brenna was required to be in attendance. Along with her surprise fiancé.

She hadn't yet mustered up the courage to break the news of her fake fiancé to her parents. She didn't think they'd be participating in today's events, but she supposed she should clue them in nonetheless.

Dad was busy in the vineyard, and Mom had been in her office all day.

Since she hadn't yet figured out what to wear, she left her room and went out to the vineyard, her blood pressure instantly dropping as she strolled the walkway among the grapes.

Being in the vineyard always calmed her. She knew herself here. This was where she grew up, where she belonged. She felt a part of this land where tiny vines grew into ripe, beautiful grapes that they turned into delicious wine.

Dad was talking to Ricardo, one of the men who worked in the vineyard, so she waited until they finished their conversation. When Ricardo walked away, she approached, reaching up to study one of the cabernet vines.

"They look so good, Dad."

He looked up at her and grinned. "*Si*. This is an excellent crop. The yield this year will be *bellissima*."

"Yes, it will. Anyway, there's something I need to tell you."

He continued to walk along the grapes. "Go ahead."

"I'm in the wedding this weekend for my friend Esther, and Allison is in the wedding, too, which means Mitchell will be here."

He frowned. "Mitchell your ex?"

"*Si*."

He straightened and looked at her. "How do we feel about this?"

"Not great. Especially about Allison. We have a bad history."

"Would you like me to talk to him?"

"To Mitchell? No. But I have a plan to deal with Allison. She's smug about marrying Mitchell and I know she'll throw it in my face and give me a hard time about being single."

He made a *pfft* sound. "Who cares? You're perfect, and much better without that *bastardo*."

Her dad was right about that. "Anyway, Finn is going to pretend to be my fiancé for four days."

"Okay. What?" His frown furrowed the lines on his forehead. "What?"

"I know it sounds crazy, but it's just for four days so I don't have to deal with Allison."

"And Finn agreed to this."

"*Si.*"

"You're not really engaged to Finn."

"No."

"This is just . . . what's the word . . . playacting?"

"*Si.*"

Dad rolled his eyes and wandered off, muttering in Italian.

That went well. She didn't think Mom would be so easy.

She explained the situation to her mother while sitting in her office. Her mother stared at her for a full minute before replying.

"Are you out of your mind?"

"No. It's a well-thought-out plan."

"Brenna. It's ridiculous. First, you and Finn aren't even dating."

"He did ask me out."

That caused her mother's brows to lift. "He did? And what did you say?"

"I said yes. We haven't actually gone out on a date yet, but we will. Eventually."

Mom shook her head. "Well, I like that idea. Your other idea is stupid. You've lost your mind. Who the hell cares what Allison thinks? Or what Mitchell thinks. You should tell them both to go to hell."

"Mom. Remember, this is Esther's wedding. Allison has stepped in as last-minute matron of honor and Esther is already stressed. We don't need any ruffled feathers, so I won't be telling anyone to go to hell."

Much as that would make her happy.

Her mother blew out a breath. "You're right, of course. Keeping the bride happy is paramount. But doing it at the expense of your comfort doesn't please me at all."

She loved that her mother thought of her first, even over the family business. "I appreciate that. But it's only four days, and having Finn by my side to run interference with Allison will alleviate any stress I might have. Then it'll be over and everything can go back to normal."

"If you say so. But I wonder if you aren't complicating things."

Brenna cocked her head to the side. "In what way?"

"Between you and Finn?"

"Finn and I are just friends."

"Who are going on a date."

She waved her hand back and forth. "That's nothing." At her mother's look, she said, "Really, it's nothing. Just a friendly date."

"Uh-huh. You know I think of Finn as my family, Brenna. Like a son. But the way he's always looked at you . . ."

She let the sentence trail off.

"What? How does he look at me?"

"Just take the blinders off, Brenna. That's all I'm asking. And don't play games with Finn."

"It's not a game. He's helping me out. For just four days, Mom. Nothing more than that."

"Okay. I just don't want to see either of you get hurt."

"I promise. No one is going to get hurt. Which is why I'm doing this in the first place. To protect myself from Allison constantly haranguing me. I'll get through being in this wedding, and after, everything will go back to normal."

"If you say so." Her mom let out a slight sigh. Brenna knew very well what that sigh meant. Her mother was concerned.

She'd just have to wait and see because it was all going to turn out fine.

Just. Fine.

In the meantime, she still had to figure out what she was going to wear for the tour and the wine tasting tonight.

At least she'd gotten the worst part over with and told her parents about her fake engagement to Finn. Now everyone knew about it.

Let the charade begin.

FINN WAS GLAD he didn't have to put on a suit every day for the next four days. Not that he minded dressing up for Brenna, but wearing a suit in late August wasn't his idea of a good time.

He'd asked Brenna about what to wear tonight. She'd said jeans and a button-down shirt would be fine. He had two types of jeans in his closet—his work jeans, which tended to be relaxed and worn. And then his going-out jeans, which were crisp and new.

He took out a pair of the crisp dark jeans, added a white button-down shirt and slid into his good boots, because a man had to have a nice pair of boots, too.

"What do you think?" He looked over at Murphy, who was way more interested in the rope he was chewing than he was in Finn's attire. But he did give Finn the once-over, then resumed playing with his toy.

He went to the top drawer of his dresser and opened the ring box for a few seconds, then pulled out the ring and shoved it in his pocket.

If they were going to do this, even if it wasn't for real, they were going to do it right.

Brenna had wanted to meet up ahead of the bridal party's arrival to go over any last-minute details. As if he needed coaching. He'd known her for twelve years. He knew how her eyes sparkled when she was happy, and shot out flares of heat when she was pissed off. He knew each of her attitudes and her moods, and what brought out the best and worst in her.

He knew he was the right guy for her. It was only a matter of time before she figured it out.

Since he didn't want to leave his new pup alone, he brought Murphy over to the main house and dropped him off with Johnny, who had already fallen in love with the pup when Finn introduced them that morning. The feeling had been mutual.

"You sure you don't mind?" he asked.

"We'll watch TV. We'll take a stroll to see the horses. Go have fun. Murphy and me will be fine." Johnny waved his hand in dismissal.

He knew his dog would be in good hands, so he left. The wine tasting had been set up in the barn. He walked in to see it decorated in shades of black and gold, with touches of pink here and there. Must be the wedding colors, because there were flowers in matching colors everywhere, along with wineglasses and wine bottles on all the tables.

Fancy. Not really his thing, but he knew a lot of couples got into this.

For Finn, give him a nice whiskey and a beautiful woman by his side and he could be happy.

He heard footsteps behind him and turned around, smiling as he saw Brenna walk in. She had on a blue short-sleeved dress that seemed to float across her skin as she walked. She had heels on that made her legs look amazing, and the dress caressed her hips and made him wonder just how his hands would feel on her beautiful curves. Her hair was down, red waves falling like a flaming-hot ocean over her shoulders.

And her bracelets chimed like magical bells, the sweetest sound he'd ever heard.

He was not a poetic guy, but damn if she didn't bring it out of him.

He stepped toward her. "You look beautiful."

"Thank you. You look hot."

He looked down. "I'm okay. Not sweatin'."

She rolled her eyes. "Hot, as in you look amazing, Finn."

"Oh." He smiled. "Thanks, then."

"Okay, in case anyone asks, we've been engaged for a year. We haven't made wedding plans yet because we're not in a hurry."

"Why aren't we in a hurry?"

She frowned. "What?"

"Why wouldn't we want to get married?"

"I don't know. I'm just trying to minimize details."

"A year seems a long time. We should set a date."

"For God's sake. This isn't a real engagement."

"No, but you don't want people to ask you questions. What month do you want to get married?"

"I don't want to get married."

He couldn't blame her for that. Not after Mitchell. "If you did. What month?"

"I don't know. September."

"Good month. September of next year it is. Now we have a wedding date."

"Great. Fine."

"You'd better ask your friend to be in your wedding, too."

"Crap. I hadn't thought about that. I'll just tell her I don't have all the details set yet like the number of bridesmaids and groomsmen. Then when I tell her you and I have broken up, no harm done."

"I'm crushed about this impending breakup, Brenna."

She rolled her eyes. "Sure you are. Okay, I think that's it."

"No, there's one more thing." He dug into his pocket and pulled out his mother's claddagh. "You should wear this."

She looked down at his hand. "What's that?"

"It was my mum's."

She lifted her gaze to his. "I can't wear that, Finn."

"We can't be engaged without you wearing a ring. My ring. It would be an insult."

She swallowed. "It's not a real engagement."

"Doesn't matter. I'd be offended."

He watched as she inhaled a shaky breath, then held out her hand. "Fine."

He slipped the ring on her finger. She gave him a surprised, almost warm look. He couldn't even define it other than it punched him right in the stomach.

"Finn."

"Yeah."

"You know this is just four days. At the end of those days, this ring is going back to you."

"Yup. Got it. But for four days we're engaged, and you wear that ring. Got it?"

She nodded and looked down at her hand. He could tell she liked wearing it, kept staring at it on her hand. For now, that worked for him.

The rest they'd figure out later.

CHAPTER

. . . . . .

eight

BRENNA HAD TO recover the ability to breathe. And to think.

It was just a ring. Not symbolic in any way.

Except their engagement was fake. And this ring was anything but. It was Finn's mother's ring. What was he thinking?

She should give it back, remind him that this was a farce.

"Food should be coming soon," Erin said as she walked in with Jason. "Hey, I like that dress on you, Bren."

Brenna whipped around, stupidly hiding her left hand behind her back, as if her sister were going to somehow zero in right there. "Oh, thanks. You look pretty, too, Erin."

"Thank you."

"You're looking pretty tonight, too, Finn," Jason said with a crooked grin.

"I like that cowboy hat you're wearing, Jason," Finn shot back.

Erin rolled her eyes. "You guys are jerks."

Finn laughed. "What? We can't throw compliments like the ladies? I mean, I really do like Jason's hat."

"See?" Jason looked over at Erin. "I told you I should wear this hat."

Brenna shot a look at Erin. "They're being ridiculous."

"I know."

"Who's being ridiculous?" Honor asked as she walked in.

"The guys."

"And I missed it? Sad."

The catering truck drove up, so conversations about cowboy hats and dresses came to a halt as they directed the caterers where to unload the food, and Brenna, though not officially on duty, couldn't help but supervise the uncorking of the wine. It was, after all, her wine. At least now she could think about something else besides wearing Finn's ring. And how hot he looked in his dark jeans and button-down shirt.

Which was ridiculous, because how could a man look so incredibly sexy in jeans and a button-down shirt?

Finn could, though. Those jeans hugged his perfect ass. She could ogle his butt all night.

Get it together, woman. That ass is not yours so quit lusting over it.

Then the cars started to arrive and her stomach knotted. She couldn't help but stare at the lineup and wish she were somewhere else right now.

She was going to deal with this. Everything was going to be fine.

When she felt Finn's arm slide around her waist, she nearly leaped.

"Take a breath," he whispered, then kissed the top of her head. "We'll get through this together."

For some reason, his voice calmed her and she smiled, leaned against him and prepared to play the part.

Esther climbed out of the passenger side of the car, her arms open wide.

"Brenna! It's my wedding weekend!"

She wasn't faking her smile as she threw her arms around her friend. "I'm so excited for you."

Esther looped her arm with Brenna's. "I know you and your fam are going to make this a killer four days. And I'm sorry for the last-minute events we threw at you."

"Are you kidding? We've got it handled, don't we, Honor?"

"Of course we do. Hello, Brock."

Esther's fiancé, Brock, stepped up next to her. "Honor. Hey, Brenna."

Brenna hugged Brock. "It's so good to see you. How are the nerves?"

"Like steel."

Everyone else followed them up to the barn and Brenna did her best to ignore Mitchell and Allison. Not that Allison would allow that.

"How very country and quaint," Allison said as she lifted her nose and sniffed as if all of this were beneath her. "Hello, Brenna."

"Allison."

Allison was dressed in a chic flowery maxi dress, her straight blond hair flowing behind her in the slight breeze. She always looked like she could grace the cover of a magazine. Then again, she was a social media influencer, so she had all the right clothes, the latest makeup, the best purses, and she knew she looked damn good. Plus she was photogenic as hell, which was incredibly annoying.

Not that Brenna followed all of Allison's social media under an anonymous account or anything.

"I'll bet this brings back some memories, doesn't it, Mitchell?" Allison asked.

"Yeah."

Mitchell looked the same. They ran into each other periodically at social events, so it wasn't like Brenna hadn't seen him since her divorce. It was just that seeing him here on her family property, knowing that she was going to have to spend four days with him and with Allison so closely tied to her made her . . .

She didn't know how it made her feel.

Annoyed? Itchy? Pissed off? Angry? Frustrated?

All of those things, probably. She decided she needed the upper hand.

"Mitchell, you know Finn, of course," Brenna said.

"Yeah." Mitchell leaned over and shook Finn's hand. "How's it going?"

"Great, thanks. You?"

"Couldn't be better."

"Finn and I are engaged."

Way to just throw it out there, Brenna. She mentally kicked herself.

Mitchell just stared.

"You're engaged," Allison said.

"Yes, we are."

Allison gave Finn the once-over, and Brenna knew she wouldn't find Finn lacking. Not with his good looks, that flowing thick hair, those enigmatic steely eyes that spoke to a woman without ever saying a word. And then his body— well, a woman would have to be dead not to notice all that lean muscle, and Allison was anything but dead. Brenna just stood there and smirked.

"You're engaged to *him*," Allison said.

"Yes."

"I didn't know that."

Brenna shrugged. "No reason you would know, since we're not friends."

"Wait." Esther leaned in. "You're engaged? Since when? How did I not know this?"

Brenna smiled. "You've had a lot on your plate."

"Still, why didn't you text me or call me or, oh my God, we should have gone out to celebrate. When did this happen?"

Crap. She hadn't thought this through all the way. She should have sat down with her sisters and made a more thorough list of *what-if*s and timelines and scenarios.

"It wasn't all that long ago," Finn said, taking Brenna's hand and giving her the kind of warm look that Brenna could have sworn was genuine. "Brenna and I kept it to ourselves for a while, and then we told the family and started making wedding plans. I think she's been keeping the news under wraps."

"You're not pregnant, are you?"

"Allison, really," Esther said, wrinkling her nose.

Allison shrugged. "Someone had to ask."

"No, not pregnant. Just in love." She tilted her head back to look at Finn, who gave her a heated grin.

"Oh my gosh, Brenna. Congratulations." Esther beamed a smile. "Looks like we have a lot to celebrate tonight."

Brenna grinned. "It's a good thing we have plenty of wine, then."

"Should we get started?" Erin asked. "Welcome to the Red Moss Vineyards."

Esther and Brock's family and friends gathered in the barn. Brenna started them out with an introduction to Red Moss and how the family got started in the winemaking business, then took them on a tour. First they toured the vineyards and Brenna told them how they chose which grapes to grow every season depending on estimates of weather and yield. The vineyard tour also contained the arbor where Esther and Brock would get married on Saturday. Honor interjected wedding ceremony details along the way to give everyone a bit of flavor for how things would happen, and as they walked Erin made sure the crowd stayed together and reiterated what Honor was saying for those in the back of the group.

It was all working out perfectly. Except for Mitchell and Allison being there, but that couldn't be helped. What was nice was Finn staying right by her side, being oh so solicitous with her, holding her hand when she wasn't gesturing about grapes or fermentation or bottling, then standing back when she gave her spiel about this year's yield and explaining the harvest that was coming up.

For a fake fiancé, he was doing a bang-up job.

After the tour they headed back to the barn where the caterers had set up the appetizers and the wine tasting could begin. Brenna had hired four staff to pour wine for the tasting tonight.

They had four different wines on hand for the group to taste—a chardonnay, a zinfandel, a rosé and a sauvignon blanc. Of course she loved all the Red Moss Vineyard wines, had a hand in creating all of them. She desperately hoped the group liked them, too.

She stood back and let the staff pour and waited, expectantly, while people tried the wines.

She wasn't pregnant, had no desire to be a mother anytime soon, but every time someone tasted their wines, it was like having one of her babies judged.

"This rosé is so smooth," Esther said, going in for another sip and leaning into Brock. "We're going to have to take some bottles home with us."

"I like the zinfandel, too." Brock clinked glasses with her. "We'll make a note to buy some of that as well."

"Good call, babe."

Outwardly, Brenna remained calm, but inside she was squealing with delight.

"I find the rosé to be a bit too cloyingly sweet," Allison said, examining her glass closely as if it held poison. "Also, the zinfandel was desert dry, the chardonnay had too much oak and the sauvignon was just . . . okay, I guess."

"I want to throw a bottle at her head," Erin muttered as they listened to Allison spout off about wine as if she had any knowledge at all. Which, Brenna knew, she didn't.

Honor nodded. "I want to pour that rosé on top of her perfect stupid head before you bean her with the bottle."

Brenna's lips twitched. "I love you both."

They all sat, noshed and sipped. "Don't pay her any attention, Bren," Erin said. "As you can see, everyone's enjoying the tasting and no one at all is complaining about the wine. In fact, several are having more glasses and I hear lots of oohs and ahhs."

Honor nodded. "Because the wine is excellent, as we all know. You chose very well."

Leave it to her sisters to pump her up when she needed it. "Thanks."

"It's good wine, Brenna," Finn said. "Even I like it and I'm a whiskey man."

Brenna looked over at him. "You have a flask stashed somewhere nearby, though, don't you?"

He shook his head. "On my best behavior tonight. Not a flask in sight."

"Shocking."

"Your whiskey is very good, Finn," Erin said. "I noticed you bottled some for Jason."

Jason gave Finn a knowing grin. "It's good stuff. You should sell it."

"Red Moss Whiskey?" Erin asked.

Finn laughed. "Not a chance. I'm happy enough just playing with it."

Brenna was actually relieved to hear that Finn wasn't interested in bottling and selling his whiskey. Not that she thought he was competition to the winery. Whiskey and wine were two different alcohols entirely. But the winery and the wedding venue had a certain ambience that fit.

Whiskey, on the other hand? Did not fit with their brand.

"You don't have an appreciation for whiskey?" he asked, the warmth of his breath teasing her ear.

"I like whiskey just fine. I like wine better."

"That's because you haven't tasted excellent Irish whiskey."

She shook her head. "I've tasted all types of alcohol, including fine Irish whiskey, not like the stuff you brew in that homemade still you've got going."

He straightened. "Now you've gone and insulted me."

She laughed. "It's impossible to insult you."

"I'd like to propose a toast," Esther's father said, diverting their attention. "To Esther and Brock, two people who are more right for each other than any couple I've ever known. With the exception of my lovely Paula and myself, of course."

He raised his glass. "To my beautiful daughter and the man she loves."

Everyone raised their glasses and cheered. Esther and Brock kissed. Brenna was so happy for her friend. Esther had had a miserable boyfriend in high school who hadn't appreciated her spunky sense of humor and intelligence. Brenna and Esther had gone to college together, and Esther had gone through a string of short, failed romances until she'd finally figured out that boys were a waste of time and focused on her studies. Now she was an amazing software developer and Brock was a hot rodeo cowboy and the best thing that had ever happened to her.

"I'd like to toast my lovely friend Esther as well," Allison said.

Brenna resisted the urge to curl her lip into a snarl. But since Allison was the matron of honor, she supposed it was her right.

"We've been friends since high school, and Esther always did have the best taste. In clothes, in music and obviously in men. Brock, you are one lucky man. To Esther and Brock."

They toasted and the couple kissed again.

As toasts went, it hadn't sucked. Score one for Allison.

"One more toast," Allison said.

Brenna thought she might groan.

"As we've discovered tonight, another of our friends is recently engaged."

Oh, shit.

Allison looked right at her as she lifted her glass. "I'm so happy that you've finally found someone, Brenna. I hated to think of you wasting away out here, all alone."

"Bitch," Erin whispered to her lap.

"I swear I'm going to poison her food," Honor said.

Brenna just plastered on a smile. Finn grasped her hand, which was now sweaty.

"To Brenna and Finn."

Brenna raised her glass and shot visual daggers at her nemesis while everyone cheered.

"Kiss, kiss, kiss," everyone yelled.

This night could not get worse. The last thing she wanted to do was kiss Finn in front of everyone. She'd never kissed him before. They'd all know their engagement was fake.

Plus, you want to be alone when you kiss him.

She pushed that thought aside and looked over at Finn, who gave her an easy smile, which meant it was up to her to decide how she was going to continue this charade.

The charade she'd invented. She was going to have to go for it. In front of all of these people.

I'll get you for this, Allison.

She gave Finn a slight nod.

He slid his hand along the side of her neck. That mere touch made her nerve endings go haywire as their lips met.

And then fireworks went off as he moved his mouth over hers. Soft, gentle, exploratory, but with intent.

Damn.

It was a brief kiss, but oh, that kiss held promise. When he pulled back, she saw the barely banked heat in his eyes.

She wanted more.

CHAPTER

· · · · · ·

nine

FINN WENT TO work on Friday, same as always. Except that kiss with Brenna lingered in his mind all day.

It had been just like he'd expected. Soft, her lips sweet and plush, making him want more. Only they'd been surrounded by a crowd of people, so he could just have a taste of her. And when he'd pulled back he'd seen the surprise in her eyes, the look that told him she'd wanted him to continue.

Which he hadn't been able to do because, again, people.

All those people. And he'd have no alone time with her for the next few days, either, because of the wedding.

He'd figure it out.

Damn. He dusted his hands off and pulled up his water jug, taking several swallows, then swiped the sweat from his brow. He pulled his phone out of his back pocket to check the time.

He needed to get ready for the rehearsal thing.

He cleaned up his workspace, put his tools away in the shed and whistled for Murphy, who hadn't wandered far.

The dog had been hanging out in the shade chewing on a bone and came running with it in his mouth. They walked back toward his house, Finn breathing a sigh of relief as the trees thickened along his path. He liked living where he did, in the thick of the woods, where the trees gave him some shelter from the harsh summer sun. He liked the pond where he could fish and the soft grass surrounding his house.

It wasn't a big place, just a one-bedroom, but it was plenty for what he needed. And it gave him privacy. He was grateful that the Bellinis had offered up this parcel of land for him to build on. It had given him the independence he'd wanted.

Not that he'd been ungrateful to live in the house with them when he'd first traveled over from Ireland. Being an orphan and lonely as hell, he'd been happy to have a roof over his head and an opportunity to use his hands and earn some money. He'd learned a lot from Johnny Bellini and the other people who worked at the vineyard.

Two years after he'd moved in he'd asked if he could build his own place. Johnny and Maureen hadn't hesitated before they said yes.

It wasn't his property. He didn't own it. But for now, it was his. And since he worked there and took care of everything, they didn't ask him to pay rent, just to take care of the house and the property and to keep watch over that part of the land, which he would have anyway.

Eventually he'd buy his own land. He banked everything he earned so he could someday make that dream come true. Until then he was happy right here.

He got to the house and stripped, took a shower, then came out and put on his boxer briefs. He fixed himself a glass of ice water and fed Murphy, who, as usual, gobbled his food up in what looked like two bites, shoved his face into his water bowl, then went off to play. Finn took a seat on the sofa to relax and unwind for a few.

His phone pinged so he picked it up. It was a message from Brenna.

What are you wearing tonight?

His lips curved as he typed a reply.

Wanna know what I'm wearing right now?

He could already imagine her eye roll.

Not particularly.

He saw the three dots as she typed. Then stopped. Then started again.
Yeah, she was imagining all right.

Anyway, we're having dinner in the barn after the rehearsal. Dress appropriately.

He waited for more. There wasn't any more.
What the fuck did *appropriately* mean?
Jason was going to be there. He pulled up Jason's number and called him.
"What's up?" Jason asked.
"What are you wearing tonight?"
Jason laughed, then paused and said, "Oh, you were serious."
"Yeah. Brenna told me to dress appropriately."
"What the hell does that mean?"

He knew his friend would be on his side. "Exactly."

"I don't know. Hang on."

He waited a few minutes, and then Jason was back.

"Erin said not jeans, and a button-down shirt would be fine. I don't even know. She either lays clothes out for me or tells me what to wear. Makes my life so easy, man."

That *would* be easy. "Okay, thanks."

"See ya."

Jason clicked off and Finn laid his phone down and went into the bedroom. His closet contained jeans, jeans and shirts. But he did have a couple of pairs of dress pants, so he pulled them out.

Would have been nice for Brenna to tell him he'd need fancy clothes for these fake fiancé shindigs.

He should probably consider buying more dress pants, in case Brenna wanted to go to places that required dressing up. Not that there were a lot of places in Oklahoma that required that. You could go to one of the finest restaurants around here and if you had on your nice jeans and a good pair of boots, you were considered dressed up.

One of the reasons he liked living here.

He put on his black pants and boots and a dark blue button-down, happy that the barn was air conditioned, because he was already hot as blazes in this getup. But for Brenna, he'd do it.

He dropped Murphy off with Johnny and Maureen, happy to see that Agatha and Puddy were also there tonight, so there was a doggie free-for-all. Murphy was having fun frolicking with the other pups. Johnny and Maureen didn't seem to mind the canine chaos; in fact, Johnny sat on the floor playing with all three dogs. He knew he loved that man for a reason.

He walked toward the barn, meeting up with Jason just outside.

"They're doing the rehearsal now," Jason said, motioning toward the vineyard and the arch where a crowd was gathered. "Erin said we could go inside the barn and wait for them where it's cooler."

"Sounds good to me."

They opened the barn doors and a blast of cold air greeted them. Finn breathed a sigh of relief and went straight to the bar and ordered a beer. Jason did the same. He noticed there were a few other people in there as well, no doubt family members or friends who weren't in the wedding party. Finn and Jason went over and introduced themselves and found out they were cousins as well as some friends of both Esther and Brock who were helping out with the wedding and had been invited to attend the rehearsal dinner.

Finn didn't know anything about weddings, rehearsals or dinners and who was invited or what went into them. He'd never been married, never gave it much thought. He figured when he fell in love and was ready to get married, then it would be the right time to start thinking about all those things. Or, the woman he was going to marry would plan it all and tell him what to do. He was okay either way.

They'd taken a seat at one of the tables near the door. "Are you involved in planning your wedding to Erin?"

Jason laid his beer on the table. "She runs her ideas by me. I say yes to everything she wants."

Finn laughed. "Sounds like a good plan."

"Hey, I've got no knowledge about weddings. Erin has everything. I'm leaving it to the expert. And she's not over the top. She isn't asking for weird shit like us coming down the aisle on giraffes, or trying to have Blake Shelton sing at our wedding or anything."

"Could she do that?"

He laughed. "She probably could. She knows a lot of people. But so far all her suggestions have been reasonable. Plus, we don't have a lot of time to plan this thing. It's going to be pretty simple."

"Simple is good. That's the kind of wedding I'd like to have. Just me, my lady and my friends and family."

"Exactly. Plus good food, good drinks and a damn good time."

"Sounds like you've got a plan."

"No, Erin's got a plan. Let's talk about your lady. You and Brenna, huh?"

He let out a chuckle. "Not really. She's just using me to get back at her ex and his wife."

Jason shrugged. "Hey, Erin used me to get over Owen. Look at us now. We all have to start someplace, ya know?"

"That's true."

"You like her?"

"I do. Probably more than she likes me." Though he had no idea how Brenna really felt about him. Sometimes she looked at him like she wanted to curl her lip and growl at him. Other times she gave him the kind of look that told him she'd like to eat him for dinner—in a good way. Women were confusing.

"She liked you enough to ask you to act like her fiancé for four days."

"True."

"Might as well roll with it and see what happens."

That was his plan. Maybe with a little more work on his part, because he wanted to see a lot more of Brenna beyond four days of acting like her fiancé.

The doors opened and people spilled in, all of them laughing and talking over one another. Finn and Jason stood and moved out of the way as the other people met up with them.

Finn spotted Brenna right away. She had on a yellow dress that clung to all of her generous curves, making him want to run his hands over her body like an explorer searching for treasure. She'd curled her hair and it waved across her shoulders. She was talking to the bride-to-be and the woman said something to her that made Brenna laugh: a full-on, tilt-her-head-back, throaty laugh that made Finn's balls quiver.

She needed to do that more often, because when she laughed like that, her whole face lit up. He liked seeing her happy.

Then she turned around and caught his gaze and motioned with her head for him to come over. Jason had already left to join Erin and he didn't know what he'd been doing just standing there watching her other than enjoying the view.

He walked to where she was. "How was the rehearsal?"

"It went fine. Everyone's prepared and they all paid attention to the instructions, which for us is always a good thing."

"Great."

He saw Allison approaching, so he slipped his arm around Brenna and nuzzled her neck.

"What are you . . . oh."

He wasn't sure whether the *oh* was her realization that Allison was coming, or the fact she liked his mouth on her neck.

"I'd like to talk to you about where I can change tomorrow for the wedding. My hotel room is way too small."

In no way was Finn going to stop paying attention to

Brenna, because it was obviously annoying both Allison and Mitchell. And Brenna was squirming, which made Finn happy as hell.

"You should probably talk to Honor about that."

"Why?" Allison asked. "Can't you handle it?"

"Honor's in charge of weddings. I handle the vineyard."

Allison made an ugly face. "I'm going to go talk to Esther about this."

"Why don't you just talk to Honor? I'm sure she'll be able to accommodate you."

"No, I want you to do it."

"Why?"

"Because. I want what I want when I want it." She turned on her heel and stalked off, Mitchell following behind her.

Mitchell hadn't said a word.

"She's kind of a bitch, isn't she?" Finn asked.

"You have no idea. I need a glass of wine. And I need to warn Honor that a blowup is about to happen." She looked around. "I don't see her. I'll send her a text."

"You tell Honor. I'll get you a glass of wine."

"Thanks. A chardonnay, please." She pulled her phone out of the pocket of her dress, her fingers flying while he walked over to the bar and got himself another beer and Brenna's glass of wine. When he got back, she had just tucked her phone back into her pocket.

"Thank you. I really need this."

"How's Honor?"

"Irritated. But she's on her way to run interference."

He looked where Brenna had pointed. Allison was wildly motioning to Esther, who was wide eyed and seemed not to know what to say. Honor came over and smiled, said something to Esther, then pulled Allison away and spoke to her for a few minutes. Allison pointed at Brenna, who smiled smugly at Allison. Honor shook her head and Allison shook hers, then started gesturing and talking again.

"My sister won't take shit from her, no matter what she demands. If she were the bride she'd get anything she wanted."

"But she's not."

Brenna took another long sip of her wine. "Nope."

Then it was Honor's turn to talk. Whatever she was saying, she was calm about it. And Allison inhaled so deeply even Finn could see it from the back of the room. Finally, she seemed to calm down and nodded, then walked away. Honor made her way between the tables toward them.

"Honestly, you'd think this was *her* wedding the way she's demanding things."

"I'm sorry."

"Don't be. I handled her. I've arranged for her to have her own changing room tomorrow. Do you know she asked for you to handle all her needs personally tomorrow?"

Brenna snorted out a laugh. "No, but I'm not surprised. She'd like nothing more than to give me orders and show off to Mitchell."

"It's not going to happen. I told her you were also in the wedding and you couldn't take the time to do things for her. And if she had a problem with that, then I was going to the bride to complain about her. I also reminded her that her job as matron of honor is to take care of Esther, to make sure the bride is calm and happy on her wedding day and has everything *she* needs."

Honor was so good at her job—as both a wedding planner and a big sister. "I love you."

"Love you, too. Gotta go." She turned and dashed between tables.

"She's kind of a force in a small package, isn't she?"

"Like you wouldn't believe."

Honor stood up on the dais and turned her mic on. "Everyone, please take your seats so we can serve dinner."

Finn slipped his hand in hers. "Good. I'm hungry."

Brenna shook her head. "Of course you are."

"Hey, I put in a full day's work today. A man works up an appetite."

"I pity the woman who marries you and has to feed you."

"Yeah, but I can do my part. I can catch fish for dinner."

"Oh. Joy."

He laughed and she led him to her assigned spot at the main table where the wedding party would sit along with their guests. There were all kinds of fancy plates and a lot of silverware. Finn didn't really do fancy, but Maureen had taught him at an early age what all those freakin' forks were for, because sometimes he would be required to attend weddings and functions that required more than a fork and a knife. So he paid attention and learned what he'd needed to learn so he wouldn't embarrass the family.

He picked up Brenna's hand and pressed a kiss to it.

"What was that for?" she asked.

"Allison is watching. Also, if you frown every time I touch you, she's going to get suspicious. So relax a little."

"You're right. Sorry." She smiled at him and leaned her shoulder into his, then grasped his chin and pulled him to her, brushing her lips across his.

He knew it was just for show, but he wasn't about to object to Brenna kissing him. In fact, she lingered just a little longer, then pulled back, her gaze meeting his. She licked her lips, then picked up her glass of wine and took a sip.

"Is that better?" she asked.

"For me? Hell yeah."

Her lips curved. "I meant for Allison."

He noticed Allison had turned her back on them and was talking to someone else now.

"She seems sufficiently bored with you now."

"Excellent."

The caterers started serving the meal, which to Finn was the most important part of the night. The food was good, too. And even better, there was a lot of it. Salad and meats and even a dessert. Of course he had to sit through toasts, which was boring since he didn't know these people, but whatever. His stomach was full so he was happy.

After dinner people hung out for a little bit. Finn stayed by Brenna's side while she visited with Esther and Brock.

"I'm strangely not nervous about tomorrow at all," Esther said. "Not yet anyway. Maybe the jitters will hit me when I wake up in the morning."

Brenna took her hand. "Or maybe you're so confident about marrying this guy that there's nothing to be nervous about."

Esther looked to Brock, who smiled at her. "That could be it. Plus, I have the best venue and one of my dearest friends is helping me handle everything. I'm more excited than nervous."

"Me, too," Brock said.

Finn knew that was the right answer. And Brock didn't look nervous at all, either. He seemed relaxed. He did have a full glass of wine in his hand. That probably helped.

"You know we'll have everything under control tomorrow," Brenna said. "You have nothing to worry about."

"You'll be at the hotel tomorrow for hair and makeup and everything?" Esther asked.

Brenna nodded. "I'll be there for sure. And Honor is coordinating with all the bridesmaids. Trust me, she'll make sure everyone shows up."

Esther inhaled and let it out. "Then I really don't have anything to stress about. Isn't that great, Brock?"

"It is, babe. The only sad thing is we have to be apart tonight."

She patted his shoulder. "Tradition. After tomorrow we'll never be apart again."

"Lookin' forward to that part."

The party started to break up about ten, and everyone left. They had a crew to clean up the barn and break everything down.

"People will be here tomorrow to set up for the reception, so it begins all over again."

Finn shook his head as he walked Brenna over to the house. He went inside and grabbed Murphy and stood on the porch with his dog and Brenna. "I don't know how you do this weekend after weekend."

She shrugged. "Part of the job."

"But wouldn't it be nice to have a weekend off every now and then?"

"Maybe. I don't know. I take days off during the week."

"What if you want to get away?"

She stood on the step of the front porch and looked at him. "Like where?"

"I don't know. Don't you want to go somewhere? Have an adventure?"

"I guess I hadn't thought much about it."

"Well, think about it. Maybe I might want to take you somewhere. After we have our date."

She frowned again. "What date?"

"The date you promised me we'd have. You know you haven't forgotten. Good night, Brenna."

He walked away before she could start arguing her way out of having that date.

Because she'd said yes. And he was going to hold her to it.

CHAPTER

· · · · · ·

ten

Wedding days, from Brenna's perspective, were always mass chaos, no matter how well prepared everyone was. Having to actually be in a wedding was a nightmare.

She'd gotten up early so she could have her coffee in peace and quiet in the library, read a few chapters of her book and just be. She knew what today was going to bring, so she needed to center herself before the bedlam began.

She had breakfast with the family, then went upstairs to take a shower. Her hair would need to be dry before she went over to the hotel, so she dried her hair but didn't put any product in it or style it since Esther had arranged to have a stylist come in and do the bridal party's hair. Which meant this out-of-control nest on top of her head was a wild mess. She had natural curl to her hair and had spent years learning how to tame it with a blow dryer and flat iron. She wished she could have just done her own hair, but whatever. The bride got what the bride wanted. And right now the bride wanted Brenna to have bird's-nest hair.

She threw on capris and a button-down shirt and slipped

into her canvas tennis shoes, then went outside and across the vineyard to check and make sure the wine order for tonight had already been pulled. Even though she already knew exactly which wines had been ordered and how many cases, she'd double-checked her spreadsheet this morning. It never hurt to be certain no mistakes would be made, especially for this wedding.

She entered the warehouse where the wines were stored, happy to see that the cases were already pulled and sitting separate for the crew to take out to the reception area later that day. She counted the cases, and of course they were correct. Her team knew their jobs. She breathed a sigh of relief and headed out, running straight into Finn.

"What are you doing out here?" she asked.

"Walking my dog. You look cute."

She smoothed her hands over her wildly uncontrollable hair. "I do not. My hair's a mess but I had to leave it this way because I'm getting it done later at the hotel. You probably don't even care, so why am I telling you this?"

He laughed. "I don't know. But your hair's not a mess. You're way too hard on yourself, Brenna. You know what you look like to me?"

She cocked her head to the side. "What?"

He wrapped his arm around her and brought his face closer to hers. "The most beautiful woman I've ever laid eyes on. Your hair is like curly pillows of amazing red. Without makeup on, I can see a sprinkle of freckles across your nose and cheeks. You look like a fairy. A sexy, desirable, seductive fairy who's got me held in her spell. You're magic, Brenna."

She momentarily lost the ability to breathe. Or to speak. What guy talked like that, wound sweet, poetic words about her appearance while holding her in his arms?

No man she'd ever known, that's for sure.

"You have a way with words, Finn Nolan."

"Do I? I just say what's on my mind. Want to hear what else is on my mind?"

She did. She most definitely did. She laid her palms on his chest, momentarily enjoying the rock-hard feel of him. But then Murphy barked and dashed toward something across the vineyard.

"Sorry, gotta go fetch my dog. We'll finish this later."

She sighed as she watched him run after Murphy and disappear around the side of one of the buildings.

She'd never been more disappointed in her life. Though it was probably for the best since they were outside where anyone could walk up on them.

And then she reminded herself that they were fake engaged, not even a real couple.

Time to face reality, Brenna. This fake romance isn't going anywhere.

And no amount of poetic words was going to change that.

She straightened her shoulders and went back to the house. It was time to pack up her things and head over to the hotel.

She checked in with Honor first to make sure she didn't need any help. As usual, Honor had everything under control.

"I've already talked to the caterers and the cake decorator and the deejay this morning," Honor said, walking so fast Brenna was out of breath by the time they made their way to the arbor, which was in the process of being decorated with beautiful flowers and vines. "The crew is here and already setting up the barn for the reception. Everything's under control. Erin and I have this, so go enjoy being a bridesmaid."

Enjoy? No, she most definitely was not going to enjoy being a bridesmaid. She wanted to be here working this wedding rather than being *in* this wedding. Having to spend the entire day with Allison was going to be like an eternity in fiery hell. But sure, she could totally handle this.

She went to her room, packed up her bag and drove over to the hotel. Esther had a suite so she took the elevator to the top floor and knocked on the door. She could already hear loud talking, likely Allison's voice because she always liked being the center of attention.

Andrea, one of the bridesmaids, answered the door. "Hey, Brenna."

"Hi, Andi. How's it going in here?"

"Utter madness. But there's champagne and snacks," she said as Brenna followed behind her.

"Brenna's here!" Esther ran over to give her a huge hug. "It's my wedding day."

"I know, honey. I'm beyond excited for you." Which she was. She was thrilled for Esther. She would have been even more thrilled if Allison weren't part of the day.

"Late as always, aren't you, Brenna?"

Speaking of Allison . . .

But Esther ignored her and looped her arm in Brenna's. "We have mimosas and pastries and we're spilling tea like you would not believe while we wait for hair and makeup to show up. And Brock's mom is giving us all the dirt about his childhood antics. Though I've heard most of them before."

Brenna grabbed a mimosa and a Danish and sat and listened to Greta talk about Brock's antics as a child. Then, since turnabout was fair play, Esther's mom, Paula, told some embarrassing stories about her. They were all innocent stories, but also hilarious.

While they all sat around waiting, Brenna got a chance

to chat with the other bridesmaids. Andrea had gone to college with Esther and Brenna, and Brenna already knew Marie from high school. Sabra worked with Esther, and Hilary was Esther's cousin.

They were all delightful and friendly. Except for Allison, of course, but Brenna planned to do her best to avoid her nemesis.

Finally, hair and makeup arrived so all the bridesmaids split up. Unfortunately, Brenna got stuck in makeup sitting right next to Allison, but she had to accept the card she was dealt because it was Esther's day. Hopefully Allison would be too busy admiring herself in the mirror to concern herself with Brenna. She listened while Allison complained about the foundation spray, then bickered about everything from the way the makeup artist did brows to the colors of eye shadow.

Brenna thought the makeup artist must have the patience of a saint to put up with her. She should draw a unibrow on her just for vengeance.

She couldn't imagine what it must be like to have to live with her.

"Brenna, I see you've been busy," Allison said, obviously running out of things to complain to the makeup artist about. "Working as a flunky for your dad. Finding such a hot guy to agree to marry you. How did you manage that?"

She took in a calming breath and let it out.

"I run the vineyard and the winery alongside my father. If you're interested in knowing more about how grapes are grown and harvested or how wine is made, I'd be happy to inform you. As far as Finn, I've known him since we were teens. We fell in love naturally. This time I have the right man."

Brenna was an excellent liar. She should probably be concerned about that.

Allison sniffed and held her head back as the woman patted powder on her face. "Whatever. It's not like you could hold on to Mitchell. He told me what happened between you two."

She shouldn't engage with Allison, who was only trying to bait her. But as tension coiled around her like an angry snake, she couldn't help herself.

"I'm sure he told you his side."

"Well, why don't you tell me yours."

She couldn't look over at Allison because her makeup artist was currently applying lashes. "What's the point, Allison? You're not really interested in my take on anything. Mitchell and I split because we wanted different things. Are you happy with him?"

"Of course I am. We're both doing amazing at our jobs, we have a house we love and we're thinking of having a baby soon."

"I'm happy for you. And for him."

Allison's sniff was her only response. Brenna would have rolled her eyes but then her lashes would end up on her eyebrows, so she did a mental eye roll instead.

It got quiet then, which to Brenna was a slice of utter heaven. Once makeup was finished, Brenna had to wait for someone to free up to do her hair, so she wandered. Allison was off in a corner on her phone so Brenna went over to see how Esther was doing. She'd already had her makeup done and was currently chatting with her mom and Greta while the stylist did her hair.

"Can I get you anything, Esther?" Brenna asked.

"Oh, you're so sweet. I'd love a glass of ice water. I went

a little hard on the mimosas and I don't want to face-plant walking down the aisle."

Brenna laughed. "Ice water coming right up."

She went over to the bar and fixed a large glass of ice water, wrapped a napkin around it so it wouldn't drip, then brought it back over to Esther.

"Thank you. What would I do without you?"

"I have no idea."

Esther grinned and squeezed her hand.

"How about some fruit and cheese? We need to keep your blood sugar level today."

"Brenna's right, honey," Paula said. "Lots of small snacks today."

"And then tonight, I get to eat lobster and filet."

"That's right," Brenna said. "I'll be right back with a plate."

She went over to the table where food had been laid out and selected some of the fruits and cheeses.

"Stuffing your face, I see," Allison said.

So it was going to be like this.

"Actually, it's for Esther. She needs to stay hydrated— not with alcohol—and well fed today with nutritious food. And maybe if you'd checked on her instead of spending all your time on your phone, you'd have taken care of the bride, since you are her matron of honor."

Brenna left Allison standing there with her mouth open and about to say something that Brenna didn't care to hear.

She delivered the plate to Esther, then was called to have her hair done, so she slid into the chair, grateful that she'd be there by herself and wouldn't have to deal with her nemesis.

She'd had enough of her. But she did notice that Allison

hovered by Esther, which was a good thing. Maybe now she'd actually do her job as matron of honor. Though Brenna didn't mind looking after the bride-to-be. Not only was Esther her friend, but Brenna and her sisters always pitched in on wedding days to help Honor, so taking care of the bride was a natural thing to Brenna.

The stylist curled her hair, then swept it into an updo. It wasn't Brenna's normal style by any means, but she had to admit it looked decent. The stylist left a curl dangling along the side of her face, and with the makeup, which hadn't been overdone like she'd feared, she looked . . . pretty damned good, she had to admit.

It was getting late so once everyone's hair was finished, they had to get dressed and make their way over to the vineyard. It would take a while to get everyone into their dresses. Everyone except the bride, who was going to get dressed at the vineyard. And Allison, of course, who had to be made to feel as special as Esther for some ridiculous reason.

Once Esther's mom was dressed, she called Esther's dad, Ron, who showed up at the suite to drive Esther and Paula to the vineyard. Along with Allison, of course. The rest of the bridesmaids would be over there later.

Brenna made sure to get dressed so she could drive over and help out in any way she could.

"Oh, Brenna," Esther said. "Would you mind hanging out here to make sure everyone is dressed and doesn't forget jewelry or anything? I was counting on Allison to do that, but since she wanted to dress at the vineyard . . ."

Brenna knew exactly what Esther wasn't saying. That her matron of honor had let her down. She nodded right away. "Of course. I'll make sure it all gets taken care of."

Because Allison couldn't do her job right, Brenna would pitch in.

Esther squeezed her hand. "Thank you so much. One thing I don't have to worry about because I know you have it."

After they left, she checked in on each of the bridesmaids as they got dressed, noting earrings and bracelets and boots—because this was a cowboy wedding, after all. Once everyone was ready, Brenna double-checked the room to make sure nothing was left behind.

They'd get their bouquets at the vineyard so she didn't have to worry about that. When she got the call that the limo was ready, she herded them all downstairs and they all piled into the car.

"What's up with Allison, thinking she's so special?" Andrea asked.

"Yeah." Marie smoothed her hands over her dress. "I don't get it. Shouldn't she be with us? I mean Esther has her mom and her mother-in-law and the bridal venue people."

"I heard she made a fuss about having her own changing room at the venue," Andi said.

"Nuh-uh," Sabra said. "Why?"

Andi shrugged. "No idea. But you know Allison."

"I definitely know Allison," Marie said. "And I believe it."

"What do you know, Brenna?" Andi asked.

All sets of eyes focused on her. No way was Brenna adding to this conversation. "I don't have any idea other than she left with Esther."

"That's too bad," Hilary said. "We need some good gossip to chew on."

They all laughed, and, fortunately, that was the end of

the Allison conversation and they moved on to the topic of everyone's cute cowgirl boots. The last thing Brenna wanted was to be accused of talking shit about her nemesis.

If the other bridesmaids saw Allison as a pain in the ass, that was fine with Brenna, but they could all form their own conclusions about her without Brenna's help.

Honor met the car at the driveway and Erin escorted the women to the waiting area, where there'd be snacks and refreshments.

"How did it go?" Honor asked as Brenna trailed behind everyone.

"About like I expected."

Honor rolled her eyes. "She's already put up a fuss about the room not being big enough for her, and wants to know why she doesn't have her own personal attendant. Do you think we could just lock her in there and tell Esther she fell down a well or something?"

"As ideal as that sounds, eventually we'd have to let her out."

Honor shot her a look. "Would we, though?"

Brenna snorted out a laugh. "Honor. You're ruthless."

"I can be, when the situation calls for it. Besides, she's on my last nerve."

Which was saying something because Honor was always the picture of calm. It took a lot to get on Honor's bad side. Dealing with overwrought brides and bridesmaids was her sister's specialty. Nothing got to her. But this was Allison. Even back in high school when they were still friends, Allison had been a handful, always having one drama after another. It was either a fight with her parents or her older sister or a boy she was dating, or she was mad at one of the friends in their group. If there wasn't drama in Allison's life, it wasn't a day ending in Y.

Clearly not much had changed.

Some women grew up and left those dramatic days behind them.

And some would continue it all their lives like they needed air to breathe.

She went into the room where the bridesmaids were, deciding she'd better eat something, because it would be a while before they ate dinner. The last thing she wanted was to feel faint tonight. She grabbed a plate and added some hummus and veggies along with a couple slices of cheese and some crackers, and poured herself a glass of juice. That would be enough. She didn't want to eat anything more filling because her dress was tight enough.

The door opened and Allison stood in the doorway as if she expected the entire group to stand in awe of her. When no one even spoke to her, Brenna noticed the disappointment shadowing her face.

Really, did she think it was *her* special day? Somewhere along the way Allison lost sight of the fact that she wasn't the bride. She almost felt bad for her.

Almost.

"Close the door, Allison," Marie said. "You're letting the hot air in."

Allison huffed out a breath and shut the door behind her.

And now Brenna really felt trapped, because the ceremony would start soon, and they would all have to stay in here until then.

"You should all be standing," Allison said. "Your dresses are going to wrinkle and you don't want to look terrible when you walk down the aisle, or for pictures. Esther will be disappointed."

Brenna knew for a fact that the fabric on these dresses wasn't going to wrinkle. And she wasn't going to get up.

She was comfortable in this nice cushy chair and her boots were off.

"Did you all remember your necklaces, bracelets and earrings?"

"I took care of that," Brenna said. "We all have everything we need."

Allison looked around, then zeroed in on Brenna. "I don't see the bouquets. Where are the bouquets?"

"They'll be at the entrance to the barn and handed out right before the ceremony, so they stay fresh."

"What about makeup? You know we're all going to need lipstick touch-ups."

Oh, she was definitely in a mood.

"The makeup artists are in with Esther right now. Before the ceremony starts they'll do a final once-over on all of us to make sure we look our best. The photographer will lead us into the bride's room to take photos with the bride as well. Is there anything else?"

Allison's lips clamped tightly together, and she went over to the refreshment center and poured herself a glass of water.

Several of the bridesmaids sent Brenna looks of gratitude as well as smiles.

Brenna leaned back in the chair and decided that maybe this day wouldn't be so bad after all.

CHAPTER
· · · · · ·
eleven

FINN HAD BOUGHT a damn suit. He never thought he'd need one, until he realized he was going to have to be Brenna's partner in crime. She was going to be all fancied up for this wedding, and him wearing a shirt and pants wasn't gonna cut it. He called Jason since he didn't have the first clue about dressing up and asked for his help. Jason went to the suit store with him and helped him pick something out that didn't make him look like a lame jackass.

He'd discovered that nice suits cost a lot of money, but Jason told him that he could wear it to several functions and it would last him several years.

He'd taken Jason's word for that, and it was a nice suit. A dark navy and he even bought a new shirt and a colorful tie. He didn't buy shoes, because he had dress boots that could be worn with anything. Even Jason had concurred with that. He could only hope he'd measure up when he stood next to the beautiful Brenna.

At least the heat had broken—a little. It was hovering in the low eighties, which for late August was like a cold snap.

Maybe Finn wouldn't sweat through his shirt and the jacket of his suit.

He'd dropped Murphy off at the house earlier, not wanting to get any dog hair on the suit. He showered and dressed and made sure he was at the vineyard early, not that he had any duties other than being Brenna's date for the event.

He also didn't know anyone there since none of his friends were attending the event. Not that that would stop him from mingling with the crowd. Some of the people were taking seats and some just standing around. He made his way to the folks hanging out at the back and introduced himself. A couple of them were there with the other bridesmaids. Brenna's ex, Mitchell, happened to be hanging with that group as well. Finn didn't mind that at all.

He met William, Marie's boyfriend; Dave, Sabra's husband; and Sue, Andrea's girlfriend. Mitchell just gave him silent looks while he learned that William was an insurance agent, Sue was a personal trainer and Dave owned a construction equipment company. Johan, Hilary's date, was a chef. Finn told them what he did there at the vineyard.

"Did you build any of the things round here?" Dave asked.

"I had a hand in a lot of it." He pointed out a few of the buildings he'd erected over the years.

"What an accomplishment," Sue said. "I love working outdoors. I do a lot of my classes outside. Nothing like building up a good sweat to make you feel like you accomplished something. Except maybe in August."

"August sucks," Dave said.

Finn nodded. "I'll drink to that."

"I grow a lot of the vegetables for my restaurant outside," Johan said. "Harvest in the late summers is awful."

"I've never been so happy to work inside an air-conditioned office," William said.

They all laughed.

"What about you, Mitchell?" Dave asked. "What do you do?"

"I'm a lawyer."

He didn't offer up any additional conversation, so that was the end of that.

Not really Mr. Personality, that Mitchell. Then again, Finn already knew that from the years he'd been married to Brenna. Whenever they'd come over for dinner with the family, he'd been quiet—or away from the table on his phone, something that had always irritated the hell out of Brenna. During the years Mitch and Brenna had been together, he had never been one to interact with Brenna's family, which was really saying something since the Bellinis were people you couldn't help but engage with. They were warm, friendly and hospitable. Mitch, on the other hand, was cold and standoffish and always seemed to hold himself above everyone else.

Finn never could figure out what Brenna had seen in him. But he could definitely see why Mitch and Allison were a perfect match.

Erin came up to them. "We're about to get started, so if you could all take your seats?"

The group ended up finding seats toward the middle. Esther and Brock had quite the group of family and friends, because the vineyard was filled.

Awesome.

Music started playing, the groomsmen took their positions next to Brock and the bridesmaids began walking down the aisle. Finn had caught a chair on the end, so he had a prime view when Brenna appeared.

She wore a violet dress with skinny straps on her shoulders, her hair all wildly curled and pulled up, revealing her incredibly beautiful neck. The dress hit just above her knees, showing off her amazing legs. And her cowgirl boots were the perfect touch. She looked dressed to kill. He didn't even notice the other bridesmaids because he was focused on Brenna, the most beautiful woman there. As she passed by him, their eyes locked and her lips curved into a hint of a smile.

Damn.

They all stood when the bride walked down with her dad. She wore a short dress, too, with sparkly white boots and the biggest smile. She looked really pretty and happy as she made her way to Brock.

The ceremony was short and emotional as the bride and groom said their vows. It was sweet. They kissed and everyone applauded. Then the bridesmaids and groomsmen led them down the aisle and everyone filed out while Honor directed the crowd toward the barn.

Finn wanted to see Brenna, but she'd already told him that she would have to linger behind for pictures, so he made his way to the barn and grabbed a beer.

"You're engaged to my wife, huh?"

He turned to Mitch. "Not your wife anymore."

"You always had a thing for her. Even when I was married to her."

He wasn't even going to dignify that with an answer, or say what he really wanted to say about men who didn't appreciate their women when they had them, so he took a long swallow of his beer and ignored Mitch.

Mitch ordered a scotch and water and the two of them moved away from the bar so other people could step in.

"The two of you have nothing in common."

Okay, maybe Finn wouldn't stay silent. "Oh, and you did?"

Mitch shrugged. "More than you do."

"We're doing great, my friend. Maybe you should focus more on your current wife and pay less attention to my relationship with my fiancée."

"Something seems off about the two of you. I just don't see her with you."

Finn took a deep breath. "Afraid she might realize that she's finally found what she was missing all those years? Because I'm telling ya, mate, she has. And it's a step up for her."

He could see Mitch's face turn a mottled red. If he had to, Finn would defuse a fight. Which would be too bad because this asshole deserved a good punch in the face.

"There you are. Did you see how I looked up there?"

Saved by Allison, because immediately, Mitch plastered on a benevolent smile and turned his focus on her. "I did. You were stunning."

"Thank you. It's amazing how your taste has improved dramatically since . . . well, since you met me." She shot Finn a scathing look.

Finn rolled his eyes, finished off his beer and wandered back to the bar, not needing to hear anything else from the two of them. He grabbed another beer and stepped outside the doors.

He paced back and forth between the barn and the vineyard for a while, drinking his beer and muttering Irish curses, wishing Mitch overly hairy, painful hemorrhoids and swollen balls that would make it uncomfortable to sit for the rest of his life.

He smiled at that thought.

He went back inside and found the table where his new friends were sitting. Fortunately Mitch wasn't there.

The deejay announced the wedding party and everyone

stood and clapped when they entered. Brenna had a smile on her face as she walked in, and then they gathered around the dance floor as the bride and groom had their first dance, joined shortly by the bridal party. After that, they took their seats at the main table and toasts were given.

Finn was hungry, so he was grateful once all the talking was done and food was served. He knew Brenna had duties to perform and she couldn't sit with him, but he had fine company at his table and they found a lot to talk about.

Mitchell had found other people to sit with, which worked great for Finn because his group was having a blast. They drank, they ate fantastic food, they shared stories about their lives and Finn didn't have to put up with Mitch's grouchy face.

All in all, a damn fine dinner. After the plates were cleared the bridal party got up and left the table. The bride and groom hit the dance floor, and the bridesmaids headed their way.

Finn stood and turned as Brenna arrived.

"Did you have a good dinner?" she asked.

"Food was amazing. Company was even better."

She laid her hand on his arm. "I'm so glad. I'm sorry I had to leave you alone for so long."

He looped an arm around her waist. Not because Mitchell was around, but because he'd missed her and he wanted to be close to her. "Don't be. These are great people. We've all had a good time."

"I swear you can make friends no matter where you are."

He cocked his head. "Does that surprise you?"

"I guess it does."

"Probably because you were previously married to Mr. Grumpy Face over there, who decided not to share a meal with us."

Her gaze tracked where he was staring. Mitch was currently introducing Allison to some people Finn didn't know.

"Other lawyers."

"You know them?"

"I know of them. I went to enough legal functions when I was married to Mitchell that I recognize the faces."

Finn looked over the group, all talking and nodding with their noses in the air. He knew a few lawyers, but the ones he knew were all easygoing, fun people. Clearly not the case with that group, though.

"Bunch of tightasses, just like your ex."

She sputtered out a laugh. "You summed him up in a single word."

"We had a few words earlier, actually."

"You did?" She tilted her head back and gave him a curious look. "About what?"

"You. He thinks I'm beneath you."

Flames of ire fired up in her eyes. "He's full of shit. He doesn't even know you. Or me, for that matter. That was half the problem in our marriage. I'd like to go over there and give him a rundown of all the ways he doesn't know me. In fact . . ."

She'd started to make a turn but he held on to her arm. "Okay, feisty, rein it in. I wanted to shove my fist in his face, too. I took a walk outside instead."

"You did? You wanted to hit him?"

"Of course I did. He's an asshole. Who wouldn't want to hit him?" He swept his hand down her arm. "Besides, how could any man not want to know everything about you?"

He felt the tension leave her body.

"Let's go dance," she said, taking hold of his hand.

"Sure."

They joined the throng of dancers bouncing around on

the dance floor. Finn had already discarded his suit coat, and the air conditioning was cranked to a nice cool level, so it wasn't too bad while he hopped around and tried to keep up with Brenna. But he was happy when a slow song came on and he pulled her into his arms, her body against his.

"Now this is more like it," he said.

"You just like having your hands on me."

He swept his fingers along her back. "No lie."

Her lips curved. "I will admit that it feels good when you touch me."

"I could do a lot more touching."

When her eyes widened, he added, "With your permission, of course. And in private."

"We haven't even had a date yet."

"We will. Besides . . ." He rubbed his fingers over the ring she wore on her left hand. "We're engaged, remember?"

"Only for one more day."

"Which means, what? That I don't get to touch you like this after tomorrow? Or lean in and kiss you on the neck like this?"

He pressed his lips to the side of her neck, felt her whole body shudder as he wrapped his arms around her and drew her closer while they swayed to the slow strains of a love song.

He thought she'd object, pull back, but she held tight to him, and he breathed in her tangy lemon scent, wishing he could run his tongue over her neck, her collarbone and all the other sweet parts of her body. He wanted to explore her, to learn everything there was to know about her body, her mind, her thoughts and what she wanted and needed.

But for now, the way they fit together was damned perfect.

He could do this all night.

. . . . . .

BRENNA SANK INTO the lull of the music, the feel of Finn's delightfully hard body pressed against hers. He smelled crisp and clean and just a little bit like something she wanted to take a bite out of, so maybe something a little dangerous, too.

When had she ever done anything dangerous in her life? Uh, never.

Mitchell had been the safe choice, the expected choice. She'd known within six months of marrying him that she'd made an epic mistake, but she'd hung on for another six months until she couldn't take his constant criticisms and never-ending phone calls and disappearances in the name of work anymore. She'd tried so hard to engage him in their relationship, in the two of them, until she'd realized that she'd been the only one putting in the work.

But that was in the past, and it was done and over with.

Now— tonight   she was being held by a seriously hot man who smelled good and felt even better and she wanted so many things she couldn't even put words to them. She wanted him to keep smoothing his hand down her back and pressing his hard thighs against her, and humming to the music with his amazingly good voice.

Sure, it was all a fantasy, but wrapping herself up in a fantasy for a little while wouldn't hurt anything, would it?

"Hey," Finn whispered.

She looked up, mesmerized by his beautiful face with all its chiseled angles. He had an amazing jaw, and what woman could resist a square jaw like that? Or his angular nose? Or those eyes that always seemed to hypnotize her.

"Mmm-hmm."

"Song's over."

She blinked and stepped back. "Oh. Of course it is. I should go do . . . something."

He took her hand. "Do you have something specific to do?"

She looked around. Esther and Brock were visiting tables, and all the other bridesmaids had disappeared.

"Not right now."

He took her hand. "We'll grab something to drink and sit at my table. You can meet all the fun people I've been hanging out with."

He seemed excited about her meeting his new friends, so she smiled and nodded. "That sounds fun."

She got a glass of wine and he ordered a beer, and then they went to the table. Everyone was laughing and having fun. She noticed Mitchell two tables away, sitting with Allison. There was a lot of nodding and talking, but no laughing or smiling.

After thirty minutes at Finn's table, she was laughing, too. Finn was right—this was a fun group of people. Sue had a bawdy sense of humor, and she'd already bonded with her girlfriend, Andi, over their shared love of books and reading.

And the entire group raved about the wines, so how could she not love everyone at the table?

Finn and Johan had discovered a mutual passion for whiskey, so apparently they were now lifelong friends.

The group was animated and boisterous. Several of the groomsmen and their wives and dates made their way over, and soon they had their own party going.

"Hey," Esther said when she came by. "Am I missing the real party?"

Brenna stood and hugged her. "Honey, you and Brock *are* the party tonight."

Esther grinned. "That's true. But after Brock and I say hello to a few more of our relatives, we're joining this shindig. It looks like you're all having way too much fun."

True to her word, Esther and Brock ended up at their table. And then the entire group went out on the dance floor together and partied their asses off song after song. Brenna was grateful that Finn not only had joined in but had been instrumental in giving her one of the best nights of her life. A night, in fact, that she had been dreading. Out of all the people here, Finn had found the fun group and dragged her right into the middle of them. And even better, whenever Brenna glanced her way, Allison looked pissed because she was stuck at a table with a bunch of people who seemingly had zero interest in dancing. Or laughing. Or having fun.

It couldn't have gone better.

The reception ended at midnight, though several people had left before then. Brenna and her sisters helped Esther's and Brock's parents load gifts into the cars, and then everyone who was left lined the driveway and blew bubbles at the newlyweds as they made their way to their car and drove off. After that the rest of the reception guests climbed into their vehicles and departed.

Brenna breathed in and exhaled.

"How did it go?" Erin asked.

"Better than expected, actually, thanks to Finn."

Finn looked over at her. "To me? What did I do?"

She smiled at him, feeling warm and satisfied for reasons she couldn't explain. "Everything right."

His lips curved.

"Okay, then. Only one more day of this and we're done," Honor said. "Just a champagne brunch, and then it's over."

Oh, right. There was still brunch to get through tomorrow morning. Today had been the longest event, and she'd survived it, thanks to Finn. She leaned against him and he instantly slipped his arm around her waist.

"It's almost over," Erin said. "We'll handle it."

"Of course we will."

"I'll make sure everything's being cleaned up," Honor said.

Erin nodded. "I'll go with you."

"I can help," Brenna said.

"No." Honor held up her hand. "You were in the wedding. You've done enough. We've got this."

"Are you sure?"

"Absolutely," Erin said. "Go get some rest."

She had to admit she was kind of wiped out. "Thanks, both of you. Good night."

"I'll walk you to the house," Finn said.

She might have objected, since the house was only a short walk from the wedding venue parking lot. But he had his arm around her and it felt good. And maybe she wasn't ready for this feeling to end. So they strolled together, neither one of them in a hurry to get to her front porch.

"I need to get Murph," he said as they walked up the steps to the door.

"Okay."

He opened the door and whispered softly, and the dog came running.

"Hey, buddy. Did you have a good time tonight?"

She watched as he ruffled the dog's fur, then let him run off into the dark to do his business.

He turned to her. "Did I tell you how beautiful you looked tonight?"

There it was again, that feeling of being blanketed by warmth. Not the oppressive-August-heat kind of warmth, but a fuzzy, low heat that spread within her, as if the stars in the clear sky tonight had sailed right through her and blasted her with their light.

She laid her head on his shoulder. "Thank you. Oh, and before I forget to tell you, you looked amazing in your suit."

"Thanks."

He tipped her chin with his fingers and kissed her, a soft, sweet kiss. He started to pull back but she wound her hand around his neck and rose up, pressing her lips to his, diving in for more.

He obliged, wrapping both arms around her, giving her the kind of kiss that made the hair on the nape of her neck stand up. His tongue slipped between her lips and her heart did a wild dance of *Oh, hell yes, we want this!* and she wished they weren't right outside the door of her parents' house, because she really wanted to be alone with him to explore, to unbutton his shirt and slide her hands all over his naked skin.

Finn was the one to break the kiss, his breaths coming out hard. His eyes were dark with desire, which only made their situation more frustrating, because she wanted to explore that desire with him—right now.

But she knew right now wasn't the right time—and so did he. Murphy had come back and was staring at both of them. He had to get his dog home. And she also knew—

What? What did she know? That this fantasy had to end? She sighed.

"See you tomorrow?" he asked.

She gave a quick nod and turned the knob and went inside the house. She closed the door and leaned against it.

It had been a good night. A really good night that had ended in one outstanding kiss. But why did it have to end? If she hurried, she could meet him on the way to his house.

She reached behind her and put her hand on the door-knob, seconds away from opening it.

But something stopped her.

What was it? Why couldn't she just go for it, have some fun with Finn and then move on with her life? Why was she always so racked with indecision?

"Dammit," she whispered, then let go of the doorknob and walked up the stairs to her room.

CHAPTER
······
twelve

When Finn first saw it, the barn looked nothing like it had the night before. Instead of all the fancy decorations and lots of tables and a deejay platform, today there were only two long wood tables decorated with glass vases filled with wildflowers, along with champagne glasses and plates, giving the room a more rustic look.

When the hell did people sleep around here? He knew they had caterers to deal with the food, but Brenna, Erin and Honor were buzzing around like a swarm of bees wearing dresses. It made his head spin. He walked up the one wide wood step, into the barn.

"What can I do?" he asked as he reached Brenna.

"The table needs straightening," Brenna said, ignoring him. "It's crooked."

"It's not crooked," Honor said. "It's perfectly straight."

"It could go a foot or so to the left." Erin eyed the table.

"No, it needs to go to the right," Brenna argued.

"I think you're both wrong." Honor glared at them. "The table is fine and it's staying where it is."

He thought the table looked fine, but he wasn't about to say anything. Having been around the three sisters for more than ten years, he knew better than to get in the middle of one of their arguments. Nobody won, least of all him. He'd learned that the first year he was here.

"What's the fuss?"

Maureen had come out and stood there, hands on her hips, giving that look to all three women.

"The table is crooked," Brenna said. "Obviously it needs to move to the right by a foot."

"The table is fine." Honor sent a deliberate look to Maureen.

Erin shook her head. "It needs to go to the left to match the other table."

Maureen sighed, then turned a critical eye to the table, walking back and forth and even bent over to give both tables a thorough examination. When she straightened, she said, "The table stays where it is. There's nothing wrong with it."

Finn waited for the angry explosion, but Brenna just blew out a breath and walked away. Erin shrugged. Honor, knowing that whooping in victory would only irritate her sisters and probably her mother, stayed silent.

Brenna came to him and tilted her head back. "The table was crooked, wasn't it?"

Now he was truly fucked. He'd never once lied to her in all the years he'd known her. But he'd never been as close to her as he was now. Would he mess that up by starting now?

"Not that I could see. It looked straight to me."

"Damn. I wanted to be right. Okay. Can you help me with some wine in the storage room?"

"Sure."

That had gone better than expected. He walked with her

to the wine cellar. She unlocked the door and they went down the steps, into the room where there were racks of wine. He wasn't exactly sure what she needed, but it was nice and cool down here.

She turned and snaked her hand around his neck, pulling his mouth to hers.

Instinctively, he wrapped his arm around her and drew her close, fusing his lips to hers, sliding his tongue inside to take what she was so fervently offering. He backed her against the cool cement wall and breathed in her citrus scent, sucked on her tongue, absorbed the moans she made as she wrapped a leg around his hip.

He was hard and pressed urgently against her center, making her moans more pronounced, and all he wanted was to lift her dress and touch her more intimately, to slide down on his knees and taste her, lick her all over until she cried out and came all over his face.

How much time did they have? Probably enough.

"Brenna? You down there?"

She tore her lips from his. "Dammit," she whispered.

Finn took a step back, his breathing heavy, his dick rock hard.

"Yes, I am," she said in response to Honor.

"People are starting to arrive."

"Be right up." She looked at him. "I thought we'd have more time."

"I wish we had. I was conjuring up plans for you."

She arched a brow as she smoothed her hair back. "Save them for later."

"Will do. Oh, shit. I should come upstairs with something." She looked around and settled on a bottle of merlot. "Esther mentioned this being a favorite of hers."

He followed her up the stairs, admiring the sway of her

hips with every step, then decided that watching her ass wasn't going to make his boner go away, so he stared at the steps instead.

When they got back to the barn, Allison and Mitchell were there. Allison looked them both up and down.

"You look sweaty. What were you two doing?"

"Are you writing an article?" Brenna asked. "Or just bored with your own life?"

She circled around Allison and Mitch and took the bottle to Esther, who squealed and threw her arms around Brenna.

"You're amazing. Thank you."

"My pleasure." Brenna sported a genuine smile. "I thought you and Brock could crack this open when you get back from your honeymoon."

"Oh, we definitely will."

Once the families and all the bridesmaids and groomsmen showed up, everyone took their seats. This time, Finn got to sit next to Brenna. There was an amazing spread of food—salmon Benedict, omelets, crepes, bacon, fried potatoes and three amazing salads along with all kinds of fruit. Plus champagne. It was all so damn good that Finn could have eaten three times. And okay, he might have overfilled his plate, but he was hungry.

After he'd made his second trip to the buffet, Brenna looked over at his plate.

"Didn't you eat last night?"

He slid his fork through his omelet. "Of course I did."

She shook her head. "I don't know where you put all that food."

"In my belly, of course."

"And yet look at you. Flat stomach. Lean. It must all turn to muscle."

He draped his arm over the back of her chair and leaned close. "Why, Miss Bellini, are you complimenting my body?"

The intent in her gaze was obvious. "Maybe."

He slid his fingers into her hair and teased them along her neck. "Maybe you might want to explore it—later."

Her breath caught and held. He knew she wasn't playing this for Mitch and Allison, because she hadn't once pulled her attention from him. No, this was all for Finn, and he was enjoying every agonizing second of it.

"You make it hard for me to breathe, Finn."

His lips curved as he whispered in her ear. "You smell like summer and sunshine. And lemons. I want to taste you, lick you all over to see if you taste like lemons, too."

Allison cleared her throat so loudly that several people—including Finn—looked across the table. She shot them both a disapproving look.

Apparently, she was a little jealous of Brenna getting attention from him. Why? Then he noticed Mitch wasn't sitting next to her. He tracked the room and saw that Mitch was huddled in the corner of the room talking on his phone. Interesting.

Finn refocused his attention on Brenna, tipped her chin up with his fingers and brushed his lips across hers.

"What was that for?" she asked.

"Just a little dagger to the heart of your nemesis. And for me, because I wanted to."

Her lips curved and she reached up to run her fingernail gently across his jaw. "It was truly my pleasure."

When brunch was over, everyone said their good-byes.

Brenna went over to Esther and Brock and hugged them.

"I hope you have a wonderful honeymoon."

"Thank you," Esther said. "Oh, and we're going to do a big thing after we get back. We're having a housewarming

party at our new house. Please tell me you and Finn will
come?"

"Oh, uh . . ." She looked over at Finn.

Finn gave Esther and Brock a grin. "We'll be there."

"Great," Brock said. "Then we'll see you after we get
back. Knowing Esther, there'll be some fancy e-vite in your
inbox, Brenna."

Brenna smiled. "I'll look for it. Now off, you two."

They wandered around to say good-bye to everyone.
Finn had actually formed a nice friendship with some of
the people he'd sat with last night. He exchanged numbers
with all of them.

"We all need to get together sometime for dinner and
drinks," Sabra said.

Sue nodded. "We definitely should. I make barbecue
ribs that would make you cry."

"Now you're just teasing us," Brenna said.

"Sabra and I have a house near the lake," Dave said.
"You all should come up next weekend. We can go out on
the boat, go fishing or tubing."

"Only if Sue makes ribs," Johan said, then winced when
his girlfriend, Hilary, elbowed him.

Finn laughed. "We'd love to come. I'll bring my homemade whiskey."

He looked over at Brenna, who nodded. "You know I'll
bring the wine."

They all started talking over each other about who would
bring what foods.

"It's a date, then," Sabra said. "Next Saturday. I'll text
everyone."

After everyone left, Brenna looked at Finn, the expression on her face surprising him.

She looked miserable and unhappy.

"Sorry about that," she said.

"About what?"

"All of it. The barbecue next weekend, and the invite to Esther and Brock's house when they get back. I didn't mean for any of that to happen."

He frowned. "Why would you think that's a problem? I like all those people."

"And all of those people think we're engaged."

"Which means, what? You don't want me to go with you? Is that what you're saying?"

"No, that's not what I'm saying at all. I just . . . I don't know what I'm saying. This was only supposed to be for four days, Finn."

What the hell? First, she acted like she couldn't wait to be with him, and now she wanted to back away? He was confused as hell by these mixed signals Brenna was throwing at him. And a little bit pissed off.

"Tell me what you want, Brenna."

She threw her hands in the air. "I don't know. I didn't want this to be complicated. And now it is. I guess I don't know what I want. I want it to be not complicated."

"It doesn't seem complicated to me at all."

"Oh, really. We have two events at least where we still have to pretend to be engaged."

"And that's a problem in what way?"

She blew out a sigh. "I don't know. I just, it just is."

"You're creating problems when there aren't any."

"I am not. And I can't believe you don't see the issue here."

Which he didn't. Other than Brenna creating this argument getting them nowhere.

"I'll tell you what. When you figure out what you want—or don't want—you let me know."

He turned and walked away before he said anything else. Like how much he wanted to be with her next weekend. And the weekend after that. Hell, he wanted to spend even more time with her.

Yeah, time for a break, because leading with his heart was only getting him into trouble.

CHAPTER
······
thirteen

BRENNA SAT SILENTLY next to her sisters as they finished dinner.

"Why isn't Finn here?" her mother asked.

No one answered. Brenna cut into her steak and lifted her fork to her mouth, pausing as she realized everyone was staring at her.

"What?"

"Where's Finn, Brenna?" Honor asked.

"How should I know?"

"Considering how close you two were at brunch, I thought maybe—"

She cut off her sister with an "I don't."

Her mother gave her a concerned look.

She finished off her steak, took her plate and glass into the kitchen and laid them in the sink, then hid out in the library where she could be alone with her thoughts and away from the expectant looks of her family.

She sat in her favorite chair in the corner and pulled her

knees up to her chest, staring out the window at the bright sunlight outside.

This was why you don't date within the scope of the family business. Not that she and Finn had been dating. They hadn't even started up anything.

Okay, they'd been getting ready to start up something, and then . . .

She had no idea what had happened. They'd gotten hit up with all these invitations, and suddenly this fun, oh-so-temporary engagement had turned into the two of them doing all these things together. Things a couple would do together.

What was she supposed to do about that? They weren't a couple. They weren't anything. This whole thing had just been playacting.

She heard a soft knock at the door, and then it opened. Honor peeked her head around it. "Is it okay if I come in?"

"Yes."

Honor shut the door behind her and took a seat in the chair across from Brenna's.

"I'm sorry about earlier," Honor said.

"Me, too. I didn't mean to bite your head off."

"I assumed, and I shouldn't have. But you and Finn have seemed so close the past few days, and I assumed—well, there I go again. Sorry."

Brenna sighed. "You're not wrong. We were getting close, and then . . . things happened."

"What things? Did he do something to piss you off?"

"No. Nothing like that. Esther invited us to a house-warming after they get back from their honeymoon, and then Finn made friends with some people in the wedding party who invited us to the lake next weekend for a bar-becue."

Honor smiled. "That all sounds fun."

"Except that all those people think we're engaged."

"Oh." Honor leaned back in her chair. "And you wanted it to be a temporary thing."

"Exactly."

"So you don't want to hang out with Finn?"

"That's not it. I mean, we got along great. Maybe too great. And that's the problem."

"You like him."

"Yes."

"And that's a problem."

"You repeating what I say isn't helping, Honor."

"Sorry. I'm just trying to understand where the dilemma is here. You and Finn hung out together for four days. Based on all the flirting and closeness I saw between the two of you, I'd say you really liked him." She shrugged. "I guess I don't see the problem."

Brenna leaned forward to emphasize her point. "The problem is . . ." And then nothing came out of her mouth.

Honor offered up a tilted smile. "Yes?"

She opened up her mouth to speak again. And, again . . . nothing.

"Dammit." There was a definite problem with her and Finn, she just couldn't articulate what a serious issue it was at the moment.

"You want to know what I think?" Honor asked.

"Not particularly, but I doubt that'll stop you."

"I think you not only like Finn, you desperately like him. Like the so-much-smoking-hot-chemistry-that-you-wish-you-were-over-at-his-place-right-now, naked-and-having-sex kind of like him."

Brenna lifted her chin, wishing her mind wasn't conjuring up those images in her head. "Do not."

Again that smug smile from Honor. "Liar. It's written all over your face, and your body language whenever you were around him this weekend said otherwise."

"What body language?"

"You leaned into him like you wanted a lot more of what he was offering."

"I did not do that." Did she? She couldn't remember. "Besides, it was all playacting for the benefit of Allison and Mitchell."

Honor shook her head. "There's acting a role and really getting into the part. You are into that man. And what's wrong with that? Finn is great."

"He's all wrong for me."

Honor laughed. "On what level is Finn wrong for you?"

"Well, first, he works here."

Honor lifted a shoulder in a half shrug. "Bren. Everyone loves him. That's a benefit right there. You already have Mom and Dad's approval."

"It's not just that. Say we start dating for real and it doesn't work out. He still works and lives on the property. How awkward would that be until the end of time?"

"I imagine you'd both be adults about it. Why don't you do something totally unexpected for you and actually go for it with Finn? Have some fun. Sex. Romance. See what happens instead of picking things apart with a guy before they even get started."

"I never do that."

Honor laughed. "You do it all the time. With every guy you go out with. You zero in on the tiniest fault and end the relationship before it ever gets off the ground."

She lifted her chin. "I have high standards. There's nothing wrong with that. After my disastrous marriage with Mitchell, I don't ever want to settle again."

Honor leaned forward and grabbed Brenna's hand. "And you don't have to marry every man you go on a date with. Aren't you entitled to have some fun, too?"

Her sister had a point. "You're right. Maybe I have been overly picky. I just don't want to get hurt again."

"I don't want you to get hurt again, either. You and Mitchell were not right for each other. But you and Finn? Now that has potential. Why don't you see where it could go and instead of worrying about next month or next year, just live in the moment with him."

"Well, we are engaged, you know."

Honor laughed. "Plan a very long engagement with him. In the meantime, how about just dating him?"

"It's a plan. That is if he's still speaking to me."

"Uh-oh. What did you do?"

"I might have in a roundabout way vacillated about all these upcoming events, giving him the impression that I might not be interested? I don't know. I was confused and not communicating well. And I'm sure he's angry with me for getting close to him, then backing off. It was juvenile behavior."

Those mixed signals? Bad, Brenna. So bad.

"Oh, Brenna. You need to go fix things with him."

"I know. I will. Tomorrow."

Honor stood and grabbed Brenna's other hand, hauling her out of the chair. "No. Fix it tonight. Go over to his place and apologize, then make your intentions clear to him."

She frowned. "You're mean. And bossy. I thought Erin was the bossy one."

"You'd like to think that." She pointed her sister toward the door. "Go."

"Okay, I'm going."

She went upstairs, slipped on her sandals, swiped her hair into some semblance of order and sucked in several breaths of self-encouragement as she came downstairs and walked out the door.

He was probably still mad at her, she thought as she made her way along the path in the dark. She'd been rude and confusing instead of excited about the prospect of the two of them spending more time together. She wouldn't blame him if he didn't want to talk to her.

She batted away mosquitoes as she wound the corner to Finn's house, then immediately started scratching her arms. She was going to be eaten alive before she ever got there, swarmed by these bloodsucking bastards. They'd find her body in the morning, bumpy and unrecognizable after the mosquitoes feasted on her flesh all night long. And she'd have never had the chance to tell Finn she was sorry.

Or maybe she was making up this revolting death story in her head because she was afraid of facing him.

"Woman up, Brenna. You can do this."

As she got to the house, she saw that the lights were on but he wasn't outside with Murphy. Maybe he'd gone out.

Maybe you wish he'd gone out, you big baby.

Just to shut up her annoying conscience, she rapped loudly on the door.

Murphy barked, and a few seconds later the door swung open.

"Oh, hey. You should have texted to tell me you were on your way over. I'd have met you halfway."

Even if he was mad he'd have done that, because that's who Finn was.

"No big deal. I thought we could talk."

"Sure. Come inside. Mosquitoes are vicious tonight."

"Don't I know it. I already have like fifty bites on me."

She followed him in and he turned as they made their way into the small living area.

Murphy came over, excitedly wagging his tail. She bent down to give him some love.

"Didn't you put repellent on?"

She straightened. "I forgot."

"Ouch. Let me get you something before you swell up. Grab yourself a drink. I'll be right back."

"That's not—" But he had already disappeared into his bedroom, Murphy trailing behind him.

She shrugged and went to the fridge. Seeing an open bottle of chardonnay, she pulled it out and found a glass to pour some into.

"I have lotion that'll kill the itch," he said as he came back in. "Where did you get bit?"

"My arms. My neck."

"Come on. Take a seat here and let me take care of you."

"I can do it."

He held some cotton balls and the lotion in his hand, then smiled at her. "More fun if I do it."

Evidently he wasn't angry with her. Or at least not as angry as she'd thought. "Okay."

She picked a spot on the sofa and he sat facing her, poured some of the lotion onto a cotton ball and dabbed it onto each of the bites on her arm. It instantly cooled and calmed the annoying itch, giving her relief. But she supposed she couldn't sit there silently, not when she'd come over with specific intentions.

"I came over to apologize for my behavior earlier."

"Is that right?"

"Yes. I was momentarily freaked out about you and me doing all these things together and continuing our fake engagement."

He patted a few spots on her shoulder. "Understandable.

You had a plan and now your plans are messed up. Unless you tell everyone we broke up, which is easy enough."

"I suppose that's true. But then there'll be all the questions about what happened. And you made all those new friends."

His lips curved. "I'm sure I'll survive if that's what you want to do. You don't need to worry about me, Brenna."

He would say that, giving her an out if she wanted one. Was that what she wanted?

"You know," he said, dabbing a spot on her cheek, "that get-together with Esther and Brock after their honeymoon means Allison will be there. Do you really want to put up with her questions about the two of us breaking up?"

"You have a point." And now he was giving her a way back in, which for some reason gave her comfort. And felt right.

He gently patted a bite on her collarbone. Damn mosquitoes. But as he got closer, the clean scent of him swirled around her, making her want to crawl onto his lap and forget all about the reason for her visit. But then things between them would be unresolved, and she hated leaving anything hanging.

"Okay, I'm sorry for the way I acted. I overreacted. And I gave you mixed signals, getting close to you during the wedding, then putting the brakes on after. It was a terrible thing for me to do."

"I'll admit it was confusing. If you want something, Brenna, you need to tell me what it is."

A million thoughts swirled through her head, so many things she wanted to say, but she couldn't form the right words. "I know. It's . . . hard for me to do that."

He cocked his head to the side. "Why?"

She inhaled, let it out. "I don't know. Just be patient with me? And forgive me for acting like an ass?"

He nodded. "You're forgiven."

She tilted her head to the side. "Just like that?"

He shrugged. "It wasn't a big deal. And I overreacted, too, so I'm sorry for walking away. I should have stayed so we could talk it out."

"In retrospect, a cooling-off period for both of us was probably the best idea anyway."

"You may be right, but I don't like leaving things unresolved."

Maybe they were more alike than she thought. "Then we're good?"

"We're good."

"And I'd like to go to those events with you, if you're okay with it."

He gave her an easy smile. "So the fake engagement continues, then."

"I guess it does. And, Finn?"

"Yeah?"

She swallowed, her throat gone dry. "Maybe we should explore the whole dating-each-other thing?"

His lips curved. "Bet that was painful to get out, wasn't it?"

"A little."

"We'll take it a day at a time. How does that sound?"

Relief washed over her. She felt warm and comfortable and finally at ease. "Good. Really good."

He laid the lotion and cotton balls on the table, then leaned in. "We should probably kiss on it. Seal the deal, you know."

Her heart rate accelerated. "Make it official?"

"Yes. Since you're wearing my ring and all, it wouldn't be right if we didn't."

She felt his ring encircling her finger. Something else she wouldn't be giving back just yet. Which was all right with her.

She moved closer and slid her hand around his neck, the softness of his hair teasing her fingers. "Then you'd better kiss me. And Finn?"

His mouth was inches from hers.

"Yeah?"

"Make it a good kiss."

His lips curved. "Good kisses are my specialty."

He wrapped his arm around her, scooted her against the arm of the sofa, and then he kissed her.

Was it a good kiss? Oh, no. A good kiss was the kind that made her feel warm and tingly.

This kiss was an inferno that melted her right to the sofa. She was swamped with so much sensation her toes curled and the hairs on the nape of her neck stood up. And then she was suddenly on her back and Finn's delicious hard body was on top of hers. She slung her leg around his and all his parts rubbed against all of hers. She grabbed hold of his shirt and held on tight as he moved his mouth over hers, slid his tongue between her lips and turned her world upside down.

He broke the kiss and looked down at her. "Good enough?"

She shook her head, needing to draw in a few deep breaths before she could speak. "No. Better than good. What else do you have in your arsenal?"

He grinned and smoothed his hand along her side, stoking the fire inside her.

"I've got a few ideas."

She definitely wanted to hear those ideas. Or even better . . .

"Show me what you've got."

He arched a brow. "You sure you're ready for that?"

She'd never been more ready. "Yes. Absolutely yes."

He hopped off the sofa and took her hand, hauling her upright. "Let's go stretch out on my bed."

Murphy followed them, but one move of Finn's palm and Murphy stopped, then curled up on the floor in the hall, laying his head on his front paws.

"I see his training is going well."

Finn's lips curved. "He's a good dog."

She liked that he gave all the credit to Murphy.

Finn closed the door behind him and pushed her against it, his body coming up to press alongside hers. He slid his fingers onto her scalp, playing with her hair.

"I've wanted to do that since . . . forever."

She drew in a breath. "What's that?"

"Touch your hair. See if it was as soft as it looked."

"You can touch any part of me you want, as long as I get to do the same to you."

"Babe, my body is yours for the taking."

She palmed his chest, raking her nails down his perfectly formed pecs, over his abs, feeling the way his body clenched in response. She smiled up at him. "Tense?"

"You could say that."

She lifted his shirt and snaked her fingers over all his perfectly formed abdominal muscles. "Then we need to relax you."

"Touching me like that isn't going to get the job done."

Then she moved her hand lower, cupping his impressive erection. "I suppose this won't, either."

He gave her a warning look. "Keep doing that and I'm going to pick you up and toss your ass on the bed."

She let out a soft laugh and rubbed his erection, unable to help herself.

In an instant, he'd hauled her over his shoulder, and now she really was upside down, and then flying through the air, landing with a bounce on his mattress.

Before she had a chance to even catch her breath, Finn

was on top of her, his hands framing her face, his mouth capturing hers in a kiss that melted her bones to liquid. She was grateful for his amazing air conditioning and the ceiling fan blowing at full force because she was hot and feverish and certain that every inch of her skin that touched his was on fire. She couldn't wait for their naked skin to slide over each other, which couldn't happen fast enough for her liking.

She wiggled her hand between them, lifting his shirt, reaching for the button of his jeans.

He lifted his head. "What's the hurry?"

"Naked. You inside me. Sex. The good stuff."

"Are you telling me my kisses aren't the good stuff?"

She swept her fingertip over his bottom lip. "Your kisses are magnificent. The best I've ever had. I'm just . . . anxious."

"About?"

"You know . . . sex. It's been a while. I'd like to get to it."

He rolled to the side, pulling her against him. Then he moved his fingers slowly down her arm, teased her rib cage, eliciting tingles of pleasure.

"You wanna know what I think?" he asked.

"Sure."

"I think we need to slow things down instead of speeding them up."

She frowned. "Whatever for?"

"Because I think you've forgotten how fun sex can be. Especially the foreplay part."

"I honestly don't need foreplay. I'm primed and ready to go."

"Uh-huh. Well I'm not."

She shifted her gaze to his sizable erection. "You lie."

He laughed. "I mean, yeah, I'm ready there. But I've wanted to touch and kiss you all over since the first time I laid eyes on you, Brenna. You wouldn't deny me that, would you?"

"The first time?"

"The very first time. When I walked in the door and your ma introduced us and there you stood, arms crossed in front of you, eyeing me suspiciously, your fiery red hair spelling out your personality without you even speaking a word."

Okay, he'd been right about that. He'd been some stranger that Mom had told them was coming to live with them and Brenna had been immediately suspicious of his motives. He'd also had the saddest look on his face and she'd had to remind herself that he'd just lost his mother and was now living in a foreign land and didn't know a single person.

It had still taken her a while to warm up to Finn because that was who she was. Fortunately, he'd had Erin and Honor and Clay and Jason and Owen to make friends with. And eventually, she'd come on board when she realized she could trust him.

She realized then that she'd trusted Finn for that long. Much longer than she trusted her ex, for that matter.

"Okay, then. We'll take it slow."

"I promise you'll enjoy it." He gave her an easy smile that made her insides quiver.

She believed him.

CHAPTER
······
fourteen

FINN HAD NEVER known a woman like Brenna. She was efficient, determined, enjoyed so many activities and kept herself so busy that she never took downtime to just—be. She was also coiled up so tight he wondered how she didn't explode.

Tonight he intended to wind her down a little, hopefully remind her that taking time to relax and savor had its benefits, especially where sex was concerned.

He hadn't been lying when he'd told her he'd wanted to touch her since he'd first laid eyes on her. He'd been eighteen then and smitten, blown away by her beauty and her smarts and fiery personality. Now, though? He wanted her like only a man could want a woman, and he intended to show her all the ways a man could make love to a woman.

He kissed her, slow and easy and for a long time until he felt her body go lax. It took a while, but he made sure to kiss her thoroughly so she could empty that highly functioning brain of hers of everything except the feel of his lips moving over hers, of his hands leisurely roaming her body.

Only then did he stroke his fingers over her collarbone, teasing lower to the swell of her breasts. She arched, but this time it was more relaxed as she eased into his touch, exactly what he'd wanted for her. He needed her to feel his fingers, every small flutter of his lips along her neck as he wound his way to her ear.

"Better?" he whispered.

"Mmm," was all she said, her eyes closed as she melted against his questing fingers.

Oh, yeah. Now he had her where he wanted her. Liquid, soft against the mattress, so when he teased his fingers along her legs and swept them above, she didn't expect him to be hurried about it. She sailed on the journey with him, let him coax and explore her body the way she needed to be explored. He took his time making his way, raising her dress, parting her legs, sweeping his fingers along her silk underwear, patting her there, stroking, then gently drawing her panties down so he could touch her.

He was hard as a rock, but she was soft, silky and damp as he rubbed her with easy, deliberate strokes.

She was beautiful as she rose, then fell with a cry of release, her body shaking with it. He continued to touch her easily as she came down from it, and then he helped her undress, revealing the most beautiful body, which he'd wanted to see for so long.

He knew she was anxious so he got up and shucked his clothes, too. She stared up at him, smiling.

"Wow, Finn," she said. "Aren't you something?"

"I'm gonna take that as a compliment."

"You definitely should."

She had one arm thrown above her head, making him wish he were an artist so he could paint her just like that.

He crawled back onto the bed, between her legs, and kissed her inner thigh.

"What? Again?" she asked.

"You think you can only come once?"

"I thought maybe it was your turn."

"We don't do turns. And I want you relaxed."

"I don't know, after that pretty intense orgasm, I'm pretty mellow."

He gave her a teasing smile. "Then let's bring you up just a little."

He put his mouth on her, and she said, "Oh." After that all he heard were a lot of moans and cries and a lot of "Yes."

She tasted sweet and tart, which fit her to a *T*, and all he wanted to do was make her come again, then sink inside her so he could feel her surrounding him. But after she came with a loud whimper, then settled back against the bed, he got up to get them both a drink of water, because he didn't want to rush it. He wanted Brenna to savor every minute of tonight. And he needed to do the same.

He handed her a glass and she took a sip, setting the glass on the table. He'd already finished half of his on his walk from the kitchen to the bedroom.

"Finn."

"Yeah."

"I appreciate this beautiful slow seduction, but I'm here, I've come twice already and you have a boner the size of California. Don't you think we should get to it?"

His lips curved. "Still in a hurry, I see."

"No, not in a hurry. But the sooner we get to fucking, the

more times we can do it. And if you're as good at that as you are with your fingers and your mouth, I figure I can get a few more orgasms tonight."

He laughed, then set his glass on the nightstand. "Oh, I see. Now you're using me for sex."

She held her arms out for him when he settled in next to her. His breath caught as she teased her fingers through the hair on his chest.

"Using you? Hardly. You are my fake fiancé, aren't you?"

"Absolutely."

"Then I'm putting sex into our nonbinding fake fiancé agreement."

"There's an agreement?"

"There is now. And it has sex in it."

He reached into his nightstand for a condom, put it on, then rolled her over onto her back and slid his hand between her breasts, sliding a fingertip around her nipple. "Where do I sign?"

She smiled up at him. "Right there. With your tongue."

He laid his tongue flat against her nipple, then flicked it, rewarded with her soft moan. He took the bud in his mouth and sucked gently, feeling it tighten against the roof of his mouth.

And when she lifted against him, he eased inside her, cupping her breast and taking her mouth in a kiss that felt like fire. She tasted like all he'd ever wanted, felt like everything he'd ever needed, and all he wanted was to stay like this, with her wrapped around him, until time stopped.

He could only hear the sound of her breathing, the feel of her body moving under his, the taste of her mouth as she kissed him with such deep passion that he had to fight the urge to release right then. He held back, wanting this to last all night, even though he knew he couldn't. But she tasted so damn sweet and the way she looked at him with such raw passion nearly did him in.

He'd always known that being with Brenna would be good—damn good. But this was more than just awesome sex. He'd been half in love with her ever since he first saw her. And now that they were one like this, he couldn't imagine ever letting her go.

She pushed at his chest and he rolled over, letting her climb on top of him, her hair a fiery cascade over her breasts as she rode him, setting the pace for both of them, making him tighten until all he could do was hold on to her hips and roll her forward and back. She tilted her head back, her beautiful breasts gliding along with her movements. And when she convulsed against him, dipping forward to kiss him as she came, he finally let go, groaning her name against her lips as he released with a shudder.

She lengthened herself along his body as they recovered, and Finn had to admit it felt pretty fine to feel her sprawled against him, her body aligned with his, her breathing soft and even. Her hair splayed across his chest and he picked up a strand, sifting it through his fingers.

Yeah. Like silk. He'd never get tired of touching her—any part of her.

"I need a drink," she mumbled, her face buried in his shoulder.

"Alcoholic or otherwise?"

"Water. All that moaning and screaming has left me parched."

He smiled as he curved his hand over her hip. "Well, I did work you over."

She lifted her head. "Hardly. You were the one just lying there on your back."

"You have no appreciation for the efforts I put in."

"I'm drowning in sympathy over here."

"I can tell by your sarcastic look."

"Who? Me?" She climbed off and he got up, disposed of the condom and went into the kitchen to refill their glasses with fresh ice water. When he came back, she was propped up against the headboard. He was happy to see she wasn't ready to bolt out of his room or his house.

He handed her the glass and she took a few swallows, then set it on the nightstand.

"Thanks."

He set his glass next to hers, then pressed a kiss to her raised knee. "So, about you insulting my manhood."

She frowned. "I did no such thing."

He raised her leg and massaged her calf, then her foot. "Oh, but you did. You said you did all the work, but I beg to differ."

"What? You're keeping score?"

"I'd never. But I don't want to be accused of being a slacker."

He moved down the bed and dragged her off the pillow so she was flat on her back, then climbed up her body, kissing every inch of her along the way.

She sighed. "Well, if you must, I guess you can try to even the score."

It was going to be a long and very fun night.

CHAPTER
······
fifteen

Brenna rolled over and stretched, realizing immediately that she was still at Finn's place. She looked out the window. The sun wasn't fully up yet, and she didn't have anything pressing to do until later, so there was time.

Except Finn wasn't in the bed with her. And she smelled coffee. She got up and, deciding not to get dressed yet, fumbled around in his closet and put on one of his T-shirts. She halted at the dresser, realizing she'd never seen the old picture that sat there. She studied it, touched by the sentimentality.

She'd seen pictures of Finn's parents before since her mom had often gone to Ireland to visit Finn's mom, but she'd never seen this particular photo of Finn's mom and dad at the water's edge. Their arms were locked around each other, their hair blown by the ocean breeze. Finn looked a lot like his dad, though Finn was taller. And he had his mom's smile, that genuine, make-you-feel-warm-and-welcome kind of smile. It must have really hurt to lose both of them. Brenna couldn't imagine her life without her own parents. How hard it must have been for him to travel across an ocean, to know no one other than Brenna's mom, to have to start over in a strange place while he was still grieving.

She smoothed her fingertip across the pic.

"You raised a great son, Mr. and Mrs. Nolan. You'd be proud of the man he is today."

She ducked into the bathroom to use the facilities and washed her hands, scrubbed her teeth with toothpaste and her finger, then looked in the mirror.

Yikes. Her hair was a wreck but there was nothing she could do about that other than finger-comb it and call it good.

She walked out into the kitchen. Finn sat at the table, Murphy sprawled at his feet.

"Hey," she said.

He looked up and smiled at her, and her heart did a little dance.

Yeah, that smile.

"Hey. Coffee's in the pot. Sugar on the counter. No cream, sorry. But there's milk in the fridge."

"That'll do." She fixed a cup and pulled up a chair at the table, took a couple of sips of the coffee and, once the caffeine kicked in, all was right in her world again.

"You hungry?" he asked.

She shook her head. "Not right now. I'll grab something at the house."

"We missed breakfast." His lips tilted. "Slept in. You kept me up late."

"No, you kept me up late. And anyway, Louise will leave food for us."

"Good," he said, curling his fingers around his cup. "I'm hungry. You made me work up an appetite."

She laughed. "You poor thing. I noticed how you suffered."

He leaned over and hauled her out of her chair and onto his lap. "Quit complaining."

"I was not complaining, asshole."

He laughed. "You're gripey in the mornings."

"I haven't had a full cup of coffee yet."

"Yeah? Too bad. I might want to take you back to bed."

"I have things to do."

"Me, too." He swept his hand alongside her neck, then kissed her. He tasted warm and inviting and she sank into the kiss, eventually forgetting everything on her to-do list. The only list on her mind now included licking along Finn's tongue and exploring every inch of his hot body with her hands. In return, he teased her breasts and nipples through the thin material of the T-shirt while continuing to kiss her until she felt dizzy. She needed him, wanted him, right now.

He had his jeans on but she'd only dressed in his T-shirt, so she straddled him and began to rock against his erection, making him groan, which heightened her sense of urgency. She reached for his belt buckle and undid his zipper.

He pulled back. "Wait. Damn, I need a condom."

With one movement he picked her up and set her on top of the table, pointing at her.

"Don't. Move."

Like she even could. Her mind felt hazy and her body was nothing but pent-up arousal. Finn was back in a second with a condom, his jeans partially undone.

He pushed her down on her back on the table and lifted his T-shirt, staring down at her with something that looked like unbridled lust in his eyes. He shoved his jeans down, put the condom on and leaned over her, grasping her hips to pull her toward him.

"I like you like this, spread out on my kitchen table like my morning feast."

She shuddered at his words, then raised one of her legs to slide her foot against his shoulder.

He grabbed her foot, kissed it, then rested it against his shoulder as he slid into her.

It was slow and easy at first, then faster, the table shaking as they rocked together. She gasped as he thrust and withdrew, then let out a moan of pleasure as he laid his fingers against her clit to take her right to the edge and over. She tilted her head back and cried out as she came. He was there with her, leaning forward to sweep her up in a demanding kiss as he shuddered with his orgasm.

They panted together and she held tight to him. What a perfect way to wake up this had been.

An amazingly built man right in her own backyard who had given her mind-blowing sex and multiple orgasms. Why had she waited all these years to jump him?

His breath blew hot against her neck and she shivered.

He raised up to look down at her. "Cold?"

"To the contrary. Quite hot."

"Hell yes you are." He lifted her off the table and set her on her feet, and then they both went into the bathroom to clean up.

Once again, her hair was a wild bird's nest. "I need a shower."

"I'll be sweating all day, so I'll pass," he said. "And you're beautiful."

He turned her to face him and pressed his lips softly against hers, then let her go so she could wind her hair up into a bun.

He stared at her in the mirror.

"What?" she asked.

"You have the most incredible freckles across your cheeks and nose."

She wrinkled said nose. "I've never liked them."

He frowned. "The hell you say. They're one of the sexiest things about you."

No one had ever said her freckles were sexy. Cute, adorable, juvenile, whatever. But sexy? Never.

She turned and lifted up on her toes to take a nibble of his chin. "And your beard stubble is hot as hell."

He slanted a hot smile at her. "Good to know you like it. I'll keep that in mind for the next time my face is between your legs."

Her entire body quivered. "Now that image will be on my mind the rest of the day while I'm working."

She got dressed and he walked with her to the door. He swept her into his arms and kissed her—a hot, long, hard kiss that heated her up and made her wish they could spend the entire day together. But she had work to do and Finn did as well, so when they broke the kiss, she sighed.

"That was nice," she said, unable to resist laying her palm against his chest, just to feel the hard muscle there. "Maybe I'll see you tonight."

"Maybe I'll be here."

She gave him a smile and walked toward the house, happy to see absolutely no one as she snuck her way up the stairs and into her room. She took a quick shower, wound her hair up and fastened it with a clip, then put on a sundress and sandals. She made her way down the stairs, stopping in the kitchen where she grabbed a cup of coffee and a cinnamon roll that Louise had left on the counter— bless her. She went into her office, answered a few e-mails and did some paperwork before it was time for the meeting.

Erin was already in the room, of course, her planners and her laptop perfectly organized.

"Is Agatha with you?"

"She was, but then she spotted Finn's dog when we got here so now the two of them are running amok outside."

"Awesome. Murphy will enjoy having a friend today."

Honor dashed in, closing the door behind her. "Sorry I'm late. I had an upset bride to deal with and once she gets talking I can't get her off the phone."

"What was she upset about?" Erin asked.

"Flower arrangements. It was a minor thing, but you know how brides get."

"Do we ever," Brenna said.

Honor blew out a breath and laid her things on the table. "She has a lot of ideas. Like, a lot of ideas."

Brenna leaned back and sipped her coffee. "Doable ideas, hopefully?"

"She wants a waterfall. In the middle of the vineyard."

Waterfalls in the middle of her vineyard were a no-go. "Oh. Not doable ideas, then."

"I assume you told her no," Erin said, shuffling her papers as she sat.

"I definitely told her we couldn't accommodate a waterfall, but I told her we could rent a nice fountain that could be placed on the arbor or next to the arbor for atmospheric and audible purposes."

"That sounds lovely," Brenna said. "What did she say?"

"She said it wasn't ideal, but she'd think about it."

Erin shrugged. "I think it's a great compromise. You're so smart, Honor."

"Agree," Brenna said. "You really try to give the bridal couple everything they ask for. I couldn't do it. I'd run screaming down the road every day if I had to do what you do."

Honor laughed. "Most couples are fabulous and super easy. It's only the occasional difficult ones that try my patience."

"Okay, let's get rolling on this meeting so we can all get to work."

Erin was always the one to call the meeting to order, mainly because she liked to be in charge, and neither Brenna nor Honor cared one way or the other.

"Before we get started," Honor said. "Brenna, you're just glowy this morning. Do you have a new facial regimen that you need to share with us?"

"Uh, no. I took a shower."

Erin studied her. "Honor's right. And I showered, too, but I don't glow like that. Did you use a new mask?"

"No. I showered. Washed my face. Can we move on now?"

"She wasn't at breakfast this morning," Honor said.

"Oh, really," Erin said.

Brenna rolled her eyes. "That's hardly earth-shattering news."

"No, it's not," Honor said. "But Finn wasn't at breakfast this morning, either."

Erin gave her a smug smile. "Oh, now that is very interesting. Couple that with the morning glow . . ."

Honor's eyes widened. "You had sex. That's a sex glow."

Erin nodded. "Yes, definitely a sex glow. A first-time-sex glow."

They were like the most annoying detectives ever. Correct, but annoying as hell. "It's freaking hot outside and I'm still sweaty from the shower. You're both being ridiculous."

Honor looked over at Erin. "Notice she didn't deny the sex part."

"She did not. Definitely guilty. So you spent the night with Finn and had so many orgasms it's written all over your face."

Her body trembled a little just thinking about all those orgasms. Which she was not about to discuss with her sisters.

"I have nothing to say."

"Oh, come on," Erin said. "You both browbeat me to death when I was first seeing Jason. Turnabout is fair play. Now spill. Did you do it in the house here?"

"Of course not. Mom and Dad are light sleepers. I would never—"

Honor pointed a finger at her. "Aha. Which means you did have sex with Finn. Obviously at his place. I knew it."

"Good sleuthing, Honor," Erin said, high-fiving her sister.

Brenna rolled her eyes. "This is juvenile."

Erin laughed. "You're just mad that you couldn't keep it a secret."

"Oh, right, like what's going on with the two of them is any secret," Honor said. "She practically drools anytime Finn gets within ten feet of her."

Now they were being asinine. "I do not. And we're not in a relationship. We're still faking."

"Did you fake it last night?" Honor asked. "Judging from how hot Finn is, my guess is no."

"I'm not dignifying that with an answer."

"Because we know the answer." Erin held out her hands toward Brenna. "Hence, the glow."

"Could we please talk about something other than my sex life now that you two have had your fun?"

"Okay, fine," Honor said with an exaggerated sigh. "But

you know we both approve of you and Finn. And you should consider making this relationship not fake. He's good for you, Bren. And he's always liked you."

Erin nodded. "He has. And I like how you are with him."

Brenna frowned. "How exactly am I with him?"

"I don't know. More relaxed. More like your old self, like you were before Mitchell."

Huh. That was interesting. She hadn't noticed that she'd changed since Mitchell. But maybe she had.

As Erin talked on about wedding budgets, Brenna thought about who she was then versus who she'd become post-Mitchell. Sure, she'd had her heart broken. She'd gone into her marriage bright-eyed and with hopes of an incredible future, only to have her hopes dashed. And sure, she'd withdrawn for a while, but she'd eventually dragged herself back up to the surface and moved on with her life, taking up all the activities she loved, like her books and her gardening and her genealogy work.

Maybe love and romance had taken a spot on the back burner. Way on the back burner. It wasn't her fault that men were continually disappointing. She'd learned a valuable lesson from her marriage, and that was to have high standards. There was no sense in wasting time with a man who couldn't meet them.

And then this whole fake fiancé thing with Finn had come about. Her idea, of course, and she had only meant it to be for four days. Now, that contract had been extended. And sex had been added to the equation, which was beneficial for both of them, right?

It was fun. No one would get hurt.

Since she had no intention of marrying Finn—and he had to know that—why not have some fun? It was pretty phenomenal sex, too.

She was long overdue for some fun and phenomenal sex.

"This Saturday night we have the garden wedding," Honor said. "Small wedding party, only thirty guests."

Brenna looked up. "That reminds me. Okay if I take Saturday off?"

Erin's lips curved. "Got a date?"

"Sort of. Finn and I have been invited to a lake barbecue."

Honor smiled. "This wedding will be easy, and we can handle the wine order. Go have some fun, Brenna."

"Are you sure?"

"Absolutely. We've got this."

"Okay, thanks. You know I'll pick up the slack anytime either of you need me to."

"We know," Honor said.

"It's about damn time, too," Erin said. "You can't work all the time."

"Oh. Look who's talking."

Erin lifted her chin. "Hey. I've got a guy. And a place to live. And a dog."

Brenna snorted. "Of course you do, Miss Perfect."

Honor waved her hands at them. "Okay, okay. Before this ends up in an all-out brawl over nothing and I have to make the two of you apologize, how about we get back to the meeting?"

Honor was right. Brenna didn't even know what they were fighting about. Of course, being sisters meant they could always find something to argue over, no matter how trivial or petty. Erin had been encouraging her date with Finn and Brenna had turned it into an argument, likely because she was still a bit unsure of herself where Finn was concerned. Which didn't mean she could take it out on her sister.

"Sorry, Erin," Brenna said.

"Me, too."

Honor nodded. "That's better. Now on to the business at hand."

They dove into the rest of the meeting, and Brenna pushed thoughts of the upcoming weekend aside.

For now.

CHAPTER

······

sixteen

Finn HAD SPENT most of the week prepping and bottling some whiskey for the weekend. It wasn't aged as much as he would have liked, but it was good and tasty and he looked forward to sharing it with his new friends.

Along with his normal daily work, he hadn't had much of a chance to spend time with Brenna. He passed her a few times during the day and they stopped and talked, but she'd said she was busy. He wasn't offended. She was often busy. And when he'd asked her if they were still on for Saturday, she smiled at him and told him she couldn't wait.

Her smile had held him the whole week.

Now he was packing up his truck with whiskey and chairs and fishing gear and whatever else Brenna kept dragging out for him to include. Which was a lot. Bags and boxes of wine and coolers and even more bags.

He tossed the current bag into the bed of the truck.

"No, that one goes in the front."

Resisting rolling his eyes, he smiled and tucked the bag into the back seat. "Sure. Anything else?"

"I don't know. Let me check."

"You do realize we're just going for the day. Not the week."

She waved one hand at him while she disappeared into the house.

At this rate, the entire day would be over before they even got there.

He leaned against the truck, arms folded, watching across the way as they set up for the day's wedding. He was actually surprised that Brenna had so quickly agreed to this, considering she always worked the weddings during the weekends.

But he couldn't deny he was happy she was coming along with him today.

She finally flew through the front door, her hair in a high ponytail. She had on a blue-and-yellow sundress with her swimsuit under it. And damn if she didn't make him catch his breath.

She slid her sunglasses down from her head onto her face and fixed him with a bright smile. "What are you waiting for? Let's go."

Since he was already wearing his shades, she missed his eye roll. "Waiting on you, princess."

She slid her hand up and down his arm. "Then let's get this party started. Hey, where's Murphy?"

"Out on the vineyard with your dad. He's watching him today. Said they were going to sit inside, have snacks and watch a baseball game later."

She laughed. "Of course they are. They'll probably nap together, too."

"No doubt."

The drive to Sabra and Dave's house took about forty minutes. They played music on low and mostly talked to each other about their week. It had always been easy to slide into conversation with Brenna. Whether it was about current events, weddings, his whiskey or an argument, they never ran out of things to talk about.

"What's in all the bags and boxes and cooler?" he asked.

"Food. Wine. Clothes. Towels. I assume you handled the fishing gear."

"I did. And I brought a fresh batch of whiskey."

"Looks like we're going to have a great day."

He took the exit off the turnpike. "Clothes?"

"Yes. So I can change out of my swimsuit. And in case I get dirty."

"You plan on getting dirty?"

She shrugged. "You never know. I like to be prepared. How about you? Did you bring a change of clothes?"

"Pretty sure there's a pair of jeans and a T-shirt back there somewhere." He tossed his thumb over his shoulder.

She rolled her eyes. "I guess that's something."

"I don't think guys need to have as much stuff as women."

"I'm amazed your species has survived as long as it has."

He figured if he laughed she'd probably throw something at him, so he kept his mouth shut. They got to the house about ten minutes later. It was a big two-story, and while it wasn't right on the lake, it wasn't far. He couldn't wait to get out on the water. He'd grown up by the sea, and being near water was one of the things he missed the most. He and his da would often go out on the boat to fish, and it was in his blood. He was aching to stretch his legs and toss his pole in the water today.

"You seem anxious," Brenna said as they started to unload the truck.

"I miss the water," he said.

"Oh, of course. You want to fish."

"Yeah."

"Hopefully you'll catch something today."

"I know I will."

Her lips curved. "I do like a confident man."

They carried everything to the door, which opened as soon as they got to it. Dave was there to greet them.

"I'm happy you two could make it," he said. "Sabra's in the kitchen making . . . I don't know. Something. Sue's out back putting the meat in the smoker and the rest of us are drinking and wishing it was already time to eat. Come on in."

They carried the bags and cooler inside with Dave's help. Andi was in the kitchen along with Hilary and Marie, who was helping Sabra slice strawberries. They all shouted out a hello.

"We're so glad you came," Sabra said. "I thought maybe you'd have to do a wedding today."

"There is one this evening, but it's a small event and my sisters graciously offered to handle it without me."

"Awesome. There's sangria in the fridge if you'd like a glass. Help yourself. And Finn, there's beer in the cooler outside."

Dave motioned with his head. "Follow me."

Finn looked over at Brenna, who waved him off, so he knew she'd be okay, and he followed Dave outside.

Brenna was happy to see that Sabra and the others were comfortable enough to let her make herself at home. And that Finn didn't feel like he'd have to sit right by her side all day.

She'd always been independent and confident enough in herself to be comfortable in a crowd of strangers. It didn't take her long to get to know the women. Sabra was vivacious and super friendly. Hilary was gorgeous and had a wicked sense of humor. Andi was smart as hell and adept at keeping the conversation moving along, and Marie was just incredibly sweet and friendly, always the one to fill drinks or pitch in to help.

They worked together to make sandwiches and fill up containers with fruit and other snacks for the boat.

"I don't know about the rest of you, but I think we make a damn good team," Hilary said. "We got that task done in record time."

"Which is good," Andi said. "Because I'm so ready to get in the water."

Brenna was as well, and she hoped Finn would get to spend some quality time fishing.

They ended up having two boats. One was at the marina, and one that Marie's boyfriend, William, had brought.

Dave, Finn, Sue, Will and Johan took one boat to fish, and the rest of them climbed onto Andi's boat so they could hang out in the water.

This wasn't exactly the day she thought she'd have with Finn, but he seemed excited about being able to fish, and that was what she wanted for him. Besides, they had coolers of booze and plenty of food to eat on each boat, so they'd all be fine. They made plans to meet up in a cove for lunch.

They started out skiing and tubing and Brenna had never laughed so much. Andi was an expert skier and Hilary had never gotten up on water skis in her life, with the rest of them falling somewhere in the middle. They gave Hilary a lot of pointers, but she still face-planted a few times, and each time came up sputtering and laughing. When she finally got back onto the boat, she was still laughing.

"Thank God I have these enormous boobs to break my fall."

Then they all started laughing so much that Andi said she was unable to maneuver the boat, so they took a break and had a drink. Brenna felt the heat from the sun and didn't want to get sick, so she drank a lot of water and drove the boat while Andi skied for a while.

The time passed quickly and they made their way to the designated meeting spot. The other group showed up about fifteen minutes later, all of them grinning, which was a good sign.

"How was the fishing?" Marie asked.

"It was good," William said as they tied their boats together. "I caught two. Finn caught four."

Brenna cast her gaze across the boat toward Finn. "Four, huh?"

He grinned. "It was a good fishing spot."

He was standing there wearing only his board shorts, his body bronzed and golden and dripping with sweat. He wore his shades and the wind blew his raven hair. It wasn't fair for a man to look so downright hot. Brenna felt a pang of regret that they weren't alone in this shaded cove so she could have her way with him about five or six times.

She dipped her sunglasses down her nose and gave him a very direct look. His lips ticked up in a knowing smile, so he'd obviously received her message.

They climbed off the boats and onto the small island, opened up the coolers and grabbed their sandwiches and fruit and veggie sticks and parked their butts in the sand.

Finn sat next to her.

"I guess it was a good fishing expedition," she said as he dug into the bag containing the carrots.

He chewed, swallowed and nodded. "Really good. I need to add 'buying a boat' to my list of things to do—someday."

"You do know we have a boat."

He shrugged. "That's your family's boat. I want one of my own so I can go out anytime I want."

She wasn't going to tell him that the Bellinis' boat was his anytime for the asking, that her father would never tell him no. She understood men and pride.

"Anything worth having is worth working for," she said.

He nodded. "Damn right."

Brenna understood that better than anyone. She chewed thoughtfully, taking a sip of her water.

"When Mitchell and I got married, I saved all the money I could, my one goal to buy a house. I hated living in that cramped one-bedroom condo."

"I sense a *but* in there."

"Mitchell liked to take trips and host parties and show off his success. One of the many things we argued over."

"Ah. You weren't on the same page, financially."

"Not in the least. But when we divorced I took the money I saved and put it away again."

"For your someday house."

She turned to him. "Yes. For my someday house."

"You'll get it. Someday."

"Just like your boat."

"Just like my boat." He smiled and smoothed a wayward hair away from her face. "Anything worth having is worth waiting for."

She wasn't certain if he was referring to his boat, her house or something else entirely. But she was lost in his eyes right then and didn't care. Whenever she looked at him, the whole world fell away.

And when he leaned in and brushed his lips across hers, she melted against him, only barely cognizant of the other people nearby. Finn was the one who broke the kiss.

"Hold that thought for later. When we're alone."

"We'll be alone later?"

"Yeah. When we get back to my place. If you wanna come over."

She pressed her fingers into his bare chest. "Oh, I want to come over."

"Good."

They all piled back into the boats after lunch and took turns tubing. Brenna ended up on the boat with Finn, and the two of them went out together.

"You ready?" he asked as Dave started the boat's engine.

"I've totally got this." Which she did, because this was not her first ride on a tube.

He grinned, and then they were off, sailing over crests like they were flying. They hit the water hard and her legs nearly flopped over her head, sending her careening off the tube. Finn grabbed on to her and tugged her against him and she fought for breath as she laughed. He held tight to her while they went catapulting over the waves.

She was dizzy by the time Dave stopped, but, hey, she'd held on. They climbed aboard and Brenna needed to get her footing. Finn stayed next to her while she downed some water.

"Feel okay?" he asked.

She looked over at him. "Exhilarated. How about you?"

He grinned. "Same. You did great out there."

"Did you have any doubt I would?"

"Nope."

Now it was Dave and Sabra's turn. Finn drove the boat and Brenna stood at the stern to watch them so she could signal Finn if one of them fell off. Sue and Andi were on their boat as well, so they all chatted while watching.

"You were a natural out there on the tube, Brenna," Sue said.

"My sisters and I went out on the boat with my mom and dad when we were kids. I learned to ski and tube as soon as I learned to swim."

"Same here," Andi said. "I grew up in Florida, and we hit the beach as soon as we could stand. We were out on the water all the time."

Sabra did a flip off the tube, so Brenna signaled Finn, who slowed and brought the boat around to pick them up.

Sabra was laughing as she climbed aboard. "I've got so much damn water in my ear I'll be floating in my sleep."

Sue and Andi went next, and they hung on for the duration of their ride.

Brenna could have done this all day, but they decided to meet up with the others and head to shore. They loaded up the boats and drove back to the house. Everyone rinsed off and Brenna took off her swimsuit and changed into her sundress, winding her hair into a knot on top of her head.

"I'm madly in love with your hair," Marie said as they stood side-by-side in the bathroom. "I've tried to get that color four times and it always ends up orange, so I gave up and went back to brown."

Marie was petite and absolutely stunning. "Your hair is lush and gorgeous. I don't know why you'd want to change it. Mine is naturally curly and drives me crazy."

Marie laughed. "We always want what we don't have."

"I guess that's true."

They went into the kitchen and dove into fixing sides while the guys went into the backyard and helped Sue pull the meat out of the smoker to get it ready to put onto the grill.

Brenna pulled out bottles of wine and they opened those, plus Andi made up a batch of sangria, so they had plenty to drink. Considering that Brenna typically worked weddings on a Saturday, it was a treat to kick back, relax and enjoy a rare day off.

They sat and drank and talked about their lives and partners. It was nice to sit with a group of women who were at similar points in their lives, who also loved their careers. She loved learning about them. They all had varied careers, from financial analyst to child development coordinator to chef.

Marie was a pastry chef, and she and Brenna had bonded right away. As they were talking she looked up Marie's shop online and was so impressed with her work. "I can't believe we haven't used you for our weddings before."

"Same," Marie said. "I'd love to create something for you."

"I'm going to pass your name on to Honor," Brenna said. "She books all the vendors. I know she'll want to give you a call and come by your shop."

Marie beamed a smile. "I'd be thrilled. Or I can bake a few things and bring them by."

"Even better. We love pastries." Total bonus. Vendors came and went and you could never have enough on your list. Honor would be thrilled, especially if Marie's pastries were awesome. Brenna just knew they would be.

They ate a smorgasbord of food and side dishes, including the fish that had been caught earlier. Brenna filled up on grilled pineapple, multiple salads and the most amazing fall-off-the-bone ribs she'd ever tasted.

"Sue, these are amazing," she said as they all piled into the kitchen and crowded around the table.

"Thanks. I've been working on the recipe for that sauce for years."

"A recipe she refuses to share with even me," Andi said, shooting her girlfriend a look.

Sue laughed. "Hey, some things need to remain a secret."

"Agreed," Finn said, tossing another clean bone onto his discard pile. "It's like whiskey. Once you perfect a method, and it tastes damn good, you can't tell everyone how you got there."

Sue pointed at Finn. "Exactly. And that whiskey you brought is outstanding, by the way. Tell no one how you did it."

Brenna caught the look of pride on Finn's face. It was the same look she had whenever someone complimented Bellini wines. Of course his whiskey making was a hobby, even though her dad had given him an entire section of the warehouse to make it.

She wasn't a whiskey kind of woman, preferring the more subtle flavors of wine. Oh, sure, she dabbled occasionally in liquor, but she always came back to the Bellini brand.

Plus, whiskey was just so . . . complicated. Then again, she'd never shown any interest in what Finn was doing in that warehouse. Nor had she ever tasted what he was concocting, figuring he was only playing around. Which he'd been doing for over ten years, well before he was legally allowed to do so. But he'd been doing it under her father's direction, and she was busy enough doing her own thing, so why should she care?

But after dinner and cleanup, they sat outside where Dave had set up torches to keep the bugs away, and Finn poured whiskey for those wanting a taste.

"I'll have some," she said as he walked around.

He arched a brow. "You. Want some whiskey."

"Sure, why not?"

"Because you don't like it?"

"Typically not, but I thought I might try it tonight."

He crouched down to pour some into a small glass for her. "Well. This will be a first."

He took a seat next to her and she thought he'd watch her, but he turned to talk to Will instead. She took a sip, instantly surprised by the smooth flavor with a hint of vanilla, making her go back for another taste, and then another.

When he turned back to her, she smiled at him. "Finn. This is exceptional."

"Thanks. It'll get better once it ages longer. This one has aged for five years. Ten to twelve is ideal."

"Do you have some that have been aging that long?"

He nodded. "I have some nearly hitting ten, but I don't know about the flavor profiles. I hadn't yet perfected my formula and technique back then."

"But you have now."

"Yeah. A better brewing system as well, thanks to your dad."

She held out her cup and he poured more in. She took a couple more sips to make sure of the flavor. It held.

"You want to be a whiskey maker."

He shrugged. "It's a passion, for sure. So, maybe. Someday. When I get all the right tools."

She'd had no clue. But she liked that he had a hobby he enjoyed.

They wrapped up about midnight and everyone packed up and said their good-byes.

"This was so much fun," Brenna said to Dave and Sabra. "Thank you for inviting us."

"Anytime," Sabra said. "Thanks for bringing the wine. It was fabulous as always."

When they got back to the house, Brenna tucked her bags inside the door while Finn quietly called for Murphy, who bounded outside and ran off to sniff every blade of grass on the front lawn.

"Want to come to my place?" he asked, moving in to sweep his fingers down her arm, making her tingle all over. "I feel like we didn't get to spend much alone time together today."

"I'd love to come to your place. Be alone with you. Talk."

His brow rose. "Talk, huh? Got some things on your mind?"

"Maybe."

"We can talk." He opened the truck door, then whistled for Murphy, who came bounding out of the darkness and hopped right into the truck.

Brenna laughed. "Ready to go, isn't he?"

"He's a smart dog."

He started up the truck and they got in, Murphy sticking his head between them from the back seat. Brenna reached over to pet him.

"Did you have a good day, Murphy?" she asked.

"Knowing your dad and how much he loves dogs, he probably had a blast," Finn said.

Brenna quirked her lips. "No doubt."

They headed down the road toward his place.

"Tell me about your whiskey."

He looked over at her. "What about it?"

"What do you like about making it?"

He shrugged. "I dunno. I guess it relaxes me."

"Why?"

"Because it's not work."

She leaned her head back against the truck's headrest. "I feel the same way about making wine. It's never felt like work to me. Watching the grapes grow, caring for them, knowing the exact right time to pick them and then nurturing them as they go through the process of fermentation, aging and bottling, realizing that I'm creating something that will taste amazing . . ."

"It's a kick, right?"

She turned her head to look at him and smiled. "Yes, it really is. It's the same for you?"

"Yeah. It's a science, really, and I always liked science. Finding the right grain, then heating it to release the sugar, adding in the right amount of yeast, almost as if you're making beer, which you are, in essence, except then you distill it and age it."

"The waiting part can't be fun."

"It's not, but the longer you do this, the easier it gets because you're doing batches, so you'll have some that's ready while you're creating others. Like today, I had some five-year-old whiskey I could share."

"Which was very good."

"It was okay. It'll get better the longer it ages. I have some ten-year-old that's better. You'll have to stop by the warehouse sometime and I'll give you a taste. It's smoother, more mellow."

She loved hearing him talk about whiskey, could feel the passion in his voice as he spoke about something he loved doing. It made her feel as if she had a kindred spirit in Finn—someone passionate about what he did, like she was about her winemaking.

He parked his truck at the side of the house and they got out. Murphy bounded out and headed to the front door.

"Think he's ready for bed?" she asked as they met at the door.

"I'm sure he's a tired pup."

Finn unlocked the door and Murphy headed straight down the hall toward the bedroom and disappeared.

"You want something to drink?" he asked.

"Just a glass of ice water, please." She'd had a full day of sunshine and more than enough alcohol. She was tired, too, and felt dehydrated.

He fixed them both tall glasses of water. She took hers gratefully, taking a couple of decent swallows.

She thought he'd lead her toward the bedroom, but he surprised her by taking her hand and sitting with her on the sofa in the living room. She set her glass on the coffee table and he pulled her against him. She kicked off her sandals and drew her feet up on the sofa.

This was nice, being held by Finn, snuggling close to him.

"You wanted to talk," he said.

"Oh, right." She yawned and laid her head on his shoulder. "I did, didn't I?"

She rested her hand against his chest, feeling the rhythmic beat of his heart, realizing this all felt just so perfect. Maybe too perfect, but she was too tired to analyze that right now, because her eyelids suddenly felt way too heavy to stay open and Finn was rubbing her arm and everything in her world felt too right to worry about anything right now.

So she closed her eyes and went with it.

CHAPTER
......
seventeen

FINN SAT OUTSIDE and sipped his coffee and watched Murphy chase a bird that flew away easily. He rolled his eyes as his dog dashed into the woods at another bird. He understood that it was the dog's nature to think he could catch it, and, hey, it was exercise if nothing else. Besides, Murph had a ton of energy and if he wanted to chase creatures he had no hope of catching, who was Finn to deny him?

The first rays of dawn were just peeking through the trees. It was Finn's favorite part of the day, when everything was quiet, the world hadn't started up yet and it was just him and nature and an outstanding cup of coffee. And now, his dog, too. What could be better?

The front door opened and Brenna came out, holding a steaming cup of coffee in her hand. She was barefoot and his gaze traveled up the length of her incredible legs, to where one of his shirts ended at her thighs. Her hair was a mass of wild curls around her shoulders. She walked over and took a seat on the porch swing with him.

He really liked seeing her wearing his shirts. Even though

they swallowed her up, there was something in that possessive part of his heart that liked seeing her wearing something he'd worn.

"You steal another one of my shirts?" he asked.

"I didn't steal it. I'm borrowing it temporarily while I'm naked because I'm too lazy to get fully dressed."

"Naked, huh?" He slid his fingers under the hem of the shirt.

She slapped his hand away. "I need this cup of coffee."

"You fell asleep last night. We were supposed to talk. And things."

She sipped the coffee and stared straight ahead. "Yes, I did. Sorry about that. Did you carry me to bed?"

"I did."

"Undressed me, too, I guess."

"You wake up with your clothes on?"

"No."

"There you go." He finished off his coffee and set the mug on the table next to the porch swing. "Besides, I've seen you naked. And you'd have been uncomfortable sleeping in your dress."

"Then thank you."

"You're welcome. I also texted Honor to let her know you were spending the night at my house so your family wouldn't worry about where you were."

She arched a brow at him, looked mad for a few seconds, then shrugged. "Okay. Thanks for that, too."

"You trying to keep us a secret?"

"Trust me, you and I are no secret where my sisters are concerned. They figured us out the first time we were together."

"Yeah?" That made him smile. Besides, he knew Erin and Honor. They could ferret out secrets in hours.

"Yes. Keeping you and me a secret wouldn't have worked for long. Not the way you look at me."

He choked out a laugh. "The way I—how about the way you look at me?"

She shifted in the swing, bringing one knee onto the swing for balance. "And how exactly do I look at you?"

"With lust. Like you want to throw me down in the vineyard and climb on top of me."

"I never look at you that way."

"Liar." He took the cup from her hands and set it next to his, then grabbed hold of her and shifted her onto his lap. With her straddling him like this, it didn't take his dick long to figure out he had a hot, mostly naked woman wriggling against him. He was hard and aching in no time.

He cupped the back of her neck and drew her mouth to his, kissing her with a hungry passion that he couldn't contain. She leaned into him, digging her nails into his shoulders, driving his desire higher.

He reached for her breasts through the thin material of his worn shirt, teasing her erect nipples, taking in the sounds of her moans against his lips, sliding his tongue along hers until he felt like he was going mad with the need for her. He slid his hand under the shirt so he could feel the softness of her skin, wrap his hand around the plumpness of her breast, roll his thumb over her silky nipple until she let out a cry.

"Make me come," she murmured against his mouth.

She didn't need to ask him twice, and since his house was out in the middle of nowhere, far away from the main house, they were guaranteed privacy.

He slipped his hand between her legs. She was wet, ready for him as he teased his fingers over her soft skin, priming her even though he knew she was ready. Then he slid two fingers inside her and found her clit with his thumb.

She rocketed against him and met his gaze as he moved his fingers in and out of her, watching her pant and grind against him.

Seeing her face, the ecstasy spread across it, made his balls hurt in the worst way. He wanted his cock pumping inside her, but God, she felt so damn good, and watching her come apart like this as he fingered her had to be the best damn experience of his life.

And when she came, she shuddered hard against him, holding on to him as if her damn life depended on it. He wrapped his arm around her and held her while she rocked through her orgasm and collapsed on him, breathing heavily.

"Damn, Finn," she murmured against his neck.

He was breathing heavily, too, only he hadn't had a release yet. He picked her up and carried her inside the house, laid her on the side of his bed and reached for a condom. He dropped his jeans down to his knees, put the condom on and spread her legs, then leaned over her, spreading his palms on either side of her hips as he slid inside of her.

Her pussy was still quivering from her orgasm, and squeezed so tightly onto his cock that he thought he might lose it right there. He stilled, sweeping his hand up to lift her shirt so he could taste her nipples.

"Mmm" was the only sound she made as he sucked and licked her while he began to move. "A lot more of that."

He gave more until she squirmed against him, lifting to give him a lot more of what he liked, which was her.

Then there were no words between them, only moans and sighs and the groans he made because damn, this was good. And when her body began to quake, he was right there with her, groaning and trembling as they both came hard. He had to hold on to Brenna as he pumped with his release, feeling as if he had given her everything he had.

And afterward, as he held her, he realized that Brenna made him feel things he'd never felt before. Like wanting to take care of her and make her happy.

For the rest of his life. So he could feel this good forever.

He kissed her neck, her jaw, her mouth.

"Hungry?" he asked.

She looked up at him with such clear eyes and a bright smile. "Starving, thanks to you."

He grinned. "How about I make us some breakfast?"

"Fabulous idea. I'll help."

They got up and cleaned up, then headed into the kitchen. Finn opened the door and called for Murphy, who came rambling in from the woods. He gave Murphy his food and set out fresh water for him, and then he and Brenna made bacon, eggs and toast along with sliced cantaloupe and orange juice.

Brenna took a slice of her toast and dredged it through her eggs. "You know we could have gone to the main house for breakfast."

"Yeah, but then I wouldn't have been alone with you."

She gave him an unfathomable look. "That's true. And everyone would have stared."

"You think so? I don't think so. I don't think anyone cares whether we're dating or not."

She snorted out a laugh. "Oh, come on, Finn. You know the family. They'll care."

"So I should expect the third degree from your dad?"

She shrugged and grabbed a slice of bacon, took a bite and chewed thoughtfully. "I don't know. Maybe. He likes you so he probably figures you and I together is okay."

"Just okay?"

"Jury's out. My mom, on the other hand, might have a few things to say about me having hot sex with the hired help."

Now it was his turn to laugh. "Oh, now I'm the hired help?"

She winked at him, then dipped her toast in his eggs.

"Hey, no stealing my food."

"I ate all my eggs."

"I can make more for you."

"I'm good."

He looked her up and down. "You sure are."

"And you're good for my ego. I might just keep you around for a while."

"You have to. We have to present our fake-engaged selves to Esther and Brock at their party or present opening or whatever it was they said."

"Right. Which means I'll have to put up with Mitchell and Allison again."

He could tell she was still bothered by that. He reached over and grabbed her hand. "Hey. We have this fake engagement down to a science now. We've got this."

Her lips curved. "Yes. We do."

And maybe, if everything went according to plan, he could arrange a few more events to keep the fake engagement going. At least until Brenna realized the two of them belonged together as a couple. Then they could forget the fake engagement and just—be.

He was looking forward to that day.

CHAPTER
......
eighteen

Brenna meandered among her Riesling grapes, checking each bundle for ripeness. She had staff to do this, but these were her babies, and it was nearly time for harvest.

Despite the oppressive heat, she enjoyed walking the vineyard and reviewing the vines. She did it every afternoon before she left for the day, making sure that every vine was secure, that pests were controlled, that nothing was out of order.

As usual, all the vines were in great shape, the leaves beautiful, the grapes plump and ready to pick.

Next week should produce a bountiful harvest. She couldn't wait.

She spotted her father out there among the grapes as well. Then again, when wasn't he out there?

"*Bellissimo*, eh?" he asked.

"*Si*, Papa," she replied. "Everything looks good. We have our seasonal staff lined up for the harvest next week."

He nodded. "Good. I'm anxious to get my hands on these Rieslings. And the sauvignon blanc not too far behind them."

As much as she knew about winemaking, her father knew ten times more. He'd been standing in vineyards since he was a child in Italy, and he was a master at his craft.

"Don't stand too long in the sun."

"You sound like your mama. I'm fine." He pointed to his head. "I'm wearing a hat. She makes me wear sunscreen."

She laughed. "Because she loves you."

He waved his hand at her in dismissal and went back to walking the lanes.

"Bye, Daddy," she said.

"Addio, bambina mia."

She smiled.

She was about to head into the main house and get a cold drink when she saw the door open to Finn's warehouse where he made his whiskey. Murphy was asleep outside in the shade. She hadn't seen Finn all day, which wasn't unusual since they were both busy, but she was curious, so she walked that way.

When she walked through the doors, she stopped, blinked and looked around, not believing what she saw.

He had an entire distillery in here, not some layman's half-assed whiskey-making apparatus, but a still and barrels and a fermentation station. It looked professional as hell. Granted, it wasn't a huge operation, but it was still an operation.

What. The. Hell?

She walked in and found him crouched down over a still, reading temperatures and writing notes.

"What the hell is going on here?"

He looked up at her. "Uh, whiskey making?"

"I can see that. Where did all this stuff come from?"

He stood and looked down at her. "Stores, mostly."

She cocked her head to the side. "You're being deliberately evasive and you know exactly what I'm asking."

"I bought it. Well, your dad and I did. He's invested in my whiskey business."

Unbelievable. She crossed her arms. "Oh, so now you have a whiskey business."

He gave her a smile, which only irritated her more. "Not yet. But someday."

There was that word again. *Someday.* Which meant nothing when one was talking about what looked like a sizable investment in equipment. "How much did all of this cost?"

"Why do you care? Your father likes my whiskey. If I recall, you liked it, too."

"I did, but that doesn't mean—"

"Doesn't mean what?" He turned to face her. "That you think I could sell it? That I could do something that's worthwhile with it? That only the great Brenna Bellini could make a sellable consumable product that people will like?"

He was twisting her words. "That's not at all what I meant."

"Then tell me what's wrong with me making whiskey."

He was mad. She could see it on his face. "I just . . . I . . ."

He waited, while she tried to form an explanation for why she felt so twisted up inside. Maybe it was because she hadn't bothered to show any interest in his whiskey making before. Maybe it was because she felt a little jealous that her father had invested in this without telling her. Before now it had always been her and her dad making magic together with wine.

Now it was Finn and her dad and whiskey?

"I don't know. I just don't like it."

"What is it that you don't like, Brenna? The whiskey, the fact that your dad invested in it? Or is it me?"

Her head was pounding and she couldn't answer him, not when he was looking at her with concern and maybe a little hurt in his eyes.

"I don't know. I have to go."

She turned and left the building, heading straight for the house. She went in through the back door, grateful not to see anyone as she headed down the hall. She'd almost made it to the stairs when she ran straight into her sisters.

"Oh, hey," Erin said. "Ooh, you look hot."

"Have you been at the vineyards?" Honor asked. "It's like a million degrees outside this afternoon."

"You want some ice water?" Erin asked.

"No. I don't want anything other than to be left alone." She circled around them and up the stairs to her room and shut the door. She paced back and forth, realizing all that did was keep her in her own head, and she didn't like the thoughts there. She stripped off her clothes, wound up her hair and got in the shower to wash off the dirt and sweat from the vineyard. Once she got out, she climbed into shorts and a tank top and flopped onto her bed, staring up at the ceiling.

What was wrong with her? Why did she jump all over Finn about the whiskey?

She heard a knock on the door and didn't even have to ask to know who it was.

"Come in."

"We brought you some ice water," Honor said, carrying a glass as she came in. "You looked awfully heated when you first came in."

"At least you showered," Erin said, coming to sit on the

edge of the bed. "Because you were heated both physically and emotionally."

Brenna pushed herself up to sit, taking the glass Honor handed her. "Thanks. I'm sorry. I was in a mood."

"I'll say," Erin said. "What's up?"

"I had a fight with Finn."

"Uh-oh." Honor pulled up the chair next to the bed. "Tell us about it."

"It was stupid. I was stupid. I said stupid things."

Erin looked to Honor, then at Brenna. "Well now we really want to hear about it."

Brenna couldn't help but laugh. "Of course you do."

Erin shrugged. "Hey, I've acted like an ass on my fair share of occasions. It's only fair you get a turn."

"That's true," Honor said, and when Erin shot her a look, she gave her an innocent shrug. "What? It is true."

"It is," Brenna said. "But this time it was me. Did you all know that Finn is making whiskey in his warehouse?"

"Yes," Honor said.

Erin nodded. "Of course. What did you think he was doing out there? Making pizza?"

"Well, no. I knew he dabbled, and that Dad let him build that big building. But there's a whole manufacturing facility in there now. A still and barrels and pipes and fermentation and everything."

"Brenna," Honor said. "Haven't you ever been in there?"

"Well, no."

"You did know Dad invested in Finn's whiskey production, right?" Erin asked.

Apparently she was the only one who didn't know that. "Uh, no, I did not. And that's what I laid into him about."

Honor shot her a look of concern. "Oh, Brenna, why?"

And wasn't that the question of the day? "I don't know. I guess it was the surprise of seeing all the equipment. I thought he was just playing around with a home still, and I expected something . . . smaller. I had no idea he had a whole potential business going."

"And that upset you . . . why, exactly?" Erin asked.

"Again, I don't know. I wish I did." She pulled her knees up to her chest, feeling shame for how she'd reacted.

"Maybe because Dad invested in Finn and didn't tell you about it?" Honor asked.

She looked over at Honor. "That's partly it. You know, Dad and I have always been about the winemaking. That's been our thing. You do the weddings, and Erin has the business mind."

"And you and Dad have always had the winemaking," Erin said. "It's been just the two of you since you were little. You always wanted to be out there in the vineyard with him."

"And now he's developed an interest in what Finn is doing," Honor said. "It's natural for you to feel a little jealous about that."

"It's petty," Brenna said. "Finn is like a son to Dad. And Finn . . . he's so proud of what he's doing. And I just stomped all over it."

Erin shrugged. "Your feelings are your feelings, Bren. You have a right to feel them, even if they are petty. But how you treated Finn, well, we don't know what you said, but if you hurt him, then you'll have to fix that."

She sighed. "Yes, I will. Thank you for hearing me out. And for not telling me I'm a terrible person."

Honor laid her hand on Brenna's arm. "We're your sisters. We'd never tell you that."

"Unless you killed someone," Erin said.

Honor nodded. "Then we'd tell you that what you did was terrible."

"After we helped you bury the body," Erin said with a smirk.

"Erin!" Honor said.

Brenna laughed and felt immensely better. But she was still going to have to apologize to Finn.

She changed into something a little more appropriate for dinner, hoping he'd be there, that they'd get a chance to talk after. Her stomach sank in disappointment when he didn't show up at the table. And when her parents asked where he was, she said she thought he was busy doing something. But after dinner, she walked over to his place, disappointed again to find that he wasn't there.

She thought about texting him, but he was obviously upset or he would have come to dinner or stayed home. He had to know she'd come to her senses and apologize.

Then again, who was she to expect anything from Finn? She'd acted like a total bitch today. He probably didn't want to see her at all.

She walked back to the house feeling more miserable than ever.

And it was all her fault.

CHAPTER
· · · · · ·
nineteen

Finn walked into the Screaming Hawk craft brewery and looked around. He spied both Jason and Clay at a corner table and headed their way. Owen was behind the bar working and waved as he walked by.

It was good to see Owen at work. He was still thin from his cancer treatments, but he was starting to get some color back in his face and he looked stronger than he had when this had all started.

He got to the table and saw that Jason and Clay already had beers.

"Be right back," he said.

He went to the bar and waited while Owen dealt with another customer. When he finished, Owen made his way to him.

"What's up, Finn?" Owen asked.

"Not much. How's it going with you?"

"Oh, you know, running a brew pub. Just living life."

Which Finn knew meant a lot more to Owen these days than ever before.

"That's great. And, hey, you're looking good. Much healthier since the last time I saw you."

Owen smiled. "Thanks. I'm feeling pretty good, too. Glad to see you guys here tonight."

"Sorry I haven't been in a while. Been busy."

"I heard. Seeing Brenna, huh?"

The one thing about everyone being close was that they always knew your business. "Something like that."

"What'll you have?"

Finn was grateful that Owen didn't press for details about Brenna and him. He wasn't in the mind-set for it tonight.

"The Back in Black IPA."

"Should have known. Let me pull it for you."

Owen drew him a draft and Finn pulled out his money and paid him.

"How's the whiskey making going?"

"Good. You should come by for a taste."

Owen scratched the side of his nose. "I try to steer clear of the Bellini property these days."

"I thought all was forgiven."

"It is, but I still think Erin needs her space."

Finn knew Owen felt bad for how everything went down with the wedding. Or the wedding that hadn't happened between Owen and Erin. But it all had turned out for the best in the end. Erin had fallen in love with Jason and she was happy.

Sometimes things just worked out the way they were supposed to. It sucked that Owen had backed out at the last minute without telling Erin he was sick, but he'd been scared and he hadn't wanted to hurt Erin, which he'd ended up doing anyway. He'd apologized to Erin and her family, and they'd all eventually forgiven him.

To Finn, it was all water under the bridge. People fucked up sometimes, and if their intentions were good, you forgave them and moved on. Holding a grudge only made you miserable in the end.

Which didn't mean Finn wasn't still irritated at Brenna. He didn't know what the hell her issue was with him making whiskey, or with her dad investing in it. But when he'd tried to get her to open up about her feelings, she'd bailed on the conversation. On him. And that was the part that pissed him off the most.

When Jason had texted asking if he wanted to go out for beers tonight, he figured getting away to clear his head was a good idea. Besides, he hadn't been out with his friends in a while, and he'd been meaning to come see Owen. He'd dropped Murphy over at the main house with Johnny and drove in to town, stopped to eat a burger, then met the guys here.

He took his beer to the table and sat.

"We were just talking about wedding plans," Clay said.

"Whose?" Finn asked. "Yours or Jason's?"

"Both, actually. Though Jason got the jump on us with their speeded-up shotgun wedding," Clay said, slanting a sly smile at Jason.

"Promise. No shotguns will be in attendance at our wedding. And my fiancée is not pregnant. That I know of."

Finn laughed. "Considering how fast this wedding is coming about, I don't think the Bellinis would be all that upset if you added a baby to the mix."

Jason held up his hands. "One thing at a time. With the wedding and moving in together, that's more than enough. We can wait on a baby."

Finn and Clay looked at each other.

"You watch," Clay said. "Erin will be pregnant by the time Alice and I get married next year."

Finn nodded. "Not even going to bet on that one. It's a sure thing."

Jason went a little pale. "Come on, guys. Give me a break."

Finn laughed and took a long drink of his beer. It was intense and had the perfect bitterness, just the way he liked it. Owen really knew how to brew beer. He was glad to see his friend back to doing what he loved again. Though he hadn't known Owen as long as Jason and Clay had, they'd become friends as soon as Finn had come to the United States.

All the guys had taken him under their wing and decided right then and there that Finn would be part of their inner circle, despite them knowing nothing about him. If the Bellinis had given him their seal of approval, that was good enough for Jason, Owen and Clay, and from then on, they'd done everything together: hanging out in the summers when everyone was home from college, going out to celebrate milestones and birthdays and hanging out at the lake or going fishing.

For someone who'd never had siblings, these guys were the closest thing to brothers Finn had ever had, and they'd come into his life when he'd needed friendship the most.

Kind of like Brenna and her sisters. He'd been lucky, and he had Maureen Bellini to thank for that. He had no idea what would have happened to him if he'd been left on his own in Ireland.

Jason nudged his shoulder. "Hey, you with us?"

Finn pulled himself out of his thoughts. "Yeah."

"You're quiet," Clay said. "Something on your mind?"

"Just thinking about when I first got here, and how you made friends with me right away."

"Well, someone had to," Jason said. "You were sad and pathetic."

Clay nodded. "This is true. We felt sorry for you. We knew no one else would be friends with you so we took pity on you."

Finn rolled his eyes. "No, you thought, 'Look at this stud. He's going to draw the ladies to us. We should make friends with him.'"

Jason looked to Clay. "I don't remember it like that at all."

"Me, either."

Owen came over and pulled up a spot. "What are we talking about?"

"How we rescued Finn from a life of obscurity when he first arrived," Clay said.

"Oh, that," Owen said. "Yeah, you were a total shitshow. You're lucky to have us."

"All of you can eat shit."

Clay grinned. "See how he loves us? Like brothers."

Finn laughed. They *were* like brothers. Insults flew regularly, but he knew that they'd always have his back.

"How's business, Owen?" Jason asked.

"Damn busy. Appreciate you all coming out. How's the beer?"

"Excellent, as always," Clay said, lifting up his glass. "This pale ale is damn good. I like the lime and lemon flavors in it."

"Good choice. It's selling well, too. I think it's the late-summer heat."

Clay nodded. "Quenching my thirst after a long day of working cattle."

"Good to hear."

"And how are you doing?" Jason asked. "Or are you tired of hearing that?"

Owen offered up a smile. "Never too tired of knowing you all care. I'm doing fine. All my scans and tests are clear. I feel good, my appetite is back and I don't have to see my oncologist for three months, so I'd say that's all good news."

Finn was relieved. "That's really great news."

"You're putting some pounds back on again," Jason said.

Owen patted his stomach. "Was that a remark about my weight?"

Jason laughed. "Only complimentary. You lost a lot of weight during your treatment and you were looking scary for a while."

"Now you're insulting my appearance."

"Well, you're ugly even on your best days," Clay said.

Finn grinned. "Yeah, we've been meaning to mention that to you, buddy."

"I can't believe I let you bastards in here." But Owen smiled.

Finn was glad they were picking on someone else. Though they eventually made the rounds so everyone was equally insulted, as typically happened. How else would they know they were friends?

"How's it going with Brenna?" Clay asked him.

Finn was hoping that was one topic that wouldn't be brought up. "It's going."

Jason studied him. "That means they had a fight. What did you do?"

Finn lifted his head. "I didn't do anything. She walked away in the middle of an argument. That she started once she found out about the whiskey warehouse and that her dad has invested in it."

"Ah." Owen nodded. "Brenna's really close to her dad. Maybe she felt threatened."

"But why? My relationship with Johnny has nothing to do with her."

"In *your* mind, yeah," Jason said. "In hers, she probably sees it as something entirely different. The two of them and winemaking have been an inseparable combination since Brenna was a kid. For as long as I can remember she was out in the vineyards with him, following him around, learning about winemaking. It was a given that she'd follow him into the business."

"That's true," Clay said. "And Johnny never showed interest in anything else. And then you come along and start making whiskey, and suddenly you have a whole operation going. An operation that Johnny's interested enough to invest in. Maybe she sees that as him showing less interest in winemaking."

"Which he isn't." Finn made the whiskey. It was damn good whiskey. Johnny just knew a good business investment when he saw one. It wasn't like Johnny was in there making whiskey with him. If there was one thing Finn knew about Johnny Bellini, it was that nothing could ever tear him away from making wine. It was in his blood and that would never change.

"Give her some time," Owen said. "She'll figure it out on her own."

"I guess. I just wish she'd talk to me."

"The Bellini women have always been quick to anger," Jason said. "But also quick to forgive and forget. Like Owen said, just give her some time to cool down and think things over."

He thought about what the guys had said all night, even as he drove by the main house on the way to his own. The house was dark except for one light, which he knew was from Brenna's room.

He ached to see her, to hold her, to just talk to her so he could figure out how she felt.

But not tonight. He'd give her that time and space that the guys had talked about, and when she was ready, she could come and talk to him.

CHAPTER

· · · · · ·

twenty

BRENNA WAS WORRIED.

Finn hadn't shown up at breakfast that morning. Or lunch. Typically he didn't miss a meal that Louise cooked. And now her parents were giving her the side-eye like she had done something wrong.

Which she had, of course, but she wasn't going to tell them that.

She busied herself with work all day, but thoughts of Finn crept in anyway. As she walked from the house to the wine cellar, she thought maybe she'd catch sight of Finn working outside somewhere. Unfortunately, she didn't, which only made her stomach knot up even more.

She needed to talk to her dad, clear her head of all that was rolling around inside it.

She found him outside checking grapes. It was eight million degrees out so she grabbed a floppy hat, put on her sunscreen and walked out there, taking time to review the grapes in the aisle where her dad was located. They were plump and ready to pick. Brenna should have been filled with joy about that, but right now all she felt was miserable.

"Hey, Dad."

"The grapes, they look good, eh?"

"They do. Can I ask you a question?"

"Si." He continued to walk, so she walked with him.

"Why did you invest in Finn's whiskey-making project?"

He stopped and turned to her with a curious look on his face. "Why wouldn't I? It's fine Irish whiskey, he knows what he's doing and the family might someday branch out and sell it, with Finn's permission. I discussed it with your mother, who agreed with me. It's a sound business investment."

When he put it like that, her entire blowup with Finn made her feel childish and petty. "Of course."

"Plus, I love the boy like my own. Why wouldn't we want to encourage his success? Especially with something he's good at?"

And now she felt even worse.

"Oh, sure. That makes sense."

She walked with him for a bit more, then made her escape, fleeing to the house, hiding out in her office with the worst feeling of guilt and dread sitting like a boulder in her stomach.

After wrapping up work for the day, she went to her room to clean up and change clothes, then headed to the kitchen.

Louise had made chicken and rice with asparagus for dinner, so she asked her to package up two servings, which Louise did with a knowing smile. Brenna ducked out the back door and made her way to Finn's place, not sure what kind of reception she was going to get, or if he'd even be there. But she had to try.

Finn wasn't outside, but his truck was there, which meant he was home—a good sign. She knocked on the door and Murphy barked.

No one answered.

Hmm.

She knocked again, louder this time. Still no answer.

Was he okay? She hadn't seen him today. Maybe he was sick. She tried the door handle and the door opened, so she walked inside.

Murphy greeted her with his tail swooshing furiously back and forth, so she bent to brush her hand over the top of his head.

"Hey, Murph. Where's your daddy? Is he okay?"

She slipped the food into the fridge, and when she turned around there was Finn, dripping wet with a towel hanging low over his hips.

"Oh. You were in the shower."

"Yeah."

"I'm sorry. When I knocked you didn't answer the door and I hadn't seen you all day and I thought maybe you were sick so I let myself in to check. Should I leave?"

He stared at her for a few extremely long seconds while she stood frozen, afraid to move at all.

"No. Give me a minute."

He turned and she couldn't help but admire his broad tanned back as he walked away from her. She curled her fingers into her palms, both nervous and helplessly turned on at the sight of an almost naked Finn, wishing she hadn't caused this rift between them. Because right now they could be out somewhere having dinner together, or even better, enjoying a night in together. Instead, she was going to have to apologize for going off on him like she had.

Rather than just standing there like a frozen statue, she

moved over to the sofa and took a seat. Murphy followed
her and curled up by her feet.

Wait. Maybe he wouldn't want to sit next to her. She
didn't want to assume, so she got up and took the chair instead.

Murphy followed.

She tapped her feet and studied the furniture. Then again,
he might think she was the one who wanted distance. That
was bad, so she got up and moved back to the sofa, taking a
spot on the far corner. Murphy got up again, followed her,
then looked up at her, his head cocked to the side, no doubt
wondering when she was going to make her next move.

Even the dog thought she was crazy.

"Playing musical chairs with my dog?"

"Oh. Uh. No." Why was Finn the only guy to ever make
her feel nervous? Maybe because she'd only made colossal
mistakes with him? "I was . . . uh . . . trying out your furniture."

He walked into the room, wearing shorts and a short-
sleeved shirt, smelling fresh and clean. And then he sat
right next to her and she wanted to lick him all over and
kiss him and do anything but have this conversation.

"You hungry?" he asked.

She tilted her head. "What?"

"You. Hungry. I'm hungry. I was going to make dinner."

"Oh. Louise made dinner and I had her put a couple of
servings in containers for us. Or for you, in case you didn't
want to eat with me."

"Why wouldn't I want to eat with you?"

"Because of the things I said yesterday." She shifted to
look directly at him. "I'm sorry, Finn. Sometimes I blurt
without thinking. I was upset about the whiskey equipment,
which I shouldn't have been. I should have checked out

what you were doing a long time ago, and I'm sorry for that, too. You've done remarkable things and I'm proud of you. Happy for you, actually. You have an amazing talent and instead of supporting you, I accused you of coming between my father and me, which was childish and petty. It was hurtful and uncalled for and I'm really sorry."

His lips curved. "As apologies go, that was a damn good one, Brenna. You're forgiven."

She hadn't realized how tight her chest was until she let go of a breath. "Thank you."

"Now I need to ask you for something."

"Okay."

"When we have an argument—about anything—I need you to stay so we can talk it out, instead of walking away from me."

She winced. "I do have a tendency to do that, don't I?"

"You do."

"I blame my first marriage on my tendency to bail. Mitchell and I would get into the worst arguments, and every time I tried to explain how I felt, he'd refuse to listen to my point of view. You can't argue with someone who won't hear your side of things. He'd drone on and on about his point of view, not at all willing to listen to mine. It got to be so unbearable that whenever we had a disagreement I'd just walk away."

Finn picked up her hand. "The whole point of having an argument is so that both sides can air their grievances. That means you both listen, and then come to some sort of understanding. It shouldn't be one person getting to air their side and refusing to listen to the other person. That's not fair."

She was so relieved that he understood. "No, it's not fair. But that's how it was. And it was tiresome."

"No wonder you don't like to fight."

"No, I don't."

"You know," he said, getting up to head to the fridge. He got out the food, then looked over at her with a smile. "A good argument can be healthy now and then."

She stood and went into the kitchen. "Is that right?"

"Yeah. Clears the air." He opened the containers and placed them in the microwave, set it and pushed the button. "You holler back and forth at each other, get everything out in the open so you each know what's bothering you. If someone was in the wrong, they can—and should—apologize. Then it's over and you kiss and make up."

"You speak like you've done this a time or two."

"Nah. Never had a long-term relationship with someone worth having a fight with, I guess. But my ma and da used to have some rows. Lots of fiery yelling back and forth."

"Really." She leaned against the kitchen counter. "And how did that work out?"

He shrugged. "Fine. They got it all out of their systems and then they'd tell me to go play outside for a half hour or so. I think they were having sex after that."

She laughed. "So fight first, and then makeup sex?"

He took the containers out of the microwave and set them on the table. "See? Key to a happy relationship. And no one holds any resentments inside."

Brenna had to admit Finn's suggestion had merit. At least both sides could get their say. And she did like the idea of makeup sex.

She ate her dinner and contemplated how easily Finn had forgiven her outrageous behavior. He was like no man she'd ever known. Certainly nothing like Mitchell, who would have used their fight against her, reminding her time and time again how wrong she'd been.

But with Finn, he'd simply . . . forgiven her. And now it was over and forgotten.

She supposed she was going to have to get used to that. Maybe even adapt his philosophy to her own way of thinking. Because she was a lot more relaxed now.

"That was good," Finn said once he ate every bite of chicken, asparagus and rice on his plate. He took a swallow of iced tea and took his plate to the sink.

She'd only eaten half of hers. "I'm finished with mine. Do you want more?"

He eyed her plate. "Maybe later."

He took her dish and covered it, tucking it into the fridge. Brenna cleaned the table while Finn washed the few dishes there were.

"I should go," she said once he hung up the dish towel.

"Now why would you do that?"

She didn't know why, other than they'd settled their argument and now she felt suddenly . . . she didn't know what she felt.

You feel out of control around him, Brenna, that's how you feel. And for someone who prided herself on always being in control, that was unsettling as hell.

But when he scooped his arm around her and drew her against him, she knew exactly how she felt. Warm, aroused and suddenly in no hurry to leave.

"I was kind of hoping we'd get to the makeup sex part of our argument."

She arched a brow. "Oh. Did we have an argument?"

"Yeah. Yesterday. Want me to rehash it for you?"

"Unnecessary." She swept her fingers over his chiseled chest, realizing how much she'd missed him.

It was only one day, Brenna. How much can you miss a guy in one day?

A lot, apparently.

She lifted up to press her lips to his. He grasped the back of her head and kissed her so thoroughly she felt that kiss all the way down to her toes.

She never knew her toes could tingle, but they did. And all her other parts as well.

This was what she had missed—his hands snaking down her back, his tongue sliding along hers, their breaths mingling in that desperate way that told her he wanted her as much as she wanted him.

This fierce desire coiled up inside her, filling her with a sense of urgency that wouldn't be denied. She lifted his shirt, feeling the heat of his skin against her hand. He tangled his fingers in her hair, tugging her head back to rain kisses along her throat and collarbone.

She wore a loose, low tank top and he dragged it down, baring her chest. She had thrown on a demi bra after her shower and he drew the cups away to kiss and lick her breasts and nipples.

Her breath caught and her legs trembled, her focus only on the sensations his mouth and tongue evoked. Her sex throbbed with the need to have his lips and tongue on her.

"Finn."

He lifted her up and carried her down the hall to his bedroom, put her down only long enough to strip off her clothes and his, then laid her on the bed, her legs dangling over the edge.

And then his mouth was on her sex, sucking her clit, his tongue taking her right to the edge—and then over. She came with a shuddering cry, her body racked with delicious spasms that seemed to go on forever.

Finn stood and grabbed a condom from the drawer, put

it on and lifted her leg, then eased inside her. She was still pulsing, her pussy wrapping around him like a glove.

"Damn," he whispered as he began to move against her.

His features tightened as he stared down at her while he pumped into her, and all she could do was hold on, because her body was fully tuned in and ready to explode again. All she had to do was reach down and help herself along.

"Yes, do it," Finn said.

His words excited her. The way he looked at her thrilled her. The way he snaked his hand up and down her leg as he twisted inside her excited her. She had to face that being here with him was the pinnacle of everything.

She was so close. And when she climaxed, he came down on top of her and gathered her in his arms, taking her mouth with his while he shuddered against her. It was a hot, passionate, intimate kiss as they both came apart together.

After, she felt his ragged breath on her cheek while she worked to take in a few deep breaths of her own. She was so sweaty that her skin stuck to his. He scooped his hand around her butt and lifted her off the bed, carrying her into the bathroom. He disposed of the condom, then turned the shower on so they could both rinse off.

She wound up her hair and stepped in after him. The water felt cool and such a relief to her tortured, hot body. Finn soaped up her back, his movements slow and tender. He rinsed her, then allowed her to return the favor. She loved the feel of his body under her hands, the way his muscles flexed with her touch. She was reluctant to let go of him, but she did and he rinsed off, and then they got out.

After she dried off, she started to grab her clothes.

"Nope," Finn said, lifting her up and carrying her to the bed. "I've got you naked now and you're staying that way."

He climbed onto the bed next to her. She rolled to her side and propped her head up on her hand.

"Oh, so you're going to hold me prisoner here?"

He trailed his fingertip between her breasts. "You're free to leave anytime you want."

As if she'd move from this spot, with him touching her and looking at her the way he was. She rolled over onto her back. "I guess you can have your way with me, then."

He moved over her, his lips inches from hers. "I love the way you suffer, Brenna."

She laughed, and then he kissed her.

CHAPTER

······

twenty-one

THE FALL HARVEST was Brenna's busiest time of year. It was crazy hectic, but also fun, especially since the entire family pitched in to help. They typically didn't have weddings that weekend because of the harvest, and because they invited the public to come out and help to pick the grapes, something the entire community enjoyed every year.

Though they hired seasonal help, it was a community outreach—and also excellent marketing for Red Moss Vineyards—to bring in friends and neighbors and put out the invitation on social media for harvest day.

Besides, who didn't want to come out and stomp grapes? Other than Brenna, of course. She'd done plenty of that when she was younger, and while it was fun, her stomping days were over. Now she directed the action rather than took part in it.

Her day began at five a.m., though the official start time was at seven. She was up early, meeting with her dad and the staff to go over everything that needed to be done and make sure all the buckets and boxes were set up at the vineyard. By six a.m. people had already started to arrive, and fortunately they had staff there to direct the visitors to parking and the waiting area.

There were large pots of coffee along with juice and water for those waiting, but Erin, Honor and Mom were taking care of their guests so Brenna could be free to deal with vineyard business today.

"Excited?" Finn asked.

She nodded. "One of our best days of the year."

He pulled her close and brushed his lips across hers. "Have a great day."

She smiled at him, relieved that he understood how utterly swamped she was going to be today. She likely wouldn't have a moment to spare. "We'll catch up later."

He nodded. "If you need something, yell for me."

By the time Brenna and her team were ready, the staging area was filled with excited people who were ready to start picking grapes and filling buckets and bins. Since her dad was not at all into public speaking, it fell to Brenna to launch the harvest, so she walked up to the front of the group.

"Good morning, everyone. Thanks so much for coming to Harvest Day at Red Moss Vineyards. On behalf of the Bellini family, we welcome you and hope you'll have a wonderful time harvesting grapes. We're going to divide the groups into pickers, fillers and stompers. If you want to stomp grapes, you can follow Finn Nolan over there to the left-hand side, and he'll lead you to the grape-stomping holding area. Pickers will be led by my father, Johnny Bellini. He and his staff will lay out all the rules about picking grapes. Then we'll have loading groups take the grapes and load them into buckets and dump them into the stomping bins.

"I want you all to know that every part of this process is vital to making wine, so we appreciate all of you showing up to help us out. Once we're finished, a champagne brunch will be served and everyone gets a T-shirt, courtesy of Red Moss Vineyards. Is everyone ready to get started?"

Cheers and claps went up and Brenna felt that initial thrill of excitement zipping through her nerve endings.

"Okay, everyone, follow your leaders, and let's have a fun harvest!"

She waited while everyone dispersed. It all went well, no one seemed confused and as she walked among the lines of the grapes, her team had everyone in order.

"Owen came today," Honor said. "I wasn't sure he would."

Brenna smiled as she noticed him having a conversation with their mom. "I'm glad he did. He hasn't missed a harvest for as long as we've known him. The breakup with Erin was hard on everyone and Owen has distanced himself since then."

Honor nodded. "Yes, he has. I think Dad calling him and asking him to come really let him know that all was forgiven."

"I hope so. Erin is over it, she's happy, and it's time for everyone to move on now."

"Exactly." Honor smiled. "Oh, Colt is here. I need to go."

Brenna squinted in the morning light to get a look at this guy that Honor had been dating. Ruggedly good-looking for sure. Honor threw her arms around him and Colt grabbed two giant handfuls of her sister's ass. Right there in the open in front of everyone.

Ugh. Brenna could only hope her parents hadn't seen that.

"What the—" Erin had come over. "Is that the infamous Colt she's been gushing over?"

"Yes."

"Handsy, isn't he?" Erin glared at him.

It was one thing to put your hands all over a woman when you were in private. But this was a public event for the Bellini family with outside guests and Brenna could tell that Honor was uncomfortable with the groping.

"Who the hell is that guy?" Owen asked as he stepped up beside Brenna.

"Colt. Some cowboy Honor's been dating."

"Uh-huh. A little publicly familiar with Honor's—parts, isn't he?"

Owen didn't look any happier about it than Brenna was.

"I'll say," Erin said.

Owen let out a disgusted grunt. "Would you like me to have a talk with him? Or maybe knock him down?"

Brenna smirked. "No, I think Honor can handle him." Hopefully.

"Fine. But I'll keep a close eye on him. Hey, good to see both of you."

"You, too, Owen," Erin said. "We're glad you're here."

Owen shot her a smile. "Thanks. It's good to be here."

Brenna watched as Owen trailed after Honor and Colt.

"Well, that was interesting, don't you think?" Erin asked.

"What was?"

"Owen was pissed about Colt getting handsy with Honor."

Brenna shrugged. "He's always been protective of us."

Erin gave her a half smile. "Maybe."

What the hell did that mean? She started to ask, but then someone needed her, and Erin ran off, so she didn't get the chance. She quickly fell into the routine of the day, and her mind was back on her grapes.

Admittedly, her grapes were her babies—as well as Red Moss Vineyards's biggest moneymaker. Having people who weren't well versed in handling them made her nervous. But between her, Dad and the staff, they kept a close eye on the pickers and made sure no one abused the grapes. Not that they would. They always had repeaters who showed up every year to pick and they loved the grapes nearly as much as Brenna did.

The system was flawless, and as she watched the bunches being placed in the buckets and carried to the stomping bins, she couldn't help the thrill of excitement. Her grapes were on their way.

As she moved from station to station, she caught sight of Finn directing staff, carrying buckets and bins or stopping to help when someone asked a question. No matter where she was, he always seemed to enter her line of sight, sweat pouring down his face on this warm day, his muscles straining from the effort of carrying full buckets of grapes by himself.

She sighed. That man was something. And he made her heart do flippity-floppity things.

She stopped for a while to watch as several people—men, women and children—stomped the grapes. It always drew a crowd and Brenna was thrilled to see that a couple of the local television crews had showed up today. She had her mom to thank for that.

What she hadn't expected were those microphones stuck in her face.

"We hear this is an annual event here at Red Moss Vineyards," one of the reporters said. "What are your planned activities for the day?"

Fortunately, Brenna was able to think on her feet, so she outlined the day's activities, then added, "If you'd like to take your shoes off, you're welcome to stomp some grapes. And we're including champagne brunch at the end."

The reporter knew a good angle when she saw it, so before long she was stomping grapes in one of the bins, with the camera person getting a great shot while the adorable reporter gave a blow-by-blow of the process. All in all, some awesome publicity for the vineyard.

"How about you, Ms. Bellini?" another reporter asked. "Will you be stomping the grapes?"

She laughed. "Oh, no. I leave that fun for our guests."

Finn came up to her and took her hand, smiling at the camera and the crowd that had gathered. "But don't you think she should?"

A round of applause followed Finn's suggestion. Since they were on camera, she couldn't shoot him a venomous look. Instead, she grinned and said, "Of course. I'd love to."

She kicked off her sneakers, dipped her feet in the wash bucket, then held Finn's hand while she climbed into one of the bins, whispering to him as she did.

"I'm going to kill you."

He just laughed in reply and said, "Have fun."

She slid into the bin. It had been years since she'd stomped grapes, but she'd done this so many times she hadn't forgotten the rhythm. Up and down, moving over the entire bin to be sure she mashed every grape. She'd forgotten how much fun it was and since the cameras were on her, she explained the process, how this was the old style of mashing grapes, how the liquid was collected underneath and how different it was from the more modern mechanical methods of extraction.

"You can imagine how much longer it took our ancestors to yield grape juice," she explained. "How hard they had to work, compared to how quickly we can get juice with today's machinery. But this is so much more fun, and an incredible amount of exercise, too."

Everyone laughed, and when the cameras turned off, she

climbed out of the bin, rinsed and dried her feet and put her sneakers back on.

Since Finn was still nearby, she went over to him. "You set me up."

"Actually, your mom did. She's the one who suggested it."

"Oh, really." She looked over at her mom, who was sitting at the table under a shade tree running grape totals. She happened to look up at the time, smiled and waved.

"You looked totally hot out there stomping those grapes. And I don't mean weather hot, either."

She looked up at him. "Thank you. It was fun. You should give it a try."

"Oh, you know, I think I hear your dad calling my name." He gave her a quick kiss on the lips. "See you later."

"Coward."

He laughed and dashed off and Brenna shook her head, then a moment later realized he'd kissed her—in public, and she hadn't shied away from it. In fact, her mom had been right there. She looked around to see not a single person paying the slightest bit of attention to her—to them.

She sighed, realizing that maybe her having a relationship with Finn was only a big deal to her, and not a single person was freaking out about it.

What did that mean?

It means you need to chill, Brenna.

Okay, then. She'd relax. A little. Maybe. Eventually.

Half the day was gone by the time picking and stomping was through. The bins were loaded up and driven to the warehouse for processing, and all the volunteers were directed to the barn where brunch was going to be served.

By then Brenna was exhausted, starving and ever-so-grateful for the catered brunch. First, she stood on the dais to talk to all the volunteers.

"My family and I would like to thank you all so much for participating today. You were a great help in harvesting the grapes, and we hope you had as much fun as we did. Now enjoy your brunch."

Everyone clapped and the food was served.

Brenna saw that Finn had saved her a seat at the main table. She smiled at that and made her way over to sit by him, again checking out her family to see if anyone smirked or looked.

Nope. Nothing. No one even looked their way.

Huh.

"It went well," he said.

She looked over at him. "Yes, it did. And you worked hard."

"Not really. Just did what everyone else was doing."

And he made it look so good.

She took a sip of her mimosa, which tasted cool and inviting, and then she went right for the food, which was just what she needed. They had multiple choices of eggs, bacon, sausage and all kinds of fruit, plus biscuits and a delectable selection of pastries to choose from. Brenna had small bites of everything. And she cleaned her plate.

"You were hungry," Finn said.

She nodded. "I nibbled on half a croissant this morning, but that was a long time ago."

He laid his hand on her thigh. "You worked up an appetite. And look at what you did. I'm so impressed."

She laughed. "I do it every year. You're always a part of it."

He leaned over and pressed a kiss to her cheek, then whispered, "Yeah, but I'm not usually as involved in everything as I was today. It was fun."

She realized as she looked around that her entire family

was watching, including her mom and dad, who both were giving them happy smiles.

Okay, *now* everyone was looking. And it made her realize that her relationship with Finn wasn't for show. This was real and happening and as she saw her sisters smiling warmly at her, too, she didn't know what to do.

Other than ignore it. That was what she was going to do. Just ignore it. Because she had wrap-up to do in the warehouse.

"I've gotta go," she said to Finn as she stood. "More work to do."

He looked up at her. "You need any help?"

She shook her head. "No. I've got this."

"Okay. I'll see you later."

As she nearly sprinted toward the cellars, she realized she'd fled the scene like some criminal on the run.

Okay, so she hadn't handled that well. But in her defense, this whole fake engagement and relationship thing with Finn had been because of Mitchell and Allison, who were not present today. And still, she'd fallen into a pattern with Finn.

It's called a relationship, dumbass. You're having a relationship with him.

"Shut up," she mumbled to herself as she haltingly descended the steps of the cellar, grateful for the coolness of the concrete wall against her hand.

Not that the slow trek helped to anchor her thoughts, which were still all over the place. She didn't know why she couldn't reconcile her relationship with Finn and accept what it was.

Fear?

Probably.

She'd been sailing along with her life just fine until Finn

crashed into it. Not that he hadn't always been there. But as a boyfriend-slash-fake-fiancé? That had changed everything.

And when had her feelings changed from let's-play-a-fun-game to it all becoming a little too real?

These were big questions. Questions she didn't have the time or the want to answer. Not today, anyway.

But would she want to answer those questions tomorrow?

Probably not. Because she'd still be afraid of the answers tomorrow.

She sighed and went to work.

CHAPTER

······

twenty-two

THIS WOULDN'T BE Finn's first time wearing a tux. He'd done it before, when Erin was supposed to get married to Owen. That hadn't exactly worked out as planned, but then she'd fallen in love with Jason and now he was going to have to wear a tux again.

Today they were just getting measurements taken. The wedding wasn't until next month, though how the hell they were getting it all done in such a short period of time was more than Finn could fathom. Then again, it was the Bellinis and if any family could put together a wedding that fast, it was them.

"Okay," Jason said, holding up a card. "Erin told me I've got three tuxes to choose from."

Clay cracked a smile. "She gave you three, huh?"

"Hey, it's not like I care. I'll show up in my underwear if it makes her happy."

Finn laughed. "It might."

"In most cases I'd say yes. On our wedding day? Not so much."

Finn looked around. "Owen's really not going to be in the wedding at all, huh?"

Jason shook his head. "Erin and I both told him we wanted him to participate, but he said that given everything that went down, he didn't feel comfortable taking part. He didn't want any bad memories to spoil our day."

Finn could understand how Owen felt, even though he'd been forgiven by both Jason and Erin. Still, it had to hurt not to stand up for your best friend. Clay was taking over best man duties, and Jason's cousin Leo was going to step in as another groomsman. It would all work out just fine.

But they were going to miss Owen.

A man came out and started taking measurements while they discussed which tux Jason liked best. Since they were guys, and fashion wasn't much of a thing that concerned them, that conversation didn't take long. Jason tried them all on, and he looked great in all three. He sent pictures to Erin and she chose the one she liked best. That was easy.

"Are you getting excited about the wedding?" Finn asked.

"I'm excited about being married to Erin. And she's excited to have the whole ceremony over with."

Clay raised his arm so the tux guy could measure him. "I thought women got into the whole wedding thing."

Jason nodded. "She was. The first time. But she said she got so wrapped up in wedding details that she lost sight of what was really important, which was being married. Now she wants to keep things simple, which works for me. We just want to be married and get our lives moving forward."

"I could see that," Finn said as the tailor motioned for him to step forward. "You two went through a lot to be together. It's time to put all of that behind you and start your married lives."

"Yeah. It was good that this early opening for a wedding date came up. Less to think about and plan for and just . . . I don't want to say get it over with, but . . ."

"But get it over with?" Clay asked with a crooked smile.

Jason laughed. "Yeah, I guess so. It's not that I don't want Erin to have the wedding day that she's dreamed about. I just saw how miserable she was on the wedding day she didn't get to have. I want this one to make her happy."

Finn pinned him with a look. "Hey. She's marrying *you*. That's enough to make her happy."

Jason smiled. "Thanks."

After they were measured and Jason got a receipt for the order, they headed out.

"Burgers and beer?" Jason asked.

"I'm down," Clay said. "But I have to pick Alice up at the airport at eight thirty."

Finn looked at his phone. It was just six right now, so plenty of time, especially since they were already in the city and closer to the airport, making it easier on Clay. "I'm game."

"Let's go."

Finn's mouth watered. They decided on Republic Gastro-pub because they had awesome burgers, as well as a big selection of craft beer.

The cold beer tasted damn good. Despite it being mid-September, it was still hot outside, and since Finn spent most of his days working outdoors, the cool AC and the beer hit the spot for him.

"How are things going with Brenna?" Jason asked. "You two still engaged?"

Clay paused mid-drink. "Wait. You're engaged? What did I miss?"

Finn set his bottle on the table. "We're not engaged. Not really. She wanted me to play the part of her fiancé for her ex-husband and his wife for this wedding she was in, so I agreed."

Jason took a long swallow of his beer, then grinned. "But that wedding is over and you're still seeing her, right?"

"Well, yeah. But there've been extenuating circumstances. It was going to be four days and done. Then there
was a barbecue with friends from the wedding. And then
we were supposed to go to the bride and groom's place after
their honeymoon, but the groom's been traveling so that's
been put off. Which means we're still fake engaged. And
while we're still fake engaged, we're dating."

"Sounds to me like those circumstances mean you like
her," Clay said. "And she likes you. So you're continuing
this whole fake engagement thing because neither of you
wants to back out of your arrangement?"

Finn shrugged. "Maybe. I don't know. We haven't discussed it. It's just there." Like a lot of things they never
talked about.

"Could it be time to tell Brenna how you feel?" Jason
asked. "And ask her how she feels? Maybe take the whole
fake thing to something real? If that's what you want."

"It's what I want. I don't exactly know what Brenna wants."

As they ate dinner, he thought about it, then thought
some more. Was this a good time to screw up a good thing?
Then again, he wasn't the type to tiptoe around something
important. Maybe it was time to bring it out into the open
and have that discussion. It had been a while. Brenna had
seemed relaxed with him, and they were having a lot of fun.

He didn't like the idea of rocking the boat, especially
with Brenna, who was shaky at best when it came to having
a relationship. But it was high time they had a conversation
about how they felt—he needed to tell her how *he* felt.

But like everything else where Brenna was concerned,
timing was everything.

He'd find the right time, and then they'd talk.

CHAPTER
......
twenty-three

B<small>RENNA</small> J<small>OTTED</small> D<small>OWN</small> notes as Honor gave her report on upcoming weddings and any changes to the schedule. Fortunately, no one had asked for changes or additions, and since Erin and Jason's wedding was on the horizon, it was good that there were no upcoming disasters. The last thing any of them needed—especially Erin—was a disaster. This wedding was going to go smoothly.

Erin went over the financials and those were all in order as well, so Brenna was up.

"The harvest went even better than anticipated. We had an excellent yield this fall."

"That's such great news," Honor said. "I thought we had a big turnout, too."

"We sold a lot of bottles of wine that day," Erin said. "Good for business."

Brenna nodded. "I'll say. We booked several wine tastings, so hopefully we'll get some repeat customers. Oh, and Honor, a recently engaged couple who was there for the harvest said they were going to contact you to set up a tour and possibly book a wedding."

"That'd be Helen Tollson and Travis Silver. Helen called me and she and Travis are scheduled to come in for an appointment next week."

"That's awesome," Erin said. "Any other business?"

Honor shook her head.

"I don't have anything," Brenna said, closing her notebook and preparing to get up.

"Let's talk about Finn," Erin said.

Brenna frowned. "What about Finn?"

"Oh, I don't know. How about the way he nuzzled you at the harvest, convinced you to stomp grapes, and how attentive he was to your every need?"

And here she thought no one had been paying any attention to them. She was wrong.

"First, he didn't nuzzle, and second, he was working the harvest like everyone else. If something needed to be done, he did it—also just like everyone else."

Erin looked to Honor. "See how she tries to deflect?"

"Hmm, I noticed. It's like she doesn't want to talk about him."

"She doesn't," Brenna said. "Are we done now?"

"No, we're just getting started," Erin said. "You know how you were just going to playact the whole fake fiancé thing with Finn for the wedding weekend? We're well past a weekend, Bren. And you're still playing with Finn. Why is that?"

"Oh, you know I meant to explain that to you, Erin, but then I realized it was none of your damn business."

Honor snickered and Erin shot her a glare. Honor held up her hands. "Sorry. Sorry. Yes, why is it that you're still playing at being engaged?"

Brenna loved her sisters. She honestly did. Except when

they butted into her personal life. "Did you miss the 'none of your damn business' comment, Honor?"

"We didn't miss it," Erin said. "We're just ignoring it, like you always ignore it when you meddle in our lives."

"I never meddle."

Erin snorted out a laugh. "Right. Like that time I was dating Jack Rutherford freshman year of high school and you thought he was wrong for me—"

"Which he was."

Erin held up a finger. "Beside the point. You had to go and tell everyone your opinion about what a jerk he was, and then Mom got wind of it and shut it down faster than a tornado."

"Well, he was kind of a jerk," Honor said. "He led you on and had another girlfriend you didn't know about."

"Again. Beside the point. Or how about that time Honor wanted to sneak out and go to the concert with Becky Black? I said she'd be fine. She had a phone."

Brenna shook her head. "Becky Black didn't have the sense that God gave her and you know it as well as I do."

"Honor does. But oh, no. You knew best and you ruined it for her."

"This is true. I really wanted to see that concert. But you told Mom."

Brenna could not believe they were rehashing old grievances. "And what happened to Becky and the other girls?"

Erin rolled her eyes. "I think her boyfriend's car breaking down can't be blamed on Becky."

"But they all got found out and grounded."

"Yeah, but at least they got to see the concert," Honor said. "I got grounded anyway."

Brenna threw up her hands. "What, then? I'm always wrong?"

"That's not at all what we're implying, Bren," Honor said. "We care about you and want what's best for you, just like you've always wanted what's best for us."

Erin nodded. "And when you shut us down and refuse to talk to us, it's concerning."

"I . . . can't talk about Finn."

Honor gave her a look of concern. "Why? Is something wrong?"

"No. I just . . . don't know where we are. Where we stand. And I'm scared to even talk about it with him because I'm afraid he'll want more than I'm ready to give him. I *know* he wants more than I'm ready to give him."

Honor reached for her hand. "What are you afraid of?"

"That I care too much already. That I'll screw this up. I'm not exactly a success in the relationships department, you know?"

"Which is a hundred percent Mitchell's fault," Erin said.

"No failure is all one person's fault. I have to take some of the blame. I was the one who decided the marriage was over. I never suggested marriage counseling or asked if he wanted to try to make our marriage work."

"Did you still love him when you ended things with him?" Honor asked.

"I don't know. I was hurt and angry and I just wanted out. I couldn't see us repairing the damage we had caused each other. There'd been so many arguments and things said that couldn't be taken back. We wanted different things, and I couldn't see it working between us. Not then and definitely not now."

"Then you made the right choice," Honor said. "And you healed and you moved forward and you started dating again."

"That's right," Erin said. "And you learned what you did and didn't want in a relationship so you could do it right the next time."

She looked at both of her sisters. "But that's the thing. I've been in a really good place. Strong and confident and knowing who I am. And then Finn comes along and—"

She couldn't seem to formulate how she felt.

"And what?" Honor asked. "Has he taken away your confidence?"

"No. That's not it at all."

"Does he make you feel less than?" Erin asked.

"No, of course not."

"Then what is it?" Honor asked.

"I don't know. I guess I felt like after what I went through with Mitchell, I just needed to figure out who I was by myself. I went from being a daddy's girl to being Mitchell's wife. After the divorce, I needed to figure out who Brenna was, all by herself. And I've been doing that, and I like who I've become as a whole person. An individual."

"Bren," Erin said. "You can be wholly independent and still love someone. You don't lose your individualism just because you're in love."

She blew out a breath. "Maybe. I'm just not sure I'm ready to take that step yet."

"Is Finn?" Honor asked. "Has he said he loves you?"

She shook her head. "No. Not at all."

"Then what are you worried about?" Erin asked. "Just enjoy what you two have and whatever happens, happens."

"Exactly," Honor said. "Why don't you live in the moment with Finn and quit worrying about the future so much? Whatever happens between the two of you will happen on its own. Shouldn't you be enjoying the now?"

Maybe she was blowing everything out of proportion, including her relationship with Finn. She should do exactly what her sisters suggested and relax, enjoy the moments and quit thinking too much into the future. "I guess you're right."

She only hoped it was that simple.

CHAPTER

······

twenty-four

FINN WASN'T A master at planning surprises, but he had come up with one for Brenna that he hoped she would like.

After work he went back to his place, fed Murphy, let him run around outside a bit while he showered, then drove to the main house. Murphy ran inside and Finn followed into the living room. He was greeted by Maureen and Johnny, who had already pseudo-adopted the dog as their own.

Maureen bent down, taking Murphy's face between her hands.

"How's my wee boy today? Did you have a good day?"

"You're spoilin' him, Maureen," Johnny said.

"Aye. He needs that."

Finn knew his dog would always be well taken care of whenever he was out. "Thanks for watching him."

Maureen came over and gave him a kiss on the cheek. "It's our pleasure."

Brenna came in, taking his breath away in a dark blue cotton dress that clung to her top half and swirled around her bottom half. Her hair was loose around her shoulders and the gold hoops she wore in her ears made him want to take a bite of her earlobes, something he kept to himself since they were standing in a room with her parents.

"You look beautiful," he said.

He saw the telltale blush creep up on her cheeks. "Thank you. Where are we going?"

"It's a surprise."

She arched a brow in suspicion.

"You two have fun," Maureen said, shooing them away with both of her hands. "Now go."

"Bye, Mom," Brenna said.

They got into his truck and they took off, heading away from the property.

"You're really not telling me where we're going."

"No."

"Am I dressed appropriately?"

He glanced over at her—okay, he ogled her legs. "You look amazing."

"Appropriately, Finn."

"Yes. You're appropriately dressed."

She sighed. "I'm very irritated with you right now."

He smiled, hoping she would enjoy the night he had planned for her.

It took a while to get to the location since it was outside the city and on the other side of town. They had twinkling lights set up and tables all around. There was already a good crowd wandering about when they climbed out of the truck.

"This is a garden center," she said.

"Yeah."

"I smell food, too."

"Yeah."

She walked over and read the sign just outside, then looked up at him. "Fall Flower Showcase and Sale?"

"Yup."

Her eyes widened. "How did you know about this?"

He shrugged. "I hear things."

"I didn't even know about this."

"I thought you might want to see what they have. Plus there's wine and dinner, too."

"Really? How fun." She grabbed his hand. "Let's go in."

Her enthusiasm was infectious. He knew how much Brenna loved gardening, and he'd come across this place the week before when he'd been out buying supplies. He saw the flyer for the dinner and sale and knew this was something she might enjoy, so he'd made sure she was going to be free tonight, then asked her out for dinner. He didn't tell her what they'd be doing, hoping she didn't already know about it. Lucky break for him that she didn't.

They'd decorated the place nicely with everything a gardener would love. There were flowers and plants and fountains, along with rocks and garden decorations, anything else you might want or need to add to your landscape. They'd added white twinkling lights outside, which brightened up the place for tonight. Brenna seemed to soak everything in piece by piece.

"Oh, look at these," she said, studying some blue flowers. "They'd be perfect for some fall color on the east side of the house."

He'd already grabbed a rolling cart, so when she pointed to an item that she wanted, he hefted it up and added it.

"We need more peonies and this is the perfect time to plant them. Look at the color of these. And these ranunculus would be amazing."

He had no idea what any of these were, but he was learning a lot just listening to Brenna talk.

"This will bloom in winter, when there's less color and

we need it most. Some of these we plant in the fall but they won't come up until spring."

He nodded, making a mental note to look for all those amazing flowers when they came up in the spring.

After he loaded the last flower she'd added, she turned to him. "Okay, now you pick something. For your place."

"Me? I don't know a damn thing about flowers, Brenna."

"I'll teach you. But first you wander and tell me if something sparks your interest."

"Okay, sure."

He hadn't intended to pick out anything for himself, though now that Brenna had suggested it, he realized the area outside of his house could use something. As he walked around, he zeroed in on one plant.

"I like this one."

She nodded. "Yucca is a good choice. It has a nice vertical design with straight shoots of flowers that would be interesting against the backdrop of the house. And it takes full sun. I like it. We could plant it on the south side. Let's get two."

"Sure." He loaded those onto the cart. "We're done now?"

She laughed. "You need some contrast. Keep looking."

He did, and found the process doubly entertaining when he was the one doing the choosing. With Brenna's expert help, he ended up with a couple of daylilies, a crepe myrtle, some evergreen shrubs, and a metal dog-shaped yard ornament that looked almost exactly like Murphy.

"He'll probably bark at it," Finn said.

Brenna laughed. "But think of how much fun he'll have doing that."

"True."

Brenna looked down at the overly filled cart. "That'll do for a start. We'll plant all of these this weekend."

"Sounds fun. Now let's go buy this stuff and then we'll have some beer and wine."

They checked out and Finn hauled everything to his truck. Once he got it loaded, he met Brenna at the center of the garden, where the bar had been set up. She handed him a beer and she took her wine from the bartender.

They wandered around and listened to the band play country music.

"This was such a great idea," she said. "Thank you for bringing me here."

"I'm glad you're enjoying it."

"I've been so busy lately, and I needed to buy some plants. They had such a great sale tonight and they had everything I wanted. I didn't even know about this place."

"From what I understand they're somewhat new to the area, so they did this as a way to introduce themselves to the community, drum up some new business."

Brenna looked around. "Hmm. They really know how to decorate. And their flowers are impeccable. I need to talk to the owner. Hold my wine and find us a seat. I'll be right back."

"Sure.

Finn grabbed them a table for two, grateful to be off his feet while he sipped his beer. The band was great, mixing new country with some classic, so the tunes kept him company while Brenna was off planning world domination.

When she came back, she had a satisfied smile on her face.

"Well?" he asked as she took her seat and picked up her glass of wine.

"I told them about us and how we're always looking for amazing florists and decorators for our weddings. They're very excited and interested so I gave them my card and took theirs for Honor to get in touch with them."

"You're a good person, Brenna."

She took a sip of her wine. "I just know a good thing when I see it. And it's great for our business, too. Our clients will love them."

And in the meantime she'd give a start-up business a big boost. He admired her for that.

Dinner was a buffet of beef and chicken along with pasta and veggies and amazing bread. Finn had worked up a hell of an appetite, so he sampled a bit of everything, and it was all outstanding.

After dinner they thanked the folks at the nursery, then headed back to the house. They unloaded the stuff for the main house first, and Brenna went inside to grab Murphy, who was, as usual, excited to see them.

"Hey, buddy," Finn said, ruffling the dog's ears. "Did you miss me?"

Murphy's tail wagged back and forth so fast it was almost a blur.

"That dog adores you," Brenna said, laughing as Murphy disappeared to go check out the trees and grass.

"The feeling is mutual."

She walked over to him and slipped her arms around his neck. "Thank you for the surprise tonight."

"You're welcome."

"I'd come home with you but I have an early meeting tomorrow morning and a woman needs her beauty sleep. And if I come home with you, I won't sleep."

"Yeah? Why wouldn't you sleep?"

She smoothed her hand down his chest. "Because we'd be naked. And I'd be on top of you. Or my mouth would be—"

"Dammit, Brenna." He stopped her from sending his imagination into further overdrive by kissing her. Which didn't help at all, but at least she wasn't fueling an already out-of-control fire with her words.

He pressed into her, needing to feel the heat of her body against his.

She moaned, and the deep, throaty sound of it caused him to groan.

He had to have her.

He knew he shouldn't. The porch light was on and anyone could walk outside and see them.

Reluctantly, he pulled his mouth away from hers. "I want you."

She took in a shaky breath. "Yes. I want you, too."

He looked around, and then an idea hit him. "Come on."

He took her hand and led her down the side steps of the porch, the two of them walking briskly over the smooth paving stones leading to the barn. Here it was dark and no one would interrupt them.

He pulled the door open and they slid inside, the cool air conditioning a relief to his heated body. He pushed the door closed, leaving the lights off, then framed Brenna's face in his hands and put his lips on hers.

He felt the warmth of her breath and the touch of her hands in the darkness, heard her whimpers as his tongue found hers. He backed her against the wall of the barn, needing to feel her body. He swept his hand around her and grabbed her ass, drawing her close to his aching erection.

"Finn," she moaned against his mouth, rubbing her body against his. "I need . . ."

She didn't finish her sentence, but he knew what she needed.

He slid his hand under her dress, cupped her sex and rubbed over her panties until she arched against him, her movements driving him wild. He pulled the top of her dress down along with the strap of her bra, drawing the cup aside to take her nipple in his mouth, sucking the bud between his lips, rewarded with her low moan of pleasure. The sounds she made shot straight to his balls, making them quiver.

He slipped his hand inside her underwear, her sex hot and damp as he explored and found a rhythm to stroke her soft flesh. In the darkness he couldn't see her, but he heard the sound of her rapid breaths, her moans and the feel of her body moving against his questing fingers. When he slipped two fingers inside her, her pussy gripped them as he began to pump, using the heel of his hand to rub her clit.

"Oh, God, yes," she said. "Just like that."

As he stroked her, his erection rubbed her hip, the ache to be inside her almost unbearable. But he wanted to get her there first, to make her come, to hear her cry out. And when she did, her whole body shaking when she came, he took her mouth to absorb her cries of pleasure.

She was still trembling when he unzipped his pants, took the condom out of his pocket and put it on. He bent to remove her panties, lifted her up and wrapped her legs around him, then slid inside her. Her pussy was still quivering from her orgasm and wrapped tightly around his cock, squeezing him so hard he could have come right then.

It felt so good to be inside her, to feel her legs wrapped around him, that all he wanted to do right now was stay in this moment with her, to feel her nails digging into his shoulder and listen to the sounds of her breathing.

And then he began to move, and it was like heaven, like this woman had been made just for him. It was perfect—she was perfect, and as she tangled her fingers in his hair and tugged his head back so she could kiss him, he'd never felt anything like the lightning strikes of need that coursed through him whenever he was with her.

Her lips were soft, her breaths coming rapidly as he drove deep and hard into her, his orgasm coming at him like a fast strike of lightning. He couldn't hold back, and when she moaned against his mouth and he felt her contracting around his cock, he went off, shuddering with his release.

He felt weak and drained and utterly satisfied.

"Was that your arm workout for the day?" she asked.

He let out a short laugh. "Maybe for a couple of days." He let Brenna down slowly, retrieved her panties and helped her climb into them, then zipped his pants back up, figuring he'd dispose of the condom when he got back to his house.

They stepped outside and he closed the barn, then walked back with Brenna toward the house. Murphy was asleep on the porch.

Good dog.

When they got to the front door, he said, "At least I didn't keep you up all night."

She reached up and curved her hand around his neck, pulling him down for a brief kiss. When she pulled back, he couldn't help but get lost in her eyes.

"It was just perfect," she said. "And exactly what I needed."

"Same here." He called to Murphy, who bounded up and followed him to the truck.

He climbed in and waited until Brenna waved and went inside, shutting the door behind her.

Then he smiled and left for his house.

CHAPTER

······

twenty-five

JASON HADN'T WANTED a big blowout bachelor party, so they decided to give Owen's brew pub some business and gathered there for a night of food and fun. Owen had closed the place down for a private party and they catered in barbecue ribs and chicken and sides, which would go perfectly with beer. Plus there was a hockey game on.

Finn couldn't think of a more perfect night with the guys. Jason seemed relaxed, eating and drinking with his friends and family while they watched the game. Finn grabbed his beer and went up to the bar where Owen was filling up glasses.

"What can I get for you?" Owen asked.

"I'm good right now, thanks. Did you eat?"

"I will, later."

"Hey, everyone's got their food. You go grab something."

Owen looked around and saw that everyone was seated, eating and drinking and watching the game. "Okay. I'll fill a plate and be right back."

Finn leaned against the bar to watch the game, groaning

along with the rest of the guys when his team got called for high-sticking and sent to the penalty box, giving the opposing team a power play.

"I can't believe Bennett got called for that," Owen said as he came back to the bar with his plate.

Finn was happy to see Owen's plate filled with chicken, ribs, beans and some cornbread.

"Yeah. Let's just hope the other team doesn't score on us."

It was a tense two minutes on the power play, but defense and their outstanding goalie held them back without a goal.

Finn swiveled on his stool to face Owen. "We got lucky."

"Sure did." Owen wiped his hands. "These ribs are great."

"Aren't they? I ate way too many."

"My appetite isn't there just yet, but I'm working on it."

Finn was glad to see Owen eating. And working. They watched the game for a while, and he noticed that Owen didn't join the group.

"Is this weird for you?" he asked.

Owen gave him a curious look. "Is what weird?"

"This. Jason getting ready to marry Erin."

"Nope. They're both right where they're supposed to be—with each other. Erin and I both realized we weren't the ones for each other. I look at that whole nonwedding debacle as setting the universe right. I mean, the way I handled it? Totally wrong and a colossal fuckup on my part. But the end result?" He looked over at Jason, who threw his head back and laughed at something Clay said. "Yeah, that worked out. They're both so damn happy together, you know?"

Finn nodded. "Yes, they are. But how about you? Are you happy?"

Owen laid his fork down and took a long swallow of

water, then smiled. "I'm surviving right now and that's all I can ask for. As far as my future? I'll just be happy to have one. Anything other than that is a bonus."

Finn lifted his beer. "Amen to that, brother."

He could see Owen's outlook—positive, and concentrating only on his health right now. The fact that he was so happy for Jason and Erin meant a lot, all things considered.

Sometimes letting the past go was the healthiest thing you could do for yourself.

Jason came over and put his arm around Finn's shoulders. "You two gonna hide out over here all night, or are you gonna join the party?"

"I'm tending bar," Owen said.

"Yeah, yeah. You might have begged off being my best man, but you're still my best bud and part of this thing tonight. So get your ass over here and talk shit about me like a best man should."

Owen gave Jason a look of pure brotherly love, then grabbed his water. "Oh, I've got some stories."

Jason and Finn both grinned.

"Now the party's getting started," Finn said, taking hold of his beer to join the group.

"I'M GETTING MARRIED!"

If Brenna hadn't restrained Erin, she was certain her sister would have climbed on top of the table at the bar and announced it to everyone.

As bachelorette parties went, this one was fairly tame. It was Brenna, Honor, Alice and Erin, along with Laurel and Mirai, Erin's college friends who lived locally. It was a bonus that those two were both loads of fun, and likely why Erin was hammered right now.

Mom had begged off, saying she was busy with other things, but Brenna figured that their mother didn't want to interfere with what she had called "the wild girl party."

Brenna had laughed, figuring they'd have dinner, go out for a couple of drinks, and Erin would want to go home.

She'd been so wrong.

The dinner part had gone well. But when they got to the bar, Erin had really let loose. Laurel and Mirai had bought the first round, toasted the bride, wished her well, then asked her if she was really going through with it "this time." From the look on Erin's face, Brenna figured that was when Erin got pissed off and was determined she was going to show her friends that not only was she actually going to get married, she was going to party her ass off tonight in celebration of the marriage she was going to go through with.

Brenna and Honor stood by and surveyed the wreckage.

"I don't know that I've ever seen her drink that much," Honor said, wincing as Erin let out a shrill whoop.

"I do. Her twenty-first birthday party. We went out for drinks that night and she overindulged."

Honor pursed her lips. "I don't remember that."

"Because you didn't go with us. You weren't twenty-one yet."

"Oh, right. Now I remember. We all went out to eat, then came home and you all went out after that without me. If it was like this, I'm sad I missed it."

"She danced on top of the bar at the dive we went to."

Alice turned her shocked face to Brenna. "She did not."

"Oh, she did. She had her cowgirl boots on that night, so at least I didn't have to worry about her doing a header off the bar because she was weaving in high heels. But she was seriously toasted. I'm surprised everyone in the house didn't hear her barfing all night long."

Alice let out a short laugh, then said, "Oh, poor Erin."

"Grateful that I missed that part," Honor said, taking a sip of her cocktail.

"Yeah, well, I was the one who had to hold her hair and listen to her drunken ramblings in between puke fests."

Honor rubbed her arm. "You're a good sister. I'll keep that in mind so I know who to call next time I throw up."

Brenna laughed.

Erin had gone to the restroom with Laurel and Mirai, and on the way back she weaved her way over to their table. "Gonna sing now. Wanna come?"

"Uh, no thanks," Brenna said. "But you go do that."

"Okay. I love you, Brenna."

"Love you, too, Erin."

Mirai and Laurel propped her up as the three of them made their way to the stage.

"Are you really going to let her do that?" Honor asked.

Brenna shrugged. "Why not?"

"Should she not sing?" Alice asked.

"She should never sing. Erin couldn't sing a note in tune if her life depended on it," Brenna said.

Honor nodded, a grim expression on her face. "Yeah, she's pretty awful."

Alice's eyes widened. "Oh, no."

The music started and Brenna cringed.

"Oh, I love this song," Alice said.

Of all things, an Adele song. And not only couldn't Erin sing, she did not have the range that song required.

Fortunately, Mirai had an incredible voice, Laurel could hold a tune and between the two of them, even drunk they managed to drown out Erin's awful tones.

They even got applause from the rather boisterous crowd.

"Okay, that wasn't the disaster I expected it to be," Honor said.

Brenna agreed. Not that her sister would have even noticed if she'd been booed given the state she was in. Okay, she might have noticed that, so she was grateful. "Yeah, Mirai and Laurel saved her butt on that one."

"I didn't even hear her over the other two," Alice said. "Next time we're together I'm busting out the tunes and making her sing."

"You're a mean friend, Alice Weatherford," Brenna said.

Alice laughed. "Hey, I can't sing, either. I need my friend to be terrible with me."

And that was friendship in a nutshell.

Brenna gave it another hour, gradually slipping glasses of water to Erin in between her cocktails, then decided at around twelve thirty that her sister had had enough. They all walked outside together and waited until Mirai and Laurel's car arrived to take them home. After that, Brenna and Honor got to listen to Erin sing to them from the back seat on the thirty-minute drive to Erin's house.

Honor slanted Brenna a murderous look, then whispered, "It's a good thing she's not still living with us, because I would murder her in her sleep."

Brenna resisted the urge to laugh, but she felt her sister's pain, because with every song Erin got louder and more obnoxious.

They got to Erin's place and the lights were on. It looked like Jason was already back from his bachelor party. He stepped outside just as they parked.

"No wild night for you, huh?"

"Nah. I got home about eleven thirty."

"Babe!" Erin stumbled out of the back seat and threw

her arms around him. "Did you know I was getting married?"

Jason gave Brenna and Honor a bemused smile before pulling Erin off him. "I've gotten wind of it. Did you have fun tonight?"

"So much fun. I sang."

He grimaced, then smiled. "You did, huh?"

"Want me to sing to you?"

"Uh, sure. Let's go inside." He threw a smile over his shoulder. "Thanks for bringing her home. And for taking her out."

"It was fun."

Erin tilted her head back. "Love you both."

"Love you, too, Erin," Brenna said.

"Love you, sis," Honor said.

They both cringed as Erin started singing a love song to Jason while they walked away.

"Poor Jason," Honor said.

"Hey, he asked for it," Brenna said. "He fell in love with her."

Brenna laughed.

They climbed back in the car and headed toward the house.

"I'm going to be honest here," Brenna said. "I was so happy to dump her on Jason."

"I guess he can be the one who holds her hair tonight, huh?"

Brenna cracked a smile. "I guess so."

CHAPTER

......

twenty-six

ERIN BENT OVER and took several fast breaths. "I knew this was going to be a disaster. We should have eloped."

Brenna rubbed Erin's back and looked over at Honor, the two of them realizing that their sister was having a meltdown on her wedding day.

"It's going to be fine, honey," Honor said. "The florist said they were only going to be a half hour late. It's no big deal."

Erin twisted her head to the side to look at Honor. "It's a nightmare. Monica double-booked herself and I don't have anyone to do makeup, and now the florist is late. What's next? The groom doesn't show up? Because I've had that happen before and I'm telling you both right now that I will lose it if Jason is a no-show."

"Of course Jason's going to show up," Brenna said. "He can't wait to marry you."

"And I've already put in three calls to our best makeup artists," Honor said. "I'm sure someone will be available."

Again, Honor gave Brenna that worried look. So there

might be a few mishaps today. But the one thing Brenna was certain of was that Jason would be there. And he wouldn't care if Erin walked down the aisle with no makeup, messy hair and wearing her llama pajamas, as long as he got to marry her today.

Though Erin wouldn't think of that as her ideal bridal look.

Honor's phone buzzed. She held up her hand and stepped out of Erin's former bedroom to take the call.

"See? That's probably one of the makeup artists right now," Brenna said.

Erin groaned. "Or maybe the caterers are canceling and we'll be forced to have grilled hot dogs for dinner."

This was why Honor dealt with brides. Brenna sucked in a deep breath and forced a benevolent smile on her sister.

"We are not having hot dogs for dinner. I'm telling you, that's one of the makeup artists on the phone."

"Yeah, likely telling Honor no. We should have eloped. I suggested eloping last week and Jason said, 'No, babe. Everything will work out fine.' Shows you what he knows. Who's the wedding expert around here? Is it him? Nope. It's me. But did he listen and hop a flight to Vegas with me? He did not. And now look. Everything is falling apart."

Brenna sighed. She was going to have to do something to keep Erin's spirits up.

Or maybe get her drunk. Tequila was the great equalizer.

"Great news," Honor said as she walked back into the room. "Ellen Pinkston has a client right now, but after that she's free and will gather her crew and be here by one p.m. to do makeup."

Erin blew out a breath. "Oh, bless her. Remind me to give Ellen a very generous tip."

"Noted," Honor said.

When Erin's phone rang, Brenna glanced at the display and saw that it was Jason. Brenna and Honor looked quickly at each other.

He wouldn't. Not Jason.

Erin put it on speaker. "Hey."

"Hi, babe. Happy wedding day. You doing okay?"

"I'm only mildly hyperventilating. How are you?"

"I'm good. Look, we have a slight . . . issue."

Erin took in a deep breath. "As long as you aren't bailing on me, we'll deal with it."

Jason laughed. "I'm marrying you today, no matter what happens."

Their sister exhaled, and Brenna felt a little bit of that relief herself. Not that she doubted Jason at all.

"What's the problem?" Erin asked.

"Leo has food poisoning."

Erin straightened. "What? What happened?"

"I don't know. Some bad oysters, I guess. But he's sick and he can't be in the wedding."

Erin blew out a breath. "Poor Leo. I hope he's going to be all right."

"He will be. But not today."

"Okay," Erin said. "We'll make this work. Get Owen. He's the same size as Leo so he can fit in the tux."

"Erin," Jason said. "Are you sure about this?"

"Of course. He should have been one of your grooms-men anyway."

"Okay. Take a minute. Think about this before you decide."

Erin looked up at her sisters. Brenna shrugged and so did Honor.

"It's up to you, Erin," Brenna said. "You and Jason."

"Jason and I have discussed this ad nauseam. Owen and

I have put that whole debacle to rest. It's all in the past, isn't it, Jason?"

"For me it is. But he didn't break up with me. He broke up with you."

"Owen and I dealt with it. And now we're all friends again. Call Owen, Jason. See if he's willing to do it. And if he's okay with it and doesn't feel uncomfortable, let me know?"

"I'll do that. And Erin?"

"Yes?"

"I love you."

Brenna was so relieved by her sister's warm smile.

"I love you, too. Bye."

Erin clicked off and looked up at Honor and Brenna. "We can only hope that's the last disaster of the day."

"Since I was the one who was paired off with Leo," Honor said, "I can always walk down the aisle alone. It won't be a big deal."

Brenna shook her head. "If Owen isn't comfortable doing it, we'll find someone else. Don't worry."

A few minutes later Jason texted. Erin looked down at her phone. "Owen's happy to fill in for Leo. We're set."

Brenna's heart did a leap at that.

"Okay, let's get you married."

Several hours and fortunately no further disasters later, they were all made up, dressed up and ready to walk down the aisle. Honor had explained to Mom and Dad about why Owen was filling in for Leo, and they were both fine with it, both of them saying the only important thing today was Erin and Jason.

Brenna took a last look in the mirror. The dress was perfect, her hair was tamed and she couldn't have asked for a more beautiful day for her sister's wedding.

Everything had come together perfectly.

It was a small gathering, with only close family and friends—along with Agatha and Puddy, Erin and Jason's dogs, who looked adorable in their bows and bow tie today. Brenna liked the intimacy of it as she walked down the aisle, spying Finn standing at the altar looking gorgeous in his dark tux. And when he smiled at her, her heart did a quick jolt.

That man did things to her.

She met up with Honor along with Erin's best friend Alice Weatherford at the vineyard altar, which had been decorated beautifully with an overflow of fall flowers on the top and sides of the arch.

Everyone stood as Dad walked down the aisle with Erin, who looked radiant and as happy as Brenna had ever seen her. She peeked over at Jason, whose eyes glistened with tears. Even Owen was smiling widely and Brenna realized that having Owen here was the best form of closure for everyone. He truly was happy for his best friends, and it was a step in the right direction for all their futures.

Dad handed Erin off to Jason, and then the pastor began the ceremony.

Brenna couldn't believe her little sister was getting married. She'd been prepared for this for a while now, but hearing Erin say her vows and listening to Jason promise to always love and care for Erin made her heart squeeze.

She'd always been the one to watch out for and take care of Erin. Now that responsibility would fall to Jason. She knew her sister had found the right man, and that Jason would love her forever.

And when the pastor pronounced them husband and wife, Brenna's eyes filled with happy tears.

She believed in their happily-ever-after. Maybe it hadn't

happened for her, and she'd been cynical about love ever since. But she could see it with Erin and Jason. These two truly loved each other.

As they left the altar, she slipped her arm into Finn's, his smile infectious.

"You look like a cat eyeing a tasty snack," Finn said.

"Maybe you're the tasty snack."

He arched a brow, then laid his hand over hers. "Filing that away for later."

She couldn't hold back the grin. "You do that."

After the guests filed to the barn, the wedding party stayed behind to take pictures. Since Honor was part of the wedding, they'd enlisted the help of an outside wedding planner to help guide the day, much to Honor's great distress. But since the entire family was in the wedding it made the most sense. They couldn't be both in the wedding and manage it, so they all had to give up control for the day.

She knew how Honor felt not having that control. It was hard for Brenna having her staff manage the distribution of the wine, but she was also supremely confident in their abilities. She'd ordered the wine and champagne for today, and all they had to do was arrange the stock. The caterers and bartenders would handle everything else.

Fortunately, the wedding party had finished with outside pics, but the photographer was going to take some more of Erin and Jason. The rest of them headed to the barn, which suited Brenna just fine. It was a little chilly outside as the sun was just beginning to set.

"I don't know about you," Brenna said as Finn held her hand while they walked. "But I'm ready for a drink."

"So ready. It was a nice ceremony."

"Yes, it was."

"Jason was so nervous today."

Jason was always calm. Nothing seemed to ruffle him. "Was he really?"

"Yeah. He wanted everything to be perfect for Erin."

"In the end, it turned out just right. And the two of them—the way they look at each other as if no one else exists . . ."

Finn looked at her, his lips curving, and it was as if time stopped. "Yeah?"

That flutter in the vicinity of her heart whenever he gave her that look was so disconcerting. She didn't know what to make of it. She pushed it aside, reminding herself that today wasn't the day to think about herself or her mixed-up feelings. "Well, that's love, isn't it?"

His smile made her heart flutter. "I guess it must be."

They took their seats at the large table in the front. The waitstaff poured wine for her, and Finn went off to grab a beer.

"I don't know about you," Honor said, leaning over to talk to her. "But it was all I could do not to sob like a baby during the ceremony."

Brenna nodded. "It was lovely, wasn't it?"

Alice came over and took Finn's seat. "It was perfect. I teared up as well. I think all of us were sniffling up there."

"You're right," Brenna said.

"Mom cried, too," Honor said. "I had to stop looking at her because then I was going to cry."

"I already knew not to look at her. You know how sentimental she is."

"See, I should have remembered that. Even Dad shed a tear."

"He did? Though that shouldn't surprise me. He's a softie when it comes to us girls."

"That's true. I still can't believe Erin is married."

"I've never seen her so happy," Alice said. "Her whole face just lit up when she was walking down the aisle."

Brenna nodded.

"How's Owen handling this?" Alice's gaze tracked to the bar where Owen, Clay and Finn stood talking.

"Like a rock," Honor said. "He's as happy for them as we all are. Now he can put it all behind him and move on with his life, concentrate only on himself."

"Which he should be doing," Alice said. "We need him healthy."

"And he needs to be happy, too," Honor said.

"Yes, he does." Brenna looked around. "Where's your cowboy, Honor?"

Honor shrugged. "Oh, well, that didn't work out."

"I'm sorry, Honor," Alice said.

She shrugged. "I'm not. He wasn't the right guy for me."

At least her sister realized that. "No, he wasn't. And, hey, now you can work the room tonight. Hit up all the single guys."

Honor laughed. "Yeah, sure. All those hot single men just wandering around at my sister's wedding."

"Hey, there are a few here," Brenna said. "Just don't pick any losers."

Honor lifted her chin. "Are you saying I date losers?"

"Yes."

"Brenna." Alice gave her a shocked look.

Brenna shrugged. "Sorry, but Honor, you've dated some choice jackasses."

"I have not. Have I?"

"Let's start with your recent cowboy who couldn't seem to keep his hands off your ass."

Alice put her hand over her mouth. "He couldn't? I must have missed that."

Honor gave Alice a squeamish look. "Yes, he did have a hands problem. Among other issues I won't go into."

"And then there was Padon," Brenna said, "who seemed to forget to show up for dates he'd made with you."

Honor nodded. "Now he was an actual jackass."

"And Cliff, who seemed to forget his wallet every time he took you out for dinner."

Honor sighed. "I don't have the best track record with men, do I?"

"Hey, we've all been there," Alice said. "Sometimes you have to go through the wrong ones to find the right one."

Brenna reached over and laid her hand over her sister's. "That's true. You just haven't met the right one yet."

Honor looked over Brenna's shoulder and smiled. "But *you* have."

Brenna shifted to see Finn approaching, along with Clay and Owen.

Honor leaned over and pressed a kiss to Brenna's cheek. "Don't let go of a good thing."

"Okay," Clay said. "You've all been talking about us, haven't you?"

Alice stood. "Honestly? Not a word about you."

"Oh, so it was me, then," Finn said.

Brenna shook her head. "Not really."

Owen grinned. "Lately if there's gossip, it's about me."

Honor laughed. "Not tonight, stud. Let's go wait at the barn entrance for the bride and groom. They should be arriving soon."

They all made their way to the doors, and just in time. Erin and Jason walked up and the deejay played a kick-ass song to get the crowd going as the new Mr. and Mrs. made their arrival in style. After the applause, everyone dispersed.

She had to go hug her sister.

"You're married," she said to Erin.

Erin had such a sweet blush to her cheeks. And the happiest smile she'd ever seen.

"I know! I still can't believe it. It's like a dream."

She took Erin's hands in hers. "The best dream. Soak it all in."

"I intend to. I love you, Brenna."

"I love you, too."

Then everyone took their seats and champagne was poured.

As the oldest sister and official maid of honor, Brenna made the first toast.

"Erin and Jason, when I see you together, I see happiness. I see joy. I see a future where you can both grow and have everything you've ever wanted. You bring out the best in each other, you calm each other in times of stress and you celebrate each other's successes. I hope you know that you can always count on your families to be there for you whenever you need us. We will always have your back. I hope that the love you feel for each other today is the same love you will feel every day for the rest of your lives. To Erin and Jason."

She lifted her glass and everyone toasted.

Then Clay gave his toast, and it was about friendship and love and brought a tear to Brenna's eye.

Finn grasped her hand under the table. "Those were some sweet words you said."

"Thank you."

"I always wished I had siblings."

"You do. You have Erin and Honor."

He took in a deep breath. "Thanks for not adding yourself as a sibling, because that would be creepy."

She laughed. "I have never once thought of you as a brother."

"You were hot for me even back then, huh?"

"I have no comment."

He looked her over. "Did I tell you today that you were beautiful?"

"No, you didn't. But thank you."

"That dress looks nice on you. And I like your hair that way, down around your shoulders, and some of it pulled up. It's very beautiful. Then again, you look pretty all the time."

He always said all the right things, and they were unpracticed, not bullshit lines. She could tell they came from his heart. She squeezed his hand, then leaned over and gave him a soft kiss. "You're so . . . I don't know . . . Finn."

He let out a soft laugh. "Yeah, that's me, *grá*."

She knew that word—it meant *love*. And didn't that set her heart to doing those flippity floppity things again.

She ran her fingers down the front of his shirt. "You in a tux? That presents quite a picture, Finn Nolan."

He looked down at himself, then back up at her. "I thought it gave me a rather James Bond kind of look."

"You look dashing, for sure." Then again he could be sweat soaked in jeans and a T-shirt, and either way he could still turn her on. It was the man himself that did it for her, not the clothes he wore.

Dinner was served next, and it was a delicious feast of steak and lobster along with a creamy potato mash and a wonderful mix of fresh vegetables.

And, of course, the wine was spectacular.

"I could have eaten that meal twice," Finn said, laying his fork and knife on the plate.

"You do like your food."

"Pretty much all food. But great food? That's the best."

"Maybe you should consider becoming a chef in your spare time."

He laughed. "I'll add that to my to-do list. Along with climbing Mt. Everest, skydiving and becoming a neurosurgeon."

"Oh, that's quite the list."

"What's on yours?"

"Actress, singer, photojournalist, prima ballerina and queen of England."

He nodded. "Ambitious. I like that about you. Don't let anything stop you from achieving your dreams."

She loved that he supported her dreams, even the ridiculously unattainable ones.

She left the table to go to the restroom, fix her lip gloss and mess with her hair.

"Stop, you're already gorgeous."

She turned to smile at her mother. "And so are you."

"That burgundy dress does amazing things for you."

"Thanks, Mom. And you look beautiful tonight."

Mom sighed and glanced into the mirror to apply lipstick, then stopped, a wistful look on her face. "I can't believe Erin is married."

All three of them were close to their mother. Brenna knew this was both a celebratory and difficult night for her. She walked over and put her arm around her mom. "You raised us all well, taught us everything you know. Erin's going to be fine."

"Oh, I know she will. Jason's a wonderful man. But it seems like it was just yesterday the three of you were getting dirty together out in the vineyard. And now, Erin's a married woman. Time moves too quickly for me these days."

She caught the telltale tears glistening in her mother's

eyes and pulled her in for a hug. "You know she's not leaving you."

"Of course not," her mother said, sniffling. "It's just a big day. I'm allowed to be emotional."

"Yes, you are."

Mom took her hand. "Come on. I think we'll be dancing soon, and we don't want to miss that."

"No, we definitely do not."

Ending on a positive note, her mom spun her around like she used to do. Brenna felt that little tug of nostalgia from dancing with her mom like she did when she was little.

Nothing like doing a little dance and twirl with your mama in the ladies' room. Brenna laughed and slipped her arm into her mother's, and they strolled back out to the reception.

"Okay, what did I miss?" Erin asked as she caught up with them.

"Mom's all teary-eyed because one of her babies got hitched tonight."

"I was not teary. Okay, maybe a little."

"Aww, Mom." Erin threw her arms around her mother. "Don't cry. It's a happy day."

"Why are we crying?" Honor asked as she came over.

"Mom's crying over Erin being all married up."

"Oh, that's sweet." Honor put her arms around Erin and Mom. Since Brenna didn't want to be left out, she joined the hug fest.

"Okay, now we're all starting to look ridiculous," Mom said, pulling away. "I love all of you. And I'm fine. It's my prerogative as your mother to cry on your wedding day. All of your wedding days. Might as well expect it."

Honor looked at Brenna. "I'm not getting married."

"Neither am I."

Mom shook her head. "Not today you aren't. But eventually you'll find the man who makes you swoon like Jason did for Erin."

Erin lifted her chin. "I never swooned."

Jason came over and slipped his arm around Erin's waist. "I seem to recall some swooning."

"You lie."

"Come on," he said. "We're supposed to dance. Then we'll see who swoons and who doesn't."

Erin waved her fingers at them as Jason led her to the dance floor while the deejay announced the bride and groom's first dance. They all followed to watch. Brenna smiled as Elvis sang "Can't Help Falling in Love." They used to watch their parents dance to that song all the time. And then they'd all join in, dancing with each other, with Mom, with Dad. Hearing that song was the sweetest memory. Brenna could understand why Erin chose that song for her first dance with Jason. It was all about love.

She heard the sniffle next to her and reached out for her Mom's hand.

"It's lovely." Mom lifted a tissue to her eyes.

After that, the bridal party had to dance along with the bride and groom. Finn took her hand.

"Ready?" he asked.

"Don't step on my toes," she said as he led her onto the dance floor.

"Babe, I'm so good we'll be dancing on clouds out there."

She couldn't hold in her laugh as he wrapped his arm around her and tugged her close. But he glided her across the floor effortlessly, and all she focused on was her hand in his, and the way he held her with such confidence, his eyes locked with hers while words of a love song filtered through her brain.

This all felt so good, so right, and yet it was dangerous to let herself fall so hard with Finn.

But what if you did fall? Would it be so bad?

A loaded question meant to be pondered later. For now she let herself be carried away by the music, by the man holding her, and the extremely happy mood she was in.

She tilted her head back. "Thank you."

He lifted a brow. "For my expert dancing skills?"

"Definitely that. But mainly for being here with me the past couple months. It's meant a lot that you've had my back."

"I always will, Brenna. You can count on it. Whenever you need me."

A strong promise. But could he keep it?

As the night progressed, she found herself staring at him as he stood across the room talking to the guys. She couldn't help looking at him all the time. It seemed to have become her favorite pastime. And who could blame her with his dark hair, those mesmerizing eyes and his incredible body? Not to mention the kind of smile that could light up a woman's world.

He'd certainly lit up hers.

What if she did allow herself to fall in love with Finn? What if she gave in to all these emotions that continued to bombard her? What might happen?

She knew what might happen. She could get hurt—again. Finn could turn out to not be the man she thought he was.

That had happened before. Mitchell had seemed perfect for her. They were both driven, had wanted things for their future that required hard work and sacrifice. They had both talked at length about what it would take to get where they wanted to be.

On paper and in conversation, it had sounded ideal. She liked to work and she appreciated a man who didn't expect her to have dinner on the table at five o'clock every night. She wasn't traditional like that, and neither was Mitchell. Sometimes she'd roll in after seven. Often he'd come in after eight. They both led busy lives and at first they jelled.

But then came the arguments. Brenna chalked it up to the two of them not spending enough time together, something she'd originally thought would work out just fine. Then she realized that Mitchell had gotten used to his routine, having things the way he wanted them, and he wasn't willing to be flexible. It was either his way or no way.

Brenna figured out fairly quickly that her reply to that was *no way*. The problem was, she hadn't seen it coming.

Or maybe she'd been so blinded by the romance of it all, she'd only seen what she wanted to see.

It would be so easy to fall into that same routine again. It was easy to see the hotness, the sweetness, the utter perfection of Finn. What she needed to do was dig into his faults, into what the traps could be, before she made the same mistake twice.

Or maybe you could quit nitpicking and just go with your heart?

She shrugged off that ridiculous thought.

No, this time she intended to do it right.

Or not at all.

CHAPTER

......

twenty-seven

Finn HAD NO idea what was up when Brenna texted Wednesday night to tell him they were both taking the next day off, she'd already cleared it with her dad and she had a surprise for him. Then she'd told him to be ready to go by five a.m. and to meet her in front of the house.

What the hell did Brenna want to do at five a.m.?

Either way, he was up, he'd had coffee, Murphy had been outside and was fed and he was ready for . . . whatever. It was cool out this morning so he put on a jacket, grabbed the dog and walked over to the front of the house, frowning when he saw the big truck parked there with the boat trailered behind it.

Brenna came out the front door with a large bag.

"Oh, good, you're here. Take this. I've got coffee inside for both of us."

"Where are we going?" He went up the steps and took the bag from her. "And where do you want me to put this?"

"In the truck." She looked down the steps.

"That's your dad's truck."

"Yes."

"And your dad's boat."

"It's the family boat. I thought we'd go out on the lake today. Maybe do a little fishing. If the idea of that suits you."

His lips curved. "It does. But don't you have work to do?"

"Every day. Today, though, we're skipping out on work to have a little fun. Any complaints about that?"

"Hey, you're the boss."

She laughed. "Not of you."

Once they put all the gear in the truck, Finn double-checked the trailer and hitch to make sure they were secure.

"I need to do something with Murphy," he said as the dog sat between them, his tail wagging wildly.

"Oh, Murph's coming with us."

"He is, huh?"

"Of course. I figured he'd enjoy a day on the boat. And there's a life jacket for him, too."

"You thought of everything, didn't you?"

She smiled. "I tried to."

They climbed in, Murphy jumping into the back seat of the truck.

"Where to?" he asked.

"I already have the coordinates mapped into the truck's GPS."

"Well, aren't you the planner today?"

"Actually, I've been working on it all week."

He tilted back a little to study her. "All to surprise me."

She shrugged. "Yes."

He liked this take-charge attitude of hers, and that she had, in fact, surprised the hell out of him. The idea of Brenna taking a day off work was practically unheard of. She had to have her fingers in everything related to winemaking. Giving that up for an entire day just to spend it with him?

He did feel special.

Hell, he felt a lot of things where Brenna was concerned, but it was too early in the morning to decipher them, so he put the truck in gear, punched Go on the GPS and off they went.

It took about an hour to get to the lake, and he followed the directions to where Brenna wanted them to go. It was a great spot to launch, so they got everything out and loaded up the boat. Finn got the boat into the water, then Brenna parked the truck and met him on the dock.

He held her hand while she climbed in. She looked amazing in her tight pants and boots, her jacket flapping in the morning breeze. She'd put her hair in a long braid this morning, and she looked so beautiful she took his breath away.

Murphy thought so, too, because he came up to her, his tail wagging so she'd pet him.

"What do you think about all this, Murphy?" she asked as she smoothed her hands over his back and rubbed his ears.

Murphy's enthusiastic tail thumping was his answer. As Finn moved slowly through the water past the No Wake zone, Murphy put his paws on the edge of the boat so he could look out over the water. Finn could tell Murph was going to enjoy this.

And Brenna? She sat in the seat next to him, wisps of her hair blowing back as he cranked up the engine and soared through the water. He'd been to this lake several times before, and he knew just the right place for fishing.

He found a nice isolated spot where they wouldn't be disturbed. Not that there'd be a lot of traffic on the water on a Thursday morning in October anyway. He killed the engine and dropped the anchor.

Brenna moved out of the chair and went to one of the bags, lifting out two sandwiches she'd wrapped in foil, and brought them over, handing him one.

"I figured you wouldn't have had any time to eat breakfast, so I made sausage and egg sandwiches."

Just the thought of food made his stomach grumble. "You made this?"

"I can cook. Sometimes. If I have to."

He gave her a look as she unwrapped her sandwich.

She shrugged. "Louise wasn't there yet so I had to do it. And it's totally edible."

"I believe you. Thanks for making this." He took a bite, and it was good. He leaned over to grab his coffee.

"Hey, this is good," she said.

"You're surprised that food you made is good. Maybe I should be scared."

"I don't cook very often. I eat out and at home we have Louise."

"But you were married before. Did Mitchell cook?"

She snorted out a laugh. "Hardly. I cooked . . . some. But we both worked a lot, and I often worked late at the house, so I took a lot of meals with the family, and he would get takeout or make a sandwich when he got home."

He nodded as he swallowed, then said, "Makes sense."

She lifted her head. "Say you're married to . . . someone. What would your expectations be about the whole cooking thing?"

"Never thought about it, honestly. I guess if she likes to cook, great. But I don't mind doing the cooking if she's not into it."

"Huh." She took a bite and chewed while staring out over the water.

"What would your expectations be?" he asked.

She pulled her gaze from the water. "Same as yours. I'm not big on one person being responsible for certain roles. Like the guy having to mow the lawn and take out the trash, and the woman having to do the cooking and cleaning."

"Nah, that's bullshit. If you live together, you share everything. Though I do enjoy mowing. I'd hate for my wife to take that task away from me."

She laughed. "Is that right?"

"Yeah. I like being outside."

"So do I."

"Okay. I'll mow. You get to be in charge of the garden."

He waited for her to laugh again, but she looked away to stare out at the water, as if she was pondering something monumental.

Or maybe she was just trying to wake up. It was still early.

He hadn't meant to plan out their future like that, to assume they'd have that life where he mowed and she gardened.

Or maybe he had. Maybe he was testing the waters to see how she'd react.

And now he knew. But he filed it away, because they were out on the water, it was a beautiful, cool fall morning and it wasn't the time for deep discussion.

After they finished eating, Finn got out the fishing poles and strung up their lines. They sat back and watched the sun come up over the hills while Murphy barked at the birds circling overhead.

"How do you feel about a working mother?" Brenna asked.

He shifted his gaze over to her. "What?"

"Say you get married, and you and your wife have a child, and she wants to go back to work after she has the baby. How do you feel about that?"

"I'd feel fine about it. Did you assume I'd want my wife to quit her job and become a full-time mother?"

"I assumed nothing. I was just asking a question."

Since the topic had never come up, it was worth pondering. "I guess if she wanted to stay home and raise the kids, we'd discuss it. Otherwise, why should she give up her career? I'm not giving up mine."

"But what about the child? Who's going to care for it? Have you thought about that?"

"Actually, no, I haven't thought about it at all since I don't currently have a kid."

She glared at him as if he'd abandoned a child he didn't yet have, but she let the subject drop while they continued to fish.

Twenty minutes later, she asked, "What if your wife makes more money than you do?"

He grinned. "Wouldn't that be fucking awesome? There's nothing better than success, is there?"

"And then what? You'll quit your job, sit on your ass and drink whiskey all day while she works?"

He leaned back to study her. "Where did I say I'd quit my job? I just said my as-yet-nonexistent-wife making more money than me would be great. That I'd be proud of her. Not that I'd sponge off her."

"Hmm."

"Did you read some article or something?"

"What?"

"Some article about the shittiest kinds of men."

"No, I didn't read an article. I'm just making conversation."

Yeah, conversation that felt accusatory, like it was directed at him and some terrible misdeeds he hadn't yet done. Or wouldn't ever do, for that matter.

Suddenly his pole had a bite, so he got distracted reeling it in, a nice-sized bass that Brenna helped him net and slide into the cooler.

"Good catch," she said.

"Thanks."

He set his pole back in the water, and it wasn't thirty minutes later that Brenna had a nibble. He let her go at it since she'd been fishing with her dad since she was little and knew what she was doing. Plus, he enjoyed watching her cuss and then laugh as the fish fought her, and Finn knew if she needed help she'd have asked for it.

She didn't need it. She pulled in a bass of her own that was just a touch smaller than the one he'd caught.

He tucked it into the cooler.

"You really did a nice job reeling that one in."

She lowered her sunglasses and gave him a look. "Was there any doubt I could? Because I'm a woman you thought maybe I couldn't handle reeling in that fish?"

Now it was time to talk. He swiveled his chair. "Okay, Brenna. What's up?"

"What's up with what?"

"You know damn well what I'm talking about. You've been grilling me all day and finding fault with everything I said. So what's wrong?"

"Nothing's wrong. We've just been having a hypothetical conversation. Just for fun, you know?"

She must have forgotten how well he knew her. And

when something was bugging her, she'd dig in her heels and come up with some stupid game like this one instead of hitting things head-on like she should. "I don't know about you, but I'm not having fun playing this game. Why don't you tell me what's actually on your mind instead of walking circles around it like you always do."

She opened her mouth, then closed it, then opened it again. Closed it again.

Yeah, there was something she wanted to say. And obviously she didn't know how to say it, which made his stomach churn.

Did she want to break up with him and she deliberately picked this circle jerk of a fight as a way to get things rolling?

No. Brenna wouldn't do that.

What the hell was this?

"I'm just in a mood, Finn. Can we let it go at that?"

"Not if something is bothering you. You should tell me—we should talk it out. Holding things inside doesn't make it go away."

"It's nothing, really. Just worrying about things I shouldn't worry about."

"Anything I can help with?"

"No, I'm fine."

She kept her gaze firmly fixed on the poles and the water—anywhere but on him. And that worried him. He reached over and swiveled her chair to face him.

"You're not fine. I know you, Brenna, and you tend to internalize things when you're worried about something. Does this have to do with you and me?"

Even though it was cool out on the water, the sun had come up bright with no clouds, so her shades shielded her eyes from him, and her eyes had always told him everything about how she felt. He wished he could pull off her sunglasses so he could really see her.

"It's a lot of things. Work stuff and personal stuff."

His lips lifted. "I'm part of your personal stuff. Talk to me."

She reached out to curl her fingers around his jaw. "I think I didn't get enough sleep last night and I woke up cranky. I wanted this to be a fun day for you and look what I did. I took out my bad mood on you. I'm sorry. Forgive me?"

He didn't think that was all there was to it, but she obviously wasn't gonna give him anything else, and he didn't want to ruin the day by pressing her. He took her hand and flipped it over to kiss it. "Always."

Then he pulled her out of her chair and onto his lap. Her body was chilled. "You're cold."

"A little."

"Want me to warm you up?"

She let out a soft laugh. "Yes."

He stood and placed her on her feet, pulled the poles out of the water and set them on the deck, then took her hand.

"Come on. Let's go below where it's warmer."

There was a small area below with a bathroom and a tiny bed, barely enough space for one person to maneuver, let alone two. Or two and a half, since Murphy had followed them down and curled into a ball at the foot of the steps, promptly going to sleep.

The tight quarters suited Finn just fine because it meant he and Brenna were cushioned together, close. She sat on the bed and toed off her boots and unzipped her jacket, shrugging it off and tossing it to the end of the bed. She leaned back, thrusting her breasts forward.

"Now I'm getting warm," she said.

"Are you? Good. Me too." He peeled off his jacket and

shirt and shimmied out of his boots and jeans, then his underwear.

"I don't think I'm that warm yet."

He gently pushed her onto the bed. "I can get you warm."

She held her arms up in invitation. "You can? Show me."

He climbed on top of her, covering her body with his, his lips meeting hers in a tangle of hot passion.

Maybe it was their earlier argument fueling his need, and maybe it was because he always wanted Brenna. He reached for her breast, cupping it through the material of her shirt.

She moaned against his mouth, his dick twitching in response to the sound. He reached up under her shirt and bra so he could feel her skin and rub his fingers against her nipple until it tightened and pebbled.

The sounds she made drove him crazy, made him want to strip her naked and lick her all over. And damn this fucking bed for being so small and so hard to maneuver around. He managed to get her pants and underwear off. She rose up, bumping her head on the ceiling and letting out a string of curses that made them both laugh. He unhooked her bra, banging his elbow on the wall as he worked to get the straps down and pull the bra off.

"This fucking boat," she said while maneuvering around the tiny bed.

"Hey, at least we're not trying to do this topside."

"Trust me, we would not be doing this topside. I'm not into exhibitionism."

He kissed her breast, taking a long lap of her nipple. "Come on, where's your sense of adventure?"

She sighed. "Down here. Where it's private."

He trailed his fingers along her ribs, down her stomach, cupping her sex and teasing her clit, then traveling lower until he slipped a finger inside her, rewarded with her gasp. "You mean if I got you all hot and bothered you wouldn't straddle my lap on the chairs topside and let me fuck you until you screamed?"

She shuddered, arching against his fingers. "Yes. I would. Do it now. Make me scream, Finn."

He moved his fingers against her, finding her clit, making sure to go slow at first, until she let him know she wanted more. And when she did, he gave it to her, her body writhing against his hand, making him sweat with all the hot sounds she made, the movements of her body, the way she looked at him, grabbing at his wrist as she came.

He held her while she shuddered, until her body relaxed. She looked up at him, her lips curving.

"Okay, done now. Let's go fish."

"You're funny. My dick is hard as a rock."

She reached between them to stroke his shaft. "Oh, and I suppose you want to do something about that."

He sucked in a breath, enjoying the feel of her touching him. "Unless you want me to go topside with a boner. Then what would our boat neighbors think?"

"It would be scandalous. We should stay down here in this tiny bed and take care of your immediate problem."

She pushed on his chest and he moved. He thought she was going to get up so he flopped onto his back on the bed. But she didn't get up. She surprised the hell out of him by straddling him.

"What are you doing?" he asked.

She wrapped both hands around his swollen cock. "Playing."

His heartbeat quickened as she inched down his body, teasing him with bites and kisses along the way.

"Brenna," he said, though her name might have come

out as a choked whisper, because her lips wrapped around his dick and he lost the ability for coherent thought.

Her mouth was warm and wet and her tongue flicked against the head of his cock, making his balls quiver. The feeling of release tightened inside him, but he held it back because the vision of her sucking him was the hottest damn thing he'd ever seen and he wanted it to last forever.

But it couldn't, because her mouth was too sweet and he was about to lose it.

"Brenna," he warned, reaching down to wrap his hand around her neck to pull her up.

She shoved his hand away and gave him more. He lost it, shuddering hard as he came.

He lay there for long minutes, his eyes closed as he came to the realization that his limbs were heavy and he might not be able to move ever again.

But then he felt Brenna's head on his chest, and her fingers trailing over his stomach.

And okay, he could still move his toes, though he might have lost a few brain cells.

Worth it.

"So, how's fishing?" she asked.

He grinned. "Best day ever."

She laughed, rolled over and lifted her head to look up at him. "I don't know about you, but I could use a drink."

He pulled her up so he could kiss her, then said, "Yeah, I'm thirsty, too."

They managed to maneuver out of the tiny bed and get dressed. Murphy had apparently given up on them and made his way topside, so they went upstairs.

Murphy was curled up on one of the cushioned benches, asleep, the breeze ruffling his fur.

"I think he's enjoying the boat," she said.

Finn wrapped his arm around Brenna and kissed her, a long, satisfying kiss that made him want to drag her back downstairs. But the cramped quarters and the lure of more fishing made him rethink that idea. Besides, there was always later.

Brenna pulled out a thermos of iced tea and poured it into their cups. They settled back into their seats and Finn adjusted the fishing poles back in the water.

After several hours they caught a couple more fish, and then the skies clouded up.

"Looks like rain's coming in," he said. "We should head back."

She nodded and they packed everything up. Finn started the engine and they headed back to the dock. They got the boat on the trailer and out of the water just in time for fat droplets of rain to start falling.

By the time they'd exited the park, it was a deluge of rain.

Finn looked through the windshield. "We left the water just in time."

"We sure did. I would have hated to be out in this."

"We could have gone below to stay dry."

She looked over him. "Uh-huh. With high waves and everything. Sounds utterly nauseating."

He laughed. "But romantic, right?"

"Sure, Finn. Totally romantic. Until I throw up on you."

"You get seasick when the boat rocks?"

"Definitely. Just ask my dad about the time the waves were high and he insisted on taking us fishing anyway. It was not a fun day for me—or for him."

"I'm sorry. Not easy when you get seasick."

"I'm sure you've never had a seasick day in your life."

"That's true, but I grew up by the sea, was out on boats

a lot, so I got my sea legs when I was old enough to stand. You're not used to being out on the water a lot. You did good today, though."

She looked out the window. "The water was calm. And we weren't at sea."

Somehow he got the idea it was more than just one bad lake adventure.

"What else happened on the water?"

She waved her hand. "Ancient history."

"Brenna."

"Mitchell and I went to Barbados for our honeymoon. We booked this catamaran cruise. It . . . didn't go well. I got so sick. Mitchell was pissed off that we wasted money and he didn't have fun."

Finn rolled his eyes. "Because it's always all about him. Didn't he care that you didn't feel well?"

"Not really. He walked me up to the room, I passed out on the bed and he went down to the bar. He ended up having dinner in the restaurant that night, and didn't even come up to check on me."

"What a dick."

"Yes. I should have seen the writing on the wall then, but I was too sick to notice."

"I'm glad you didn't waste too long on him. See? You're smart."

She laughed. "Not smart enough. I still married him."

The worst of the storm had passed just as Finn got on the expressway, but there was a lot of water on the road so he stayed in the right lane since they were towing a boat. He glanced quickly at Brenna. "Don't you think it's time you let it go?"

She frowned. "Let what go?"

"Mitchell. So you married him and he turned out to be

a jackass. That wasn't your fault, Brenna. Quit beating yourself up over it. Lots of people end up with bad marriages. You got out of yours quickly, but you haven't really moved on yet."

"Sure I have."

"Have you? It's like every decision you make revolves around what happened in your marriage. It's as if it defines you."

"No, it doesn't."

"Really? This whole engagement thing came about because of Mitchell and Allison. How you didn't want to be seen as single, which shouldn't have mattered because you're smart and successful and gorgeous as fuck. You should have been rubbing that in their faces instead of dragging me along as some kind of trophy fiancé."

She went dead silent and he knew he shouldn't have said it, but fuck it, he had and it was the truth. She was an amazing woman who should be proud to stand on her own.

When he pulled up in front of the house, he figured Brenna would bail for the front door as soon as the truck stopped. He grasped her hand before she could make a run for it. "Brenna, look. I'm sorry if I hurt your feelings. You know I would never want to hurt you. I care about you. But I also want you to be free."

"Free of what? Of you?"

He frowned. "No, not of me. Of the pain you keep holding on to from the past. Of Mitchell and whatever hold Allison seems to have on you. You deserve better. But you and I seem to keep getting into these arguments that don't make any sense, and I think it's because you're afraid to feel too deeply."

She blinked. "Oh, now you're going to explain to me how I feel."

Shit. He was screwing this up. "No, that's not what I meant at all."

"I'm tired, Finn, and I've got some things to do. Let's regroup and talk about this later, okay?"

"Yeah. Sure. I'll take care of cleaning the boat and storing it."

"Okay, thanks."

She slipped out of the truck and he went around to her side to help her with the bags. He walked with her up the steps.

"Brenna."

She turned, but didn't look at him. "Yes."

"Thank you for today. I really did have a great time."

She nodded and went inside.

He walked down the steps and climbed back into the truck, put it in gear and drove toward the garage.

Way to fuck up a perfect day, Finn.

But he wouldn't take back what he'd said, because it was the truth.

Dammit, he was in love with Brenna. And if that meant digging at her layers to get to the truth of how she felt, he'd keep digging. Even if it pissed her off.

Because she was worth it.

CHAPTER
······
twenty-eight

BRENNA RUBBED HER temples where the headache had taken up permanent residence the entire day. This meeting with her sisters wasn't helping. It especially wasn't helping that Erin, freshly back from her honeymoon, was tanned and in a gloriously happy mood, while Brenna was still smarting from her not-so-fun outing with Finn a few days ago.

She'd been avoiding him ever since, despite his efforts to get together with her for some one-on-one time. She'd begged off, claiming work or previous engagements with Honor or her mom, and even though she knew Finn wasn't buying any of her excuses, she just wasn't ready to deal with him.

"Oh, and the Belgrave/Monticelli wedding this weekend wants four additional cases of the merlot, plus three additional cases of champagne. Did you get that, Brenna?"

"Brenna? Did you hear what Honor said?" Erin asked.

Brenna snapped her head up. "I got it, though I'm getting tired of all these last-minute order changes. Why can't people just leave it alone? Why is everyone pushing at me?"

Erin looked at Honor, then back at Brenna. "Somehow I don't think we're talking about wine orders anymore."

"What's wrong, Brenna?" Honor asked.

"It's nothing." She waved her hand, hoping they'd get back to business and away from her.

"It's not nothing," Honor said. "You've been out of sorts for days."

Erin studied her. "You have? What happened?"

Knowing her sisters, Brenna knew she wasn't going to get out of this without an explanation. "Finn and I sort of had a fight."

"You did?" Honor looked shocked. "About what?"

"He accused me of living in the past, of using my relationship with Mitchell to inform all of my decision making."

The room went quiet, and Erin and Honor started shuffling paperwork.

She gaped at her sisters. "What? You two think the same thing?"

Erin looked at her. "You're the one who came up with the fake fiancé because you couldn't stand the thought of facing Mitchell and Allison on your own."

"That's different. That was more Allison than anything. You know how she is."

"And maybe some of it was proving to Mitchell that you'd moved on, that you were happy without him?"

Brenna looked over at Honor. "I *am* happy without him."

"We both know that," Erin said. "But your marriage left scars that you haven't allowed to heal."

"Which was why you always found fault with men you dated," Honor said.

Erin nodded. "And maybe why you're having so much

trouble settling in with Finn, who's the greatest guy I've ever known—short of my husband, of course."

"He really is, Bren," Honor said. "He cares deeply for you. He would never do anything to hurt you."

"And he sure as hell is nothing like Mitchell. He doesn't put work first, he goes above and beyond to spend time with you. I mean, what exactly is it that you're looking for?"

She wished she knew the answer to that question. "I don't know. Maybe he and I just aren't a match. This was what I was afraid of when everyone was pushing at me to have a relationship with him. That it wouldn't work out."

"Why isn't it working out, though?" Honor asked. "Is it because you don't have the right feelings for him, or is it because you're afraid you do?"

That question sailed straight to her heart, shutting her down completely.

"I don't know. We haven't discussed it."

"Which means you haven't spoken to him," Erin said. "Since when?"

She stared at her laptop instead of her sisters. "I don't know. A few days ago."

"Brenna," Honor said. "That's not like you."

She sighed. "I know. But it scares me. He scares me. My feelings scare me."

"Just . . . talk to him, Brenna," Erin said. "Nothing gets resolved without a conversation."

"That's true," Honor said. "You have to deal with things head-on. Ignoring the situation only makes it worse."

"I will." She looked up to find two pair of disbelieving eyes staring at her. "I will. I promise. Now can we get back to the meeting?"

She'd deal with all things Finn later.

Much later.

Though *much later* turned out to be a lot sooner than she wanted it to be, because after she left the wine cellar that night she literally ran right into him on the walkway between the buildings and the main house. Finn had his head down and so did she, so neither of them saw it coming and she almost fell on her ass. Would have, actually, had Finn not caught her in his arms to steady her.

"You okay?" he asked.

"Yes, I'm fine."

Murphy ran circles around her in his excitement to see her, so she bent to pet him, then straightened.

"What are you up to?" she asked.

"Just putting things away for the night. You?"

"Same."

"Working late."

She nodded. "I had a meeting, and then I needed to check on a few things."

"I see."

This conversation was painfully awkward—all because of her. She needed to do something to fix that.

"Finn, look. About the other day. I was out of sorts and in my head. And I know there are things we need to talk about. Deep, important things. But I'm just not ready yet. I need some time to sort through it all in my head. I'm confused and just working through it gives me a headache. Can you give me some time? I promise I'm not blowing you off or trying to avoid a conversation. I just want to make sure I have coherent thoughts when we do have it."

He nodded. "That's fair."

She hadn't expected him to acquiesce so quickly. "Thanks."

"In the meantime, I'm starving and Louise told me she was making lasagna for dinner. How about we go eat?"

She smiled. "That sounds like a great idea."

He held his arm out for her and she slipped her arm in his, and all that tension she'd been holding inside suddenly melted away, along with her headache.

They walked toward the house together.

CHAPTER

......

twenty-nine

Finn knew that Brenna wasn't looking forward to being around Mitchell and Allison again, but she was going to go through with seeing them tonight, because she'd agreed to go to Esther and Brock's housewarming party. He knew she'd been happy when Esther had to delay the party because Brock had to take several out-of-town business trips, but now it was finally happening.

She'd even obsessed over buying them a gift, dragging him out to shop with her so he could offer an opinion. Which was nice, but she was the one with taste, not him, so whatever she chose would have been fine. But she wanted to put both their names on the card since they were still supposed to be engaged, so she chose a decorative something or other for their living room and asked him what he thought.

To Finn it looked like a curved bluish bowl, so he said it was fine. Apparently *fine* was the wrong word because she gave him a head tilt and a look. He offered up that it was pretty, and that seemed to satisfy her. When the salesperson rang it up, Finn nearly choked at the price.

Damn, fancy bowls were expensive as hell. But he dug out half the cost from his wallet and handed her the cash.

She looked down at the money. "What's this?"

"My share."

"Unnecessary."

"It's from both of us, right?"

"Yes, but it was my—"

"No *but*s. I pay half." He gave her a firm look.

She sighed. "Then you should have taken more of an interest in the decision making."

The salesperson handed him the bag and they walked away from the counter. "No shit. I wouldn't have spent that much money."

She laughed and slipped her arm through his. "I guess I don't have to ever worry about you spending all our money once we're fake married, huh?"

He gave her a curious look, but she didn't seem to notice.

It had been two weeks since their boat trip, and they still hadn't had a deep conversation about the issues they needed to talk out.

Finn wasn't much for letting things hang unresolved, but Brenna didn't seem to want to talk about it, and since they'd been getting along well and Brenna had seemed to move past whatever the problem had been that day, he hadn't wanted to push it.

People got moody. Hell, he got moody sometimes, all up in his head with thoughts and worries. He knew how that went. But that day when they'd been out on the water, there'd been something else going on besides just a mood. And at some point they'd have to hash that out. Until they cleared the air, it would never be resolved. And you couldn't move forward in a relationship with issues that were left unsettled.

After they left the store, they drove over to Esther and Brock's house, a nice-looking white ranch-style with a big yard, a good-sized driveway and lots of space between neighbors. There were already several cars in the driveway, so Finn parked behind one of them and they got out. He grabbed the bag with the gift, then took Brenna's hand as they walked up to the front door. He glanced over at her. She looked amazing tonight in a yellow dress with a coral sweater over it, her hair loose and flowing over her shoulders.

"Did I mention how beautiful you look tonight?"

Her cheeks brightened and her lips curved. "Thank you."

Brock opened the door and leaned against it, looking relaxed with a beer in his hand.

"Hey, you two. Glad you made it. Come on in."

The inside of the house was open and spacious, with a vaulted ceiling in the living room that led to a good-sized kitchen where Esther was pouring wine for Allison, Hilary and Sabra, along with Brock's mom, Greta, as well as several other people Finn didn't know.

Esther looked up as they entered. "Oh, hey, you're here. I'm so glad you could make it."

Brenna went over to hug Esther. "Wouldn't miss it."

"I thought you'd be busy doing your . . . whatever it is you do," Allison said, her nose pointed so high in the air Finn thought she might get it stuck to the ceiling.

Brenna didn't take the bait. Instead, she listened as Esther introduced her to a few people they didn't know.

"Your house is fabulous, Esther," Brenna said.

"Thank you. We loved it on first sight. The owners had

only lived in it for two years before they had to move due to a job transfer. It's perfect for us. Four bedrooms. Plenty of space for any kids that come along, plus an office for Brock and me to share. Would you like a tour?"

"I'd love one."

Greta took over wine duties and snack prep while Esther led them on a tour.

The bedrooms were all good-sized, there was a bath in the hall and the main bedroom was killer huge with an attached bath that anyone would like. Finn watched Brenna's eyes light up as she wandered the bathroom, her fingers lingering over the soaker tub.

"It's amazing," Brenna said as they made their way back toward the kitchen. "You must be so happy."

"Incredibly. We saved for two years to get this house, living with Brock's parents, who were so sweet to let us stay with them."

Greta gave Esther a smile. "We loved having you with us."

"At least they had a good reason to be living with their parents." Allison shot Brenna a smirk.

Finn knew better than to get in the middle of Brenna's ongoing feud with her former friend, but it took everything in him not to say something.

And again, Brenna didn't take the bait. He admired her restraint.

She picked up the bag they'd brought in and handed it to Esther. "We brought you and Brock a gift. Again, congratulations on your new home."

"Oh, thank you." Esther hugged her. "You didn't have to do that. Brock, could you come here for a second?"

Brock walked over and Esther pulled the bowl out of the bag, her eyes widening. "Oh, I love this bowl. I wanted it so much."

Brock smiled. "I remember you eyeing that at the store. I believe you squealed."

Esther laughed. "I did squeal. Thank you both so much." She hugged Finn, then Brenna. "I'm going to put it on the table right now."

Finn didn't get the appeal of a bowl, but he was happy Esther liked it. And Allison seemed to be irritated over how much everyone exclaimed over the bowl, so that part was good.

He got a beer and sat with some of his friends to catch up with them but still kept one eye on Brenna, who sat in the kitchen with the women. Mitchell seemed quiet tonight, not engaging much in conversation. Then again, that was pretty much Mitch's personality—aloof and above everyone else.

Fortunately he had other people to talk to besides clammed-up Mitch, so tonight should be fun.

BRENNA HAD BEEN reluctant to come tonight, which was ridiculous because she loved Esther and Brock, and she'd be damned if Allison and Mitchell would keep her from seeing them. Besides, with all the delays in organizing this, it had been a while since she'd seen her friends.

She was so glad she had, because she was having a great time. And it seemed as if Allison was having a not-so-great night, which put Brenna in an even better mood. As she was sitting in the group of women and catching up on their lives, she'd noticed Allison being silent, while also shooting glares at Mitchell. Something must be off with the two of them tonight.

Maybe they'd had an argument. Brenna knew all about

what it was like to have a fight with Mitchell. It could be exasperating.

When Allison went into the kitchen, Brenna followed. She didn't know why because getting in the middle of Allison and Mitchell was just asking for it.

"Allison, is everything all right?"

She swiveled and pasted on a fake smile. "Everything's fine. Why would you ask?"

"You're quiet tonight. Not your normal vivacious self. You only threw two insults at me when I first walked in, and then you went dead silent."

"Oh. Well. Uh . . . no, everything's perfect. Thank you for asking, though." She took a swallow of her iced tea. "And I didn't insult you."

Brenna laughed. "Of course you did. You always do. You have ever since high school."

"I have, haven't I?" She sighed and swiped a finger across her brow. "I'm sorry. I'm such a bitch."

Allison apologizing? Okay, this was new. It took a minute for Brenna to gather her bearings before she replied. "You need to let it go, Allison. It was a long time ago. And I never meant to hurt you. I'm sorry, too."

Allison leaned against the kitchen counter, tears welling in her eyes.

Was Brenna living in some alternate universe? Allison showing actual emotion?

"Can we talk for a minute?" Allison asked. "Outside, maybe?"

"Sure." They stepped out back and took a seat on the patio chairs. Brenna waited while Allison took another few sips of water.

"I'm pregnant, Brenna."

No wonder she was drinking iced tea. Allison did love her wine. "That's wonderful. Congratulations."

"Thank you. I think it's wonderful, too. But Mitchell isn't happy about it."

Brenna frowned. "What? How can he not be?"

"Because I screwed up his perfectly crafted timeline. He wanted to wait two more years and I guess I forgot one or two of my birth control pills a couple of months ago and now, here I am, having messed with his grand plan. He's really upset with me."

What. A. Jackass. "Well. Shit happens, you know. But how exciting. A baby."

Allison tried for a smile but only made it halfway. "I was excited. I *am* excited. When I told him, I expected him to be happy about it. He gave me this stern look and accused me of getting pregnant on purpose just to screw him over."

That was so how Mitchell would think, making it all about him. "He's an asshole."

Allison laughed. "At least we have a common frame of reference. I'm just so disappointed in him, Brenna. I don't know what to do. We're having a baby. He kind of has to get on board with this. And I want him to be happy about it. Like genuinely happy."

She reached over and grasped Allison's hand. "He will. Just give him some time. Mitchell has his faults, but I'm sure once he realizes this is happening—timeline or not—he'll be over-the-moon excited about it."

"I hope so."

"And try not to worry. Surround yourself with the people who are happy for you. That'll help lift your mood."

"Thank you. I needed to hear that. And please keep this to yourself, if you would."

Brenna nodded. "Of course."

"And Brenna?"

"Yes?"

"Thank you. I've been an awful person to you for so long, over ancient history. You could have told me I deserved what I got. You didn't. I appreciate that more than I can say."

She squeezed Allison's hand. "Hey, whatever animosity was between us is over. Now we move forward, okay?"

Allison nodded. "Okay."

Esther and a few of the other women wandered outside, and then some of the guys followed, so the conversation ended. Brenna went in to refill her glass. She poured wine, then noticed Mitchell in the living room on the phone.

Of course he was on the phone. Brenna was surprised his phone wasn't permanently fused to his ear by now.

She rolled her eyes, then thought for a few seconds. She should stay out of it. Then again, when had she ever stayed out of things she should have? As soon as he hung up she walked over to him.

"What do you want, Brenna?"

"I hear you're having a baby. Congratulations."

He frowned. "Who told you that?"

"Allison did. She's really happy about it. Maybe you could be, too."

"She told you I wasn't happy?"

"She did."

"She told *you* I wasn't happy."

"Yes."

"Damn." He sat on the sofa and stared down at the floor. "It was a shock. I wasn't expecting it."

Brenna took a seat in the chair. "Neither was she. But

she's so thrilled and she obviously loves you, so maybe you can show some excitement about it. You love her, don't you?"

He lifted his gaze to hers. "I really do."

She saw the truth of that on his face and realized she was happy to see it. Allison wasn't his trophy wife or his rebound. He loved her, and she was relieved, for Allison's sake.

"Then it's time for you to get ready to be a daddy, Mitchell. And show your wife some actual emotion about it. I know it's not what you expected, but wow, you're going to be a dad. How thrilling is that?"

He sucked in a deep breath. "Yeah. I can't believe she talked to you about it."

"I'm a good listener."

His lips curved. "That means the two of you made up, huh?"

"Yes."

"Then I won't have to hear her complain about you anymore?"

"Mitchell . . ."

He held up his hands. "Fine. I'll be the excited father-to-be. And I'll buy my wife some flowers tomorrow."

"You do that. Maybe consider a baby gift to go along with the flowers."

He frowned. "Baby gift? Like what?"

She pulled out her phone and quickly looked up generic but adorable onesies at a local baby store. "Like this. At this store."

He grabbed the link and put it on his phone. "Okay. Good idea. Thanks, Brenna."

"You're welcome."

"And Brenna?"

"Yes?"

"I'm sorry."

She frowned. "For what?"

"For . . . everything, I guess. I did it all wrong with you. I'm trying to do it better with Allison, even though it doesn't appear that way."

"Hey, don't worry about it. I want only the best for you and for Allison. And I'm really happy about the baby."

He managed a smile. "Thanks."

She stood and walked away, shaking her head. Mitchell would always be who he was, but maybe fatherhood would mellow him.

One could only hope.

She went back outside where the entire group had gathered. The night was cool and it was absolutely perfect on the patio.

Finn appeared by her side and slipped his hand around her waist.

"Where've you been?"

"Mending old wounds and doing a little damage control."

At his curious look, she added, "We'll talk later."

He kissed her temple. "Okay."

They all snacked on amazing food and chatted and Brenna finally relaxed and had a great time. She felt an immense sense of relief because she and Allison had finally cleared the air. She could only hope that Mitchell would come around and start acting like a human being capable of feelings.

The party wound down around ten since it was a work night. They said their good-byes and headed out to Brenna's car. Finn only had one beer earlier while Brenna had a few glasses of wine, so he drove them back home.

On the drive home she thought about Mitchell, of all the ways he had never changed. And how hard it was to make relationships work. Brenna and Finn got along so well. But would that last? She and Mitchell had started out on a good path, and then it had all gone to hell in a matter of months. Wouldn't it stand to reason that the same thing would happen to her and Finn?

They still had so much to talk about. And that conversation scared the hell out of her.

Finn parked in front of her house, then turned to face her.

"Wanna tell me what went on with you and Allison? I saw the two of you talking. Did you have a big fight?"

She unlocked her seat belt so she could shift around to look at him. "The opposite, actually. We had a long talk and everything's good between us now."

He gave her a dubious look. "Just like that."

"Well, it wasn't exactly like that, but she had a problem and asked for my help."

"And you didn't tell her to stick it."

She offered up a smile. "No."

"What kind of problem would she need your help with?"

"It had to do with Mitchell, so we talked it over for a while and hopefully things will resolve for the two of them."

"Oh. She's having issues with her marriage."

"I didn't say that."

"You're not really saying anything."

"She asked me not to. I'm sorry."

"Okay. I get it. I won't ask you to betray a confidence. Do you feel better about Allison now?"

"Yes."

"Nothing else matters, then."

They got out of the car and Finn walked her up the steps to the front door, popping it open to gently call for Murphy, who came bounding out.

"Thanks for coming with me tonight," she said.

"Hey, no problem."

She twirled the claddagh ring around her finger. She'd gotten used to wearing it, to seeing it on her finger every day. It had become a part of her. And every time she looked at it, felt it, it gave her a feeling of permanence. She felt Finn whenever she saw it.

But it didn't belong to her. He didn't belong to her. And every day since that day on the boat, she had felt a sense of unease, a feeling that any moment this whole thing was going to come crashing down on top of her.

She hesitated, then pulled the ring off and held it out to Finn.

He frowned. "What the hell did you do that for?"

"The reasons for wearing it are over. Allison and I made up, Esther and Brock's wedding is long past and we don't have to pretend to be a couple anymore."

"Is that what we've been doing, Brenna? Pretending to be a couple?"

"I—" She looked at him, not knowing what to say, wishing he would say something so she wouldn't have to. "I don't know. Maybe. We're not engaged, Finn. We were just playacting."

"So this whole time with you there were no real feelings involved. You just needed me to act like your fiancé, and now that it's over, we're done."

This wasn't going like she planned. Maybe seeing Mitchell tonight, and Allison so miserable, reminded her of all she'd gone through before, of what she never wanted to go through again. "I didn't say that. We could still—hang out, you know."

"Hang out. Like buddies."

"Something like that."

"I've got bros, Brenna. You're not one of them. I thought there was more to us than just being friends. Was I wrong?"

Her heart pounded against her chest as she realized she was dangling at the edge of a cliff. She could do two things right here—tell him how she really felt about him, or walk away. And the thought of opening her heart to the possibility of hurt again was too terrifying to contemplate.

"I don't know, Finn. I have a lot going on in my life. I'm set in my ways. And you have ambitions and things you want to do with yours. I just don't think we're compatible."

"I see." He fisted the ring in his hand and shoved it into his pocket. "I'm so glad you made this decision for us, Brenna. That you know I have ambitions and things I want to do with my life. Because you're right about that. And clearly you don't see yourself in my life anymore. Good to know."

"Finn—"

"No. You're always the one who has things to say. Now it's my turn. I do have plans for my life. I want to start a whiskey business. Buy some land of my own. Build a bigger house. Get married and raise a family. And I thought at some point you and I could talk about those plans together, because I love you, Brenna. I've probably been in love with you since I was eighteen years old, since I first stepped foot on the property here and saw you standing there, all mad and defiant about some strange boy coming to live in your house. I fell in love with your spirit and your beauty and how smart you were. And then you married that jackass and I tried not to love you then, but I still did.

"I was still in love with you after your divorce when I'd catch you crying out in the garden or holed up in the library for hours on end. And when you and I got together it was like a dream to me. Your sassiness, your laugh, all of that wrapped around me and made me the happiest man around. And I thought—okay, we've got a chance, you and I. A chance to have something amazing together. But you never really gave me the chance, Brenna, because you were too afraid of your past to build a future with me.

"And if you want out, then I feel bad for you because I'm the best damn thing to ever happen to you. You go live your life and I'll go live mine. Good-bye, Brenna."

He turned and walked down the steps of the porch, Murphy wagging his tail as he followed behind him.

Brenna waited for the words to come out to yell at Finn to stop, to tell him that she'd made a huge mistake. But the words never came. She just stood there and watched him drive away while she rubbed the naked spot on her finger where Finn's ring used to be, those sweet words he'd said to her still ringing in her ears, still wrapped around her heart. And she still couldn't move her feet, couldn't take those steps to stop him.

Finally, after what seemed like hours, she went inside, closed and locked the door and walked upstairs to her room. She sat on the bed, feeling as empty as she had ever felt in her life, as if there were a hole right through the center of her heart.

What had she done?

CHAPTER

......

Wait ... WHAT? SHE broke up with you?"

Finn nodded at Jason and took another long chug of his ale.

"What the hell did she do that for?" Clay asked.

"I guess she doesn't feel the same way I do."

"That's bullshit," Owen said. "Hang on, I've got a customer."

Owen wandered off while the rest of them sat at a table at the Screaming Hawk.

"Okay," Jason said. "Tell us everything that happened."

He went over it again, step-by-step—at least the steps he could piece together since none of it made sense to him.

"But you love her," Owen said.

He stared miserably into his glass. "Yeah."

"Then fight for her," Jason said. "Don't let her go that easily."

"Brenna's stubborn. She thinks she knows what she wants."

"Then . . . maybe make it harder for her to have you," Clay said.

Finn frowned. "What? Nah. I don't play games like that. She either wants to be with me or she doesn't. That's her choice. The last thing I'm gonna do is start dating other women and parade them in front of her. That would hurt her and I don't want to do that."

"No, I don't mean it like that. You've been there at the vineyard the whole time, since you were eighteen. She knew you were always there for her. If she changes her mind, you'll be right there. Like always."

"Oh, I get it," Owen said. "What if you weren't there, ready to take her back in a hot minute?"

"Yeah," Jason said. "You know what they say about absence. What if you're not there when she decides she wants to talk this all out? Make her realize what she's missing. Who she's missing."

Maybe not a terrible idea. And Finn could use a break. Clear his head. He never took time off. And he had just the location in mind.

He looked up at his friends and smiled for the first time in days. "You're all very smart."

"We have to be," Owen said. "Because you're a dumbass."

He laughed, and started to formulate a plan in his mind.

IT HAD BEEN a week since Brenna had broken up with Finn. Three days since she'd even seen him wandering around the property. She appreciated that he hadn't come around to talk to her, that he'd given her space.

But did she really appreciate it, or was she just trying to convince herself of that? Because the next day she figured he'd come around and tell her again what a colossal mistake she'd made. And then they'd talk and she'd agree with him, tell him yes, she'd been afraid and she'd apologize.

She'd beg him to take her back. He'd forgive her, they'd kiss and make up and all would be right again.

Instead, he'd been nowhere to be found. Or the day after that or the day after that. Not that she'd gone looking for him or anything, because she wouldn't do that. After all, they were broken up. And he needed his space as much as she needed hers.

But where was he, anyway?

He hadn't shown up to the house for meals, which she could understand given how awkward that would have been, facing each other at the table. But still, where the hell was he?

And why was Murphy staying at the house? Shouldn't he be at Finn's? For the past few days the dog had been at the house—her constant companion—following her around like he was a little lost, not knowing what to do without Finn. Very odd. Though she found Murphy's presence comforting.

She knew exactly how Murphy felt. She'd asked her dad why the dog was here and his only response was to say they were dog sitting, making her wonder what was going on.

Not that it was any of her business, she decided as she finished up her paperwork for the day. She put everything away and wandered into her mother's office.

"What's up?" she asked her mom.

"Nothing much. Just working on these balance sheets. What's up with you?"

"Oh, nothing." She leaned against the doorway. "I noticed Murphy has been staying here."

"Mmm-hmm." Her mom studied her laptop.

"Any reason why?"

"Why what?"

"Why is Murphy here, Mom?"

"Oh. We're watching him for Finn."

"I see." She studied her nails. "And why is that?"

Nothing. Her mother ignored her. Damn.

"Mom."

Her mother tore her gaze from her laptop. "What?"

"Why are we watching Murphy?"

"Because Finn isn't here."

"Obviously." It was like pulling teeth. "Where is he?"

"He took a vacation, Brenna. And if you hadn't broken up with him you'd be aware of that."

Ouch. *Straight to the heart, Mom.*

"You didn't even ask me if Finn had done something terrible to me. If he'd broken my heart or cheated on me."

Her mother's response was to cock her head to the side and give her a look that told her she was being ridiculous.

"Really, Brenna? It's like you think I don't know Finn as well as I know my own three daughters. *Did* he break your heart or cheat on you?"

Now she was backed into a corner. "Well, no."

"Do you want to talk to me about what happened? Because I don't recall you coming to me wanting a heart-to-heart talk about breaking up with the man you love."

She lifted her chin. "I don't recall saying I loved him."

Her mother slanted a look her way. "You were just playing with the boy this whole time."

"I didn't say that, either."

"Then what are you saying?"

Defeated, she walked in and flopped into the chair. "That I'm a disaster and I made a mess out of my relationship with Finn."

"He wasn't too happy about it, either, when he came to your father and me. Asked us for some time off to travel and clear his head. Do you know he's never once taken a vacation, despite your da and I asking him to?"

She sighed, feeling guiltier by the second. "I was not aware of that."

"He asked for three weeks, Brenna."

Her heart sank. "Three weeks?"

Her mother nodded.

Three weeks was a very long time. He could be anywhere. With anyone. Doing anything. Was he with someone else? No, he wasn't. That wasn't Finn.

"Do you know where he went?"

"Aye, I do. But I'm not sure I should tell you. You gave up that right when you broke up with him."

Her stomach hurt. Her heart hurt. And the realization hit that she couldn't hide from her feelings any longer.

Tears pricked her eyes and she couldn't hold them back. "I love him, Mom. I haven't even admitted that to myself until right now. And I miss him so much it feels like my heart is breaking in two. I need to find him and make this right, if I can."

Her mother nodded. "Now you're starting to make some sense."

She wound her hands together. "So you'll tell me where he is?"

"Yes. All right, go get your man back, Brenna. You'll have to swallow your pride."

She could do that. She'd do anything to have Finn back in her life. In any way he wanted her.

If he wanted her back.

CHAPTER
· · · · · ·
thirty-one

Finn inhaled and let the sharp sea breeze blow over him, bringing him the calm he'd needed so badly. He stood at the edge of the cliff for the longest time, then walked back to the cottage.

He'd been lucky to find this place situated on the cliffs with an incredible view of the water. It was isolated, which was just what he'd needed so he could take the time to be by himself, to reflect and figure out his next steps.

Not that he'd figured out what those steps were just yet. But he would. Soon.

A light rain began to fall, the taps on the roof reminding him of his childhood. A fire roared in the fireplace, keeping the small cottage warm. Perfect. He sat on the sofa and put his feet up, sipping the coffee he'd poured.

Being alone wasn't so bad. He liked it out here—a chance to commune with his homeland again, to breathe the sea air and remember what it felt like to be in Ireland.

The first few days he'd stayed in the village where he'd grown up, though he didn't know but a few people there anymore. Still, it felt good to reconnect, to go visit his parents' graves, to feel closer to them somehow. It had been so long.

He'd spent some time at the cemetery talking to his ma, telling her about his troubles with Brenna. Just talking it out had helped give him some perspective. Then he came up to this place and had fallen instantly in love with the seclusion and the beauty of it. He drove down to the village for groceries, but otherwise, he was completely alone.

Alone and missing Brenna so much he thought his heart might shrivel up and die from it. But he couldn't change how someone else felt, he could only manage himself.

Still, he intended to go back and fight for her, convince her that what they had together was the real thing. And if it took him the rest of his life to convince her, then that was what he intended to do. Because that was what you did when you loved someone—and you knew that that someone loved you back, even though she might be afraid of love.

He was a patient man. And Brenna needed him.

There was a knock on the door and he frowned.

No one should be up here.

He walked to the door and opened it, shocked as hell to see a totally soaked Brenna standing there, suitcase on wheels trailing behind her. She looked utterly miserable and pissed as hell.

"Really, Finn? You had to come all the way to Ireland to get away from me?"

"You think this trip was all about you?"

"Wasn't it? I'm wet. Can I come in?"

He stepped aside to let her drag her suitcase in. She left it at the door, shook off the water from her raincoat and undid the buttons, hanging it on the hook by the door.

Finn went into the bathroom and grabbed a towel, then brought it out to her.

"Thanks." She sat on the bench and pulled off her boots.

"Want some coffee or tea?"

"Coffee would be great, thank you."

He poured a cup for her, then carried it into the living area where she'd taken a seat on the chair by the fireplace.

"Thanks. Nice place."

"It works for me. What are you doing here, Brenna?"

"Oh, we're getting right into it. Okay."

"No reason not to, is there?" What he wanted to do was grab her up into his arms and hold her, kiss her and tell her how he felt. But he knew she'd made this trip to talk to him, so he was going to let her do that.

"I guess not." She took a sip of the coffee, then set it on the table and stood, coming over to stand in front of him. "You left without saying anything. I missed you."

His heart pinged, but he pushed it away. "I left so I could have some time to think."

She tilted her head back and he tried not to get lost in her eyes. "Think about what?"

"Next steps. My future. What I want."

He jammed his hands in his jeans pockets to keep himself from reaching out to touch her. He'd spent the past week reconciling in his head how he was going to deal with seeing her every day, working with her every day, and not touch her, not kiss her, not think of her as his. And now she stood right across from him, having traveled thousands of miles to see him. He was confused as hell.

"What do you want, Finn?"

He dragged his fingers through his hair. "Honestly, Brenna? I don't know yet. Right now I just want some peace."

He walked away from her and stood at the door to look at the sea, at the rolling waves and the rain coming down, the fierceness of nature mimicking the storm roiling inside him.

And then she was next to him and her hand was on his shoulder, her touch burning him from the inside out.

"I'm sorry, Finn. Sorry for hurting you so badly that you felt you had to leave. This is all my fault. I was so scared about how I felt, about how much you made me feel. I've never felt like this before, so consumed by love that I was afraid it would overwhelm me. And you were right when you told me that the mistakes of my past had led me to make all my decisions. I had to let that go because I'm not the same person I was then, and you're not at all like the man I was once married to.

"You're kind and gentle and open with your feelings. You even argue with me and tell me when I'm wrong, which I don't often appreciate at the time, but in retrospect I realize I need so much in my life. But you also listen to my point of view and I can't tell you how much I appreciate that. I love you, Finn, and my heart will break if I can't spend the rest of my life with you."

His heart filled to bursting, and as he turned to face her he saw the tears streaming down her cheeks. He swiped them away with his thumb, then took her hand in his.

"I love you, Brenna. And one of the things I came to terms with while I've been out here is that you're worth fighting for. Even if it was you I had to fight with. I was never going to let you go. Because you're everything I've ever wanted. You're a smart, funny, beautiful, sexy, oh my God, stubborn-as-hell woman, but you're the perfect woman for me. And *my* heart will break if I don't get to spend the rest of my life with you."

"Finn," she sobbed.

He pulled her into his arms and kissed her, tasting the

salt of her tears and releasing the emotion he'd held in check since the last time he'd seen her. God, he loved this woman so much he was never letting her go.

Except for just a minute. "Go on, sit by the fire and warm up. I'll be right back."

BRENNA HADN'T EXPECTED that Finn would even open the door for her, let alone that the two of them would make up—that he would tell her he loved her, not after all the mistakes she'd made. But she'd told him the truth—she loved him. And she'd keep on telling him that for as long as he let her, because she was never going to make the mistake of letting him go again.

Every word he spoke to her was like magic. She realized how she'd ignored the truth all along, how she hadn't seen the wonderful man standing right in front of her all this time.

He came back into the room and she stood.

"I've been holding on to this," he said. "Hoping I'd get the chance to give it back to you."

And then he knelt in front of her and held out the claddagh ring, the one she'd missed having on her finger since she'd stupidly removed it.

"Brenna Bellini. The first time wasn't real. This time is. I love you—everything about you—the way your smile lights up my day, the way your beauty knocks me off my feet, the way you love your family that's become my family, too. I love how smart you are and how hard you work. I love your moodiness and your sarcastic wit and the way you challenge me. I love that when we fight you still come back to me, because we belong together. I want to build a future with you, a family with you, forever with you. Marry me."

Her entire body trembled at his declaration of love. She

held out her hand. "My hand was cold and my soul was empty without that ring—without that part of you. I love you now and forever, Finn Nolan. Yes, I'd be honored to marry you."

He slipped the ring on her finger and stood. "I'll get you a diamond—"

"You absolutely will not. This is the only ring I'll ever need. And you're the only man I'll ever want. Now and forever. Now kiss me."

He did, and her heart was full. He picked her up and carried her to the bedroom, and with the storm raging outside, they made their own storm rage inside as they hurried with removing their clothes, touching each other as if it had been months instead of just weeks without each other.

And when he was inside her, she looked into his eyes and knew she had found her forever.

Afterward, he brought her suitcase into the bedroom so she could put on dry clothes, and then they wandered into the kitchen to make some food.

"How much longer do you have this place?" she asked as she peeled potatoes while he cooked the meat.

"Another week." He leaned against the counter. "Can you stay?"

She thought of all the work waiting for her at home, and things she'd need to juggle, and then she looked out the window. The rain had ended and she had a clear view of the cliffs and the sea.

Wow.

She looked over at him and smiled. "I'll e-mail my sisters and my mom and let them know. They can carry on without me. I think you and I could use some alone time."

He slipped his arm around her and kissed her, and she melted into his embrace.

She could have never imagined that what started out as a fake engagement would end in finding the love of her life.

She would never take this amazing love for granted again. She couldn't wait to start their future together. It was going to be an incredible life.

NEW YORK TIMES AND *USA TODAY*
BESTSELLING AUTHOR

JACI
BURTON

"Jaci Burton's stories are full of heat and heart."

—#1 *New York Times*

bestselling author Maya Banks

For a complete list of titles,
please visit prh.com/jaciburton